Preface

'Dancing to the Pizzica' is a story of intrigue, romance, vendetta and the malevolent hold of the mafia in Italy and abroad. The narrative takes a humorous look at the incidents and circumstances surrounding the lives of the protagonists and the colourful characters they meet on the way. The events are set in the Salento region of Puglia, in the southernmost part of Italy's heel as well as, briefly, in London.

The 'pizzica' is a traditional dance from Salento and is peculiar to the area around Lecce – the beautiful, baroque city which is the region's provincial capital. The pizzica is part of the family of dances known as the 'Tarantella'. Its intensely rhythmical strains are infectious and reveal undercurrents of paganism which the modern world has failed to erase. The origins of the dance are ancient. Traditionally, it was a cure for the bite of the Tarantula spider – 'pizzica' means a bite or sting. By analogy, the dance became a way of chasing out the Devil from those thought to be possessed. The dancers would gyrate round and round in a frenzy to music supplied by the local inhabitants – the pace becoming faster and faster as the dance progressed.

This traditional dance has become the mainstay of folk music in Salento. It has retained its captivating and intense rhythm even though, nowadays, it is danced only for pleasure. There is nothing like witnessing the 'pizzica' being performed by and for local people in a crowded southern Italian piazza as darkness falls. Should you wish to get an idea of what the 'pizzica' looks and sounds like, you can log on to Youtube and type in *Pizzica Salento BTQ'* or the musical group *'Schiattacore'* which features in this narrative.

The characters in this novel are based on real people. Many of the events are drawn from the characters' real life experiences, including some of the more unlikely incidents described: the episode of the stolen purse in the disco, the identical dream dreamed by two members of Rosaria's family, and all the incidents that happened to Adam in his precarious career as a teacher. The ultrasound scan episode is also factual, but drawn from another source. Fortunately, the family tragedy described did not happen to Rosaria's family. But similar unsolved crimes are frequently reported by the Italian media.

Descriptions of the various places visited by Rosaria and Adam during the course of their travels are authentic – although place names which might reveal the identity of the real life *'Rosaria'* have been altered. There really was a night when the whole of Italy suffered a total blackout, all because of a fallen tree, it is said, which interrupted power supplies from Switzerland. It took well over twenty-four hours for electricity supplies to be restored – even longer in Salento.

The novel is dedicated to friends in Salento – and to one woman in particular who is my inspiration for Rosaria, the heroine of the story. The hero, or perhaps the *'anti-hero'*, is a fifty-year-old Englishman called Adam, caught up in events for which his previous experiences leave him singularly ill-prepared. His learning curve is steep and the profound changes to his personality and outlook on life are irreversible as he is carried along by the tide of events.

The author would like to point out that specific references to businesses and people affected by mafia activities in London and Italy are fictionalised. However, the criminal activities described are *far from being fictitious. It is enough to read articles such as 'The British Connection: Italian mafia finds UK good for doing business,' to realise that the presence of the mafia on the streets of London is already well-established. (The Observer, Sunday 27th December 2009)*

Names chosen for the characters in the novel are common names in Italy – there is no intentional reference to anyone who might bear the same name. To the inhabitants of a certain road in St John's Wood, I apologise but I took care to ensure that the house number chosen does not exist.

1: *The Mystery of the Missing Cousin*

Rosaria Miccoli was standing in the street outside the family home. She was peering through the narrow slit in the letter box to see if there was anything of interest inside before ferreting for the tiny key which would be somewhere in the depths of her handbag. Yes, there *was* a letter there instead of the usual flyers which the local supermarkets constantly distributed, depicting the current week's irresistible discounts on anything from Parma ham to toilet rolls. The unemployed teenagers who were paid a pittance to deliver the leaflets could not usually be bothered to push them inside the letter boxes, so they flew off into the gutters or became wedged in the bushes. Rosaria decided that it was worth going to the trouble of unlocking the letter box to see who had written to them.

As she was delving into the bottom of her handbag, she was wolf-whistled and hooted at by a pair of youths driving past in a battered Alfa Romeo a good few years older than they were. At twenty-nine years of age, Rosaria did not deign to turn round in acknowledgement of the intended compliment from a pair of spotty, vulgar boys. This form of tribute happened so many times in the space of a day whenever she walked down the street that it had become merely tedious. In the council offices where she worked, the admiring looks were usually more covert and the compliments more subtle. Not always, she had to admit. For a time, when she had first started working there, she had had to put up with 'help' whenever she used the photocopier from a lascivious younger colleague who pressed his attentions on her – literally – in his desperation to assist this beautiful newcomer to decipher the complexities of the machine's electronic display. Even by local standards of male permissiveness, his self-indulgence went well beyond the bounds of acceptability. After a week of his unflagging devotion, Rosaria had smiled sweetly at him and said in a voice loud enough to be heard throughout the office, 'Thank you, Giovanni, but I definitely need to *reduce* the size of everything today!' There were audible titters from her other colleagues. Giovanni had blushed to his roots and had become aloof towards her. No matter, thought Rosaria. There were plenty of other men in the office who were willing to fetch her life-saving coffees from the local bar at strategic moments during the course of a working day.

Rosaria found the tiny silver key and retrieved the letter. It was as she had surmised – a letter from England and it was addressed to her. As she turned to open the gate and began to mount the steps that led up to the front door, she heard the Alfa Romeo driving past again. The boys had apparently thought it worth their while to reverse the car and have a follow-up run on the nearside approach to get a better view. They were shouting out, asking if she was free that evening. Rosaria had the satisfaction of hearing the screech of brakes as the Alfa Romeo narrowly missed colliding with a second car which had pulled out of a side road into its path. The youths started to yell at each other and at the other driver in the coarse language of the local dialect. Rosaria's legs disappeared from view as she reached the level of the double front door.

Once in the peace of her own bedroom, she opened the envelope with great care, ensuring that the postmark was not torn. It was the fifth such letter that she had received in the space of eight or nine months from her cousin, Diletta, who had been living and working in London for the previous five years. Just under two years ago, Diletta had come back to Campanula for her summer holidays to see her family and to spend time on the miles of unspoilt sandy beaches and rocky coves which line the Salento coast. Rosaria and Diletta had grown up together and formed a bond of friendship which had survived through childhood, first boy-friend experiences and university days. They would go out together alone or with a group of mutual friends. Whenever Rosaria's sister, Martina, was home from Rome, where she was completing her Master's degree in psychology, the three of them would spend hours together on the beach or gossip endlessly over a pizza in the evenings.

It had come as shock when Diletta had announced out of the blue that she was intending to get married in the very near future. To Rosaria, the news had seemed as devastating as the outbreak of a war. The man was called Enrico and he was from Calabria. 'A Calabrian – not so good!' Rosaria had commented ironically to herself. They had met by chance, Diletta explained, while she had been visiting the Italian embassy in London where Enrico worked. Diletta was tall and attractive, with long dark hair and a perfect olive complexion. In London, at least, she stood out in a crowd. Diletta had shown her a photograph of Enrico. He could be considered handsome, she supposed, but his rough good looks carried a hint of cruelty with them. 'Capable of violence,' she had thought at the time.

'I didn't think you would choose someone like that,' she had commented to her cousin.

'Someone like *what*, Rosy?' Diletta had retorted. 'I'm twenty-eight now. I can't wait for ever. And he seems to be very secure financially,' she had added defensively. Rosaria remained unconvinced for motives that she could not quite identify.

3

Diletta and Enrico had got married soon afterwards in neighbouring Campanula, where most of her family lived. It was a relatively modest affair by Italian standards – paid for entirely by the husband. During the ceremony and the reception, Rosaria had been struck by the fact that Enrico seemed ill-at-ease whenever his photograph was taken. He was courteous enough to Diletta's mother, Rosaria's Auntie Flavia, a lady already in her fifties and a mother of five children whom she had brought into this world at regular intervals.

Rosaria had felt uncomfortable at the wedding and even more so at the reception, still unable to translate her misgivings into precise thoughts. It was significant, considered Rosaria, that none of Enrico's relatives had been present. It was as if the event had been a charade staged for the benefit of Diletta's family. After the wedding, Diletta and her husband had stayed on in Puglia for another week, during which time Rosaria and Martina had seen their cousin only once. The transformation had been disquieting. Diletta had looked cowed, edgy and scared.

Then the couple had left unexpectedly one morning without explanation. Enrico had phoned Flavia, Diletta's mother and said in his incomprehensible Calabrian dialect that he had been called back on urgent business.

'But can't I say goodbye to…?' began Diletta's mother.

'We'll be in touch as soon as possible,' Enrico said abruptly and hung up. Auntie Flavia had come straight round to see Rosaria, deeply distraught. 'There's something wrong,' she said to her niece between her tears. Rosaria knew from that moment that her own fears were not just a figment of her imagination.

The only news that they had received were these occasional letters sent sometimes to the mother but usually to Rosaria. There was never an address or phone number. The postmark was always from London but not always from the same district. The letters were written in handwriting that seemed like Diletta's but in a register that was not remotely hers. Now Rosaria was looking at the fifth such letter, which also contained a photocopied image of an ultrasound scan showing two tiny foetuses. Rosaria read the letter attentively:

Mia carissima Rosaria,

Great news! I am expecting twins as you can see from this picture. Enrico and I are thrilled. Life in London is good, so different to what you are used to in Salento. You will soon be able to come and visit me – visit the four of us! We are going to be moving house soon. Then I shall send you my phone number and address. Be patient, dear cousin. I miss you.

Hugs and kisses.

Tua Diletta x x x

It just wasn't Diletta. In the first place, Diletta had always used the familiar form of her cousin's name – Rosy – as did all of Rosaria's family and closest friends. Rosaria showed the letter and the scan to Martina and to her mother, who was a nurse. Martina tended to think that her elder sister was being paranoid. But Rosaria's mother looked at the scan and immediately said: 'These scans *always* show the mother's name above the image. There is *no* name on this one. It's been cut off. That *is* strange!'

Her mother's words were decisive for Rosaria. Now she was certain there was something seriously wrong. For the first time, she feared that her cousin might be in real danger. However, she needed to convince her sister too.

Rosaria and Martina gave strength and moral support to each other in ways that only close sisters can do. They were both enviably beautiful but quite different physically. Martina was smaller boned than Rosaria, taking more after their mother. Martina had jet black hair whereas her sister had brown hair. This posed a daily problem for Rosaria, who was never quite sure which shade of brown to try out whenever her hairdresser came round. Looking very closely at Rosaria, it could be seen that she had an ever-so-slightly crooked nose – the result of a childhood accident when Martina had hurled a wooden shoe across the room. By sheer fluke, the shoe had struck her sister smartly across the bridge of her nose. More than twenty-five years later, this tiny blemish went by unnoticed by all except Rosaria herself. She had forgiven her sister ages ago. Martina had a harder edge to her character – undoubtedly the result of living away from home for a number of years.

A photograph of Martina hung on the wall in Rosaria's bedroom. She was wearing professionally applied make-up which highlighted the precision of her features and the oriental slant of her charcoal black eyes. Martina had recently taken part as an 'extra' on a film set – a TV hospital drama series called *Mio padre è medico* – My Father, the Doctor. There is a brief shot of Martina as she pushes a trolley laden with medicines along a white corridor, giving rise to the fleeting illusion to viewers that a hospital must be a desirable place in which to suffer. One of the other extras on the

6

film set, a gormless youth lying on a bed with his head bandaged, had said to Martina: 'I would contract a serious illness tomorrow if I could be nursed by someone like you!'

'Why wait until tomorrow?' Martina had retorted and walked scornfully away leaving the crestfallen young man protesting feebly that he had only wanted to pay her a compliment.

Martina slipped into her sister's bedroom where Rosaria was looking pensively at the letter and the scan. Her brow was deeply furrowed.

'What are you thinking about, Rosy?' she asked, knowing full well what the answer would be.

'I'm thinking about how to save Diletta, Marti. I just *know* there's something wrong.'

Martina was momentarily tempted to smile at the dramatic manner in which Rosaria had expressed herself. But her mother's matter-of-fact comment about the scan not bearing the expectant mother's name had given her serious pause for thought. Maybe her sister's fears were, after all, justified.

'Well, *you* are the detective among us, Rosy. I trust your instincts,' said Martina with a shade more conviction than in the past.

2: The Making of Inspector Miccoli

Rosaria's reputation as a 'detective' was well-established amongst her circle of friends and even with a number of her work colleagues. She had earned herself the nickname of *Commissario Miccoli*, a title which she dismissed modestly but felt secretly flattered by. It had all started quite by accident a few years ago when a group of them had gone to a discotheque in nearby Gravino. Rosaria, Martina, Diletta, Benedetto – Rosaria's *fidanzato* of ten years' standing – and a number of other friends were present.

Diletta had trustingly left her handbag on the long padded bench next to a pink anorak belonging to one of the girls in another group while she, Diletta, went on to the dance floor to 'warm up' as she put it. When Diletta and the others returned, she opened her handbag to look for a paper tissue.

'Rosaria,' she said with alarm in her voice, 'my purse has gone. I had everything in it – money, keys, credit card, my ID card...' Her voice tailed off close to tears.

Rosaria had not wasted time with pointless questions. She remembered seeing the girl wearing the pink anorak going off hurriedly in the direction of the cloakroom only minutes beforehand while her party was on the dance floor. When she returned, she had no pink anorak with her. The girl sat down again, laughing and chatting to her group of friends. Rosaria concluded within seconds that she must have taken her anorak to the cloakroom. 'Why?' she wondered. There was only one explanation possible.

'Come and dance, Rosy,' ordered Benedetto imperiously.

'Not for the moment, Benedetto. I don't feel like dancing. You go!'

With a sour look on his face, he went on to the dance floor again with Angela, a decidedly podgy girl in her late twenties who obviously had a serious crush on him. '*And* you, Diletta,' Rosaria added with authority. 'I need a minute or so on my own. I think I know where your purse is.' Diletta looked strangely at Rosaria but did as she was told.

Rosaria waited until the group of girls, including Pink-Anorak-Girl, had decided to return to the dance floor. There was a popular number playing and everyone headed instinctively towards the rhythmic mass of dancing bodies. Pink-Anorak-Girl even smiled at Rosaria and looked meaningfully at her handbag, as if to say: 'Keep an eye on it for me, please'.

Rosaria returned the smile and nodded guilelessly at her. It took ten seconds for Rosaria's nimble fingers to open the handbag, find the numbered cloakroom ticket and snap the handbag shut again, taking care to leave it in its original position. She strode with a confidence that she did not feel towards the exit and the cloakroom. 'Toilet,' she said mouthing the word to Benedetto, who was watching her resentfully from the dance floor. Angela was trying to dance as close to him as her ample bosom would allow, to Benedetto's obvious discomfort.

When Rosaria reached the cloakroom, the attendant was nowhere to be seen. He was in a kitchenette at the back of the cloakroom whence he had lured a newly acquired boyfriend of seventeen whom he was in the process of softening up prior to seduction. Rosaria could not afford to hang around. She could plainly see the pink anorak with its fluffy white collar barely an arm's length away from her. In an instant, she had lifted the hatch and was feeling through the pockets. She had worked out logically that, if there was a purse in the anorak pockets, it could only belong to Diletta. She had discovered Pink-Anorak-Girl's own purse – a pink one – in her handbag on the padded seat. Success! She was removing the purse when the cloakroom attendant, alerted by some movement, emerged from his cubby hole. He was a good-looking lad of about twenty-two. Rosaria noted with interest the obvious erection through his tight jeans and saw the look of frustration and mild embarrassment on his face. She smiled her most dazzling smile and stepped towards him, the cloakroom ticket already proffered.

'I'm sorry,' she said, all sweet innocence. 'I thought there was nobody here. I needed my purse, you see.'

The young man, being of the opposite persuasion, had not taken a lot of notice of the dark-haired girl who had handed in her pink anorak only minutes beforehand. But he was not unintelligent in a predatory way and Rosaria could see the shadow of doubt that crossed his face. Rosaria smiled again taking another step towards him, near enough for him to take an involuntary step backwards.

'Don't worry,' said Rosaria in a confiding manner. 'I won't tell anyone the cloakroom was unattended.' Before he could react, she had let herself out through the hatch without a backward glance. The cloakroom attendant shrugged and returned to more engaging pursuits. But his concentration had been broken and he had to keep a more obvious lookout from his post at the back of the cloakroom, thereby delaying a boy's complicit corruption for a while longer.

Rosaria returned to her seat. Good! Everybody was still busy dancing. But Benedetto noticed her return and broke free from the devouring eyes of Angela with a gesture that was supposed to indicate that he was tired. Pink-Anorak-Girl was still deeply involved with her gyrating body and Rosaria managed to slip the cloakroom ticket back into her handbag. She clipped the clasp shut just as Benedetto reached her.

'What are doing, Rosy?' he asked reprovingly. 'Going through other people's belongings?' It was rare for Benedetto to be able to feel morally superior to his *fidanzata* and he was hoping to savour the moment. Rosaria glared at him with the most withering look at her disposal.

'Trust *you* to jump to conclusions without thinking first,' she snapped.

'But I'm not blind, Rosy,' he persisted unwisely.

'Mentally, you are!' she retorted. Rosaria reserved her triumphant smile for Diletta and the rest of the group as they arrived. 'Here you are, Diletta – your purse. Check to see if there's anything missing.'

Diletta beamed at her cousin. 'Rosy, you're amazing. How did you...? Where did you...?'

Rosaria could see Pink-Anorak-Girl returning with her friends. 'I'll explain later,' she said.

Benedetto looked crestfallen and attempted an apology. 'I'm sorry, Rosy. I didn't realise... Of course, I knew you wouldn't really...'

She cut him off by standing up and heading resolutely for the dance floor, her close-fitting skirt and the movement of her legs and buttocks far more eloquent than any reproof. Benedetto followed as if attached to an invisible leash. Rosaria soon became caught up in the next dance. She danced with a natural rhythm, every muscle in her body responding to the beat of the music as if she had become an extension of each pulse of the melody. Benedetto danced well for a man and soon Rosaria managed a forgiving smile. After all, she realised, she would have come to the same conclusion if circumstances had been reversed. There would be time for recriminations later on when she might need the excuse not to succumb to his amorous advances on the way home.

Rosaria and company continued to drink coca-colas and dance well into the early hours. Pink-Anorak-Girl and friends had left soon after midnight. They were still of high school age so their parents had obviously set a time limit on their outing. Pink-Anorak-Girl reached the cloakroom to reclaim her garment. The cloakroom attendant looked at her more keenly this time. No, it was definitely not the same person whom he had caught going through the pockets earlier on. Pink-Anorak-Girl put her hand into the pocket. The expression of mild shock on her face was palpable.

'Is there anything wrong?' asked the attendant anxiously.

'My...' she began. But the complications that would arise flashed through her mind in an instant. 'No, nothing wrong,' she said.

Back inside, Diletta looked at Rosaria and asked her what had happened. Rosaria explained publicly what had led her to the conclusion that she had arrived at and how she had retrieved the purse. She was roundly applauded by the whole group for her powers of observation and her prompt action.

'You should have been a private investigator, Rosy,' another girl in their group, Sara, had joked with admiration in her voice. Angela entertained the mean thought that the whole episode had been too pat, that Rosaria had staged the whole episode for dramatic effect. Or worse…! Rosaria understood by the expression on Angela's face what was passing through her mind. But she knew that it was her envy which had provoked the thought rather than mistrust.

'No, Angela,' she said quietly. 'Don't worry. It wasn't like that.'

'*Mio Dio!* She can read minds as well,' thought poor Angela.

On the way out, the cloakroom attendant gave Rosaria an accusing look. Rosaria merely wagged her finger from side to side and gave him a shrewd look of accusation as if to say: 'I know what you are thinking and you are mistaken.' The attendant merely shrugged and said nothing.

So it had come about that the germ of an idea had been sown in Rosaria's mind. Discovering the secret motives that drove people's desire to conceal the truth fascinated her. She was shrewd and a very good judge of character. Being an amateur sleuth had become a sort of hobby when her regular job did not present a sufficient challenge. She became very adept at using modern technology to aid her 'investigations'. Whereas most people found electronic gadgets daunting, Rosaria had the knack of understanding how to use them after a few exploratory attempts.

It had taken one more public incident, shortly after thwarting Pink-Anorak-Girl, to establish Rosaria's reputation among her immediate entourage. After that, all sorts of people would come to her with minor problems that they were unwilling or unable to solve on their own – from suspected infidelities to checking their tax returns.

The same group of friends had gone out to a pizzeria one evening, to celebrate somebody's birthday. Rosaria was waiting for Benedetto to return from Lecce where 'his' team had been playing a home match against Rome. She knew from experience that the result of this football match would determine Benedetto's mood for the remainder of the evening. If Lecce had lost – which happened quite often – Benedetto would expect sympathy or else he tended to become even more overbearing than usual.

That evening, there was a girl in the group called Cinzia accompanied by her *fidanzato*, Andrea. She was tall and very pretty but a little willowy, in Rosaria's opinion, and easily dominated by her more extrovert fiancé. At one juncture, Andrea's mobile rang. As soon as he had said *'pronto'* into the mouthpiece, a look of guilt had momentarily crossed his face. He excused himself from the group and, turning to Cinzia, he said to her, with a forced expression of remorse: 'It's my boss.' This was unlikely, thought Rosaria, as it was a Sunday evening.

Cinzia looked anxiously at Rosaria. 'I'm worried, Rosy. I'm sure Andrea is seeing someone else.' The look of appeal on her face was a cry for help which Rosaria could not resist.

'Leave it to me, Cinzia,' she said.

As soon as Andrea returned to the group, Rosaria pointedly went through the act of making a call on her mobile. *'Accidenti!'* she said, addressing Andrea. 'What a nuisance! I haven't got any credit left. Can I borrow your mobile for a minute, Andrea? I'm a bit concerned about Benedetto. He should be here by now.'

Rosaria had such a natural and beguiling manner when asking for small favours that other people felt it was almost a privilege to help her. She beamed her thanks excusing herself as she moved away from the group to make her 'private phone call'. From that distance, she appeared to be   dialling a number for an outgoing call. In reality, her nimble fingers had selected the incoming calls key. She had developed the ability to memorise numbers instantly. All she needed to do after that was to go through the pretence of having a brief conversation with Benedetto before handing back the mobile to an unsuspecting Andrea. She entered the memorised number on her phone while it was still fresh in her mind.

Benedetto obligingly arrived a few minutes later. '2-1 to Lecce!' he announced triumphantly to everybody. Rosaria breathed an inward sigh of relief and began to consider how she should proceed with the next step of her new investigation.

Before the group split up for the night, Rosaria led an unsuspecting Cinzia to one side and spoke to her quietly. 'Are you sure, Cinzia, that you want to know who Andrea was phoning? Of course, there is probably a perfectly innocent explanation for the call he received, but there again...'

Cinzia was clearly hesitating, tempted to leave matters as they were and continue to hope for the best. To Rosaria's surprise, she plucked up the courage to say:

'Rosy, we are supposed to be getting married in September. I have to know if he is seeing someone else, don't I? I just have an uneasy feeling, that's all. Yes, Rosy, I want to put my mind at rest.'

Rosaria smiled at her friend and gave her a *bacio* on each cheek. She was undecided whether to risk a direct phone call to the number she had lifted from Andrea's phone or whether to send a subtly worded text message. She decided she should sleep on it. *La notte porta consiglio* seemed a very wise saying at that moment late in the evening. She managed to avoid anything more serious than a good night kiss from Benedetto, who seemed more excited by Lecce winning a match than by the prospect of a hurried coupling in the back of his old FIAT *Cinquecento*.

When she woke up the following morning, Rosaria had a clear plan in her mind. She would phone the unknown caller directly, choosing the right moment. Rosaria had learnt that people were generally less on their guard when they were at home in the morning. She would phone just after eight o'clock. Any earlier and the person would be irritated by the intrusion. Any later and they would be on their way to work. It was best to catch people as they were enjoying their first coffee of the day.

Rosaria took a deep breath and at exactly seven minutes past eight, as she was drinking her own first cup of coffee, she dialled the number of Andrea's unknown caller. She prayed silently that she had remembered the number correctly as the ringing tone began to sound.

'*Pronto,*' said a young woman's voice.

'May I speak to Andrea, please?' asked Rosaria in her most engaging voice?

'Andrea?' replied the girl abruptly. 'There is nobody by...' Rosaria had been ready for that.

'Yes, Andrea di Giorgio,' she interrupted giving Andrea's surname There was a marked pause on the other end of the line as the girl tried to digest this unexpected information. Then the girl made the unconscious mistake of saying: 'Andrea doesn't live *here.*' Rosaria picked up on the subtle shift of intonation and it told her what she wanted to know.

'Oh dear,' said Rosaria with embarrassment in her voice. 'Andrea must have given me the wrong number by mistake.'

'Yes, I think he *did,*' replied the girl, irritation rising in her voice. Rosaria was on the point of making a tactical withdrawal when an extra piece of good fortune came her way. A male voice in the background could be heard saying: 'Who is it, Valeria?'

'Shhh!' the girl said urgently. But it was too late. Rosaria apologised once more saying that she would have a stern word with Andrea when she next saw him. Then she rang off quickly before the girl began to become suspicious. Valeria had been taken off guard. Rosaria had managed to confirm that, yes, the number belonged to another girl and that this Valeria knew Andrea and did not want to admit it. Finding out her name had been an extra bonus.

The information that Rosaria had extracted was put to excellent use. After a showdown that left Andrea with a markedly higher level of respect for his *fidanzata,* he had promised to take his pre-nuptial commitments seriously. The couple had duly become man and wife, with Rosaria a guest of honour.

* * * * *

And now, sitting on the bed with Martina by her side, Rosaria was frowning deeply. She was wondering where on earth she was going to begin. Uncovering the mystery surrounding the disappearance of her cousin and closest friend, Diletta, would be infinitely more challenging than any investigation that she had so far undertaken. Martina silently placed her hand over her sister's hand. She could think of nothing helpful to say.

It might have helped them both to know that the course events would take, from that moment onwards, was already ordained to happen in that nebulous time zone which we think of as the future. In some small measure, the unfolding of these events would involve an unsuspecting Englishman currently living just outside London.

3: A Man Called Adam in Search of a New Life

'But why on Earth would you want to go and do *that* again, Adam? Last time you did it, you got the sack and swore you would never go and teach in Italy again.' declared Adam's ex-wife with the usual note of scorn in her voice. This was the tone which she adopted whenever she considered that his behaviour bordered on the irrational, or worse, was the direct result of his severe mental and emotional instability. In her opinion, her ex-husband had displayed all of these traits every time he had been unfaithful to her, leading inexorably to the breakdown of their marriage.

Adam, naturally enough, did not share this interpretation of his moral waywardness. He had managed to convince himself that his infidelities were provoked by the notable lack of compatibility that existed between himself and his spouse, despite the existence of two beautiful sons. It had to be admitted that, to date, his quest for an ideal partner had not yielded the soul-mate he so desired. At heart, Adam belonged to that dangerous category of men, erroneously described as 'romantic'. Consequently, he tended not to form relationships that were based on anything concrete or realistic. Thus, his subsequent partners had been either too young or married women who had wanted to escape for a while from the routine of conjugal life. He was disturbed to discover that none of his new relationships lasted more than a couple of years. Had he been more astute and understood his own nature a bit better, he would have realised that his choice of 'ideal partner' had a built in expiry date, which guaranteed that he would never actually have to commit himself long term.

At fifty-one years of age, Adam was passably good-looking – even if he himself was singularly unaware of the fact. He had lost the skinny, boyish, acne-inflicted aspect of growing up that had haunted him throughout his adolescence and early adult years. As a teenager, he had nurtured a secret longing to look like Paul Newman, but had ended up looking more like a watered-down version of George Clooney. His self-esteem regarding his physical appearance had not been helped by teaching school children who nicknamed him Mr Bean. He was assured by the few colleagues who cared for his feelings that the nickname was intended to be affectionate and was born out of his pupils' fascination with the various facial contortions that became manifest whilst he attempted to make them pronounce French and Italian words convincingly.

Adam's arrival to manhood had been retarded by being brought up by a loving but religiously over-zealous Catholic mother, who had inflicted on her impressionable son, regular visits to the confessional, weekly pudding-basin haircuts, long shorts reaching just below knee-level and an insistence that he should become an altar boy – all for the good of his immortal soul. Although Adam had superficially rejected these unwelcome impositions by his early twenties, there remained a deep-seated belief that sexual attraction was taboo and that he himself was largely repulsive to the opposite sex. He was, therefore, often filled with something akin to disbelief and excessive gratitude when any woman showed signs of being physically attracted to him.

Having reached adulthood – at least in terms of years spent on Planet Earth - the only aspect of his life which he felt remotely confident about was the fact that he had become a good teacher. Adam's skills in the classroom were, unfortunately, not enough to endear him to the school's recently appointed head teacher – a gentleman called Mr Norman, who had hailed from an army background. As a result, the new head had inherited very rigid ideas about uniforms. As far as Adam was concerned, if school children were universally expected to adopt this remnant of England's glory days as a military force, there was little he could do about it except feel sympathy towards his pupils. But when, during summertime, the temperatures in badly ventilated classrooms soared to 28 degrees Celsius, Mr Norman insisted that male teachers must continue to wear ties, Adam went immediately and fatally into rebellious mode.

Adam had conceived a dislike for Mr Norman from an early stage. He had the distinct impression that this gentleman found disciplining his teaching staff a softer option than bringing recalcitrant pupils to heel. He could always wield the threat of dismissal over his staff, whereas the average miscreant pupil did not particularly care which secondary school regime he (or indeed she) had to suffer under. Mr Norman conceived an equal dislike for his maverick Head of Languages, whom he regarded as a spanner in the works of an otherwise smoothly running machine. After one particularly bad and very public run-in with Adam, Mr Norman was purported to have said to his two deputies: 'Who will rid me of this turbulent teacher?' or words to that effect.

The trouble had flared up at a staff meeting during which the main item under discussion had been precisely the matter of enforcing the rigid dress code during the 'unusually hot summer'.

'Boys should continue to observe the rule about the wearing of ties,' insisted Mr Norman.

'What - even during sports' lessons?' Adam had unwisely piped up. He was gratified to see the colour of the head teacher's face turn a shade of puce.

'Don't be facetious with me, Mr Knight! And naturally, in order to set a proper example to the boys, teachers will be expected to wear ties as usual,' persisted Mr Norman, his military blinkers firmly back in place.

'That amounts to sexual discrimination,' declared Adam, whose risk-taking sense of injustice had been aroused. 'Why should I wear one metre's worth of strangulation round my neck when the ladies are allowed to go around with open top blouses?' It might have been the case that Mr Norman had a strong preference for Imperial measurements. But whatever his reasons, he roundly accused Adam of being 'unprofessional' and said that he would see him in his office later. Adam took this as a dismissal, and left the staff room amidst a deadly hush.

The threatened summons did not arrive until three weeks later. Adam was harangued by Mr Norman plus his male and female deputies, who subjected Adam to a verbal drubbing which, they hoped, would reduce him to a humiliated pulp. No such luck! Adam, roused, had no fear of authority imposed from above. The subsequent exchange of words was heated and mutual recriminations rebounded off Mr Norman's study walls like a ball in a squash court. The conflict revealed no outright victor.

In the end, it was Adam himself who managed to overstep the mark without any outside help, thereby giving Mr Norman the excuse he needed to rid himself of this intransigent member of staff. Adam had decided to take his revenge on Mr Norman by putting on a cabaret evening in French for parents and pupils –

plus anyone else who wished to attend. It was a very successful, though marginally *risqué* evening, enjoyed almost universally. However, Adam had failed to appreciate that asking a sixth form girl to perform a mock striptease would give Mr Norman just the ammunition he needed. In point of fact, the girl, wearing a leotard throughout her short performance, was backlit onto a white screen, so that all the audience could see was her appealing silhouette. After a minute or so of miming the removal of a few outer garments, she was chased off the scene by a cat-like shadow to the signature tune of the Pink Panther. The performance was greeted with enthusiastic applause by young and old alike – with the exception of Mr Norman, who, nevertheless, came to both performances just to be sure that the act really *was* bordering on the indecent. The local press had not been invited.

The following week, Adam was invited by Mr Norman to apply for a vacant post at the local Further Education College. He was successful at the interview, but was greatly helped by the fact that he was the sole candidate. Mr Norman had given the college principal a glowing report as to Adam's professional abilities, stressing how cooperative he was towards those in authority.

Adam was delighted to be rid of Mr Norman in equal measure to Mr Norman's pleasure at seeing the back of Adam. Working in a college environment was akin to paradise – at least for a few years. There were no bells at the end of each lesson, no uniforms and no detentions. Above all, there were no morning assemblies, which had been a frequent bone of contention between Adam and his superiors. It had not been judicious, Adam had to concede afterwards, to make public claims whenever he had been forced to conduct an assembly that the Catholic church was the only true church – especially not in a Church of England school. His papist tendencies were added to the list of his other failings. At least, he had ensured that he would never have to conduct another assembly.

At the college, all the students were over sixteen and addressed their teachers by their first names. Even better, he found himself teaching adults in the evenings. It was as near to paradise as a teacher could hope for, thought Adam, grateful for his stroke of good fortune. Even his new Head of Faculty was the world's perfect boss. Adam respected him unreservedly and found he had lost the desire to be conflictual.

The cliché that 'all good things come to an end' is, regrettably, very true and was certainly true in Adam's case. The College Principal had retired and was replaced by a new one who nobody in charge saw eye to eye with. This was doubly true of Adam's Head of Faculty, Bernard, who became increasingly critical of the new regime. Bernard was such a 'comfortable' person to work for. Even his name conjured up images of dogs carrying life-saving cognac barrels round their necks, or friendly uncles always there to encourage their nephews. The new managerial strata took umbrage at the criticism levelled against them by this outspoken Head of Faculty. It was suggested that there was no place for the likes of anyone called Bernard in the great new scheme of things. Bernard agreed and accepted a retirement deal.

This left Adam and the languages section at the mercy of a scheming harpy called Marjory. His old antagonism towards those in authority over him was immediately rekindled. He nicknamed her Marjory 'Rubberstamp' which was a neat corruption of her real surname and one which coincided with Adam's conviction that she had been appointed by the new senior management to carry out their directives without question – regardless as to whether they had any relevance to education.

Her first act of tyranny was to move all the modern languages section into an office in the remotest part of the college she could find. The room had formerly been a boys' toilet. His staff moved meekly into their new quarters without a word of protest. Adam refused to budge on the grounds that their new cubby hole contravened fire regulations. 'There should be a glass window in the door and the fire alarm should be audible,' he told Rubberstamp haughtily. 'Until that is put right, I refuse to move into that cupboard that you have seen fit to allocate us. It is patently obvious,' he added, delivering the *coup de grâce* as far as their working relationship was concerned, 'that you do not speak a word of any other language and have no concept at all as to the importance of foreign languages in the college curriculum.'

She fumed and swore vengeance but was obliged to go to the new management to ask them to carry out the modifications, since it was obvious that Adam was technically correct. Adam duly moved into his new accommodation. His next step was to point out to his new boss that the room, having been nothing more than a toilet with a lick of paint on the walls, had no number on the door. 'Without a number, our students can't find us because they don't know where to look,' he told her.

'SO GIVE IT A NUMBER, ADAM!' snorted Rubberstamp in reply.

Adam did just that and, after due research, became famous, or notorious, throughout the college, for attaching the numbers SIX followed by a NINE on to the door of their 'toilet'. It is doubtful whether Rubberstamp ever appreciated the significance of the number '69' – but nearly everyone else did. He cherished the hope that she would remain in perpetual ignorance of such secret intimacies.

Matters would have continued to deteriorate but, once again, Adam had a stroke of good fortune. It was at a time when the government was offering early retirement to any lecturer over fifty – based on the short-sighted view that a lot of money could be saved by getting rid of the better paid and, incidentally, more experienced members of the profession. After a great deal of soul-searching, Adam accepted the generously compensated offer. Rubberstamp claimed that she was delighted for him and became almost friendly at the prospect of his imminent departure. Adam decided that he preferred her hostility to the hypocrisy of her cloying friendliness. He left without a single word in her direction. Silence, he reckoned, was more eloquent than words.

4: *Re-educating Adam*

Adam felt a free man all of a sudden. He was under no obligation to teach another lesson in his life. So, naturally, he decided to carry on teaching. In essence, it was just like Mr Norman making him wear a tie. As soon as he began working in the college, where nobody bothered how teachers dressed, Adam had felt free to wear a tie whenever he felt like it. However, he decided that it was time to stop teaching other people's languages. With a few thousand pounds sterling safely tucked away in his bank account, Adam set about gaining a qualification as a teacher of English as a Foreign Language - the passport to almost anywhere in the world. He assumed, rather over-confidently, that obtaining this qualification would be a doddle for an experienced languages teacher such as himself, used to organising school trips abroad, striptease shows and so on.

There followed four long, arduous weeks of almost total humiliation. The first week was rendered even more traumatic since it coincided with an all-out tube strike, which made the trip up to London to reach the Teacher Training Centre near Piccadilly more like an orienteering course. He felt drained even before the course had begun.

The first thing that struck Adam was the age of his fellow students. They were all 'sweet young things' who had barely graduated from university. They had swotted up beforehand on their Present Perfects, Past Simples and Past Posteriors and so on, leaving Adam feeling inadequate. The teaching staff were, on the whole, five minutes older than the students and fired up with something akin to religious zeal. It was their mission to convert all those ignorant, tenderfoot, would-be English teachers to the doctrines of Teaching English as a Foreign Language.

After his first practice session with a group of mixed nationality students, he was publicly shamed by a High Priestess of the school who used Adam's fifteen minute contribution to the lesson as an excellent example of how not to conduct an English lesson. The sweet young things sat in their chairs nodding sagely at the High Priestess's divine utterances. Adam was praying that the floor would open up beneath him.

'What did you do before you came on this course, Adam?' asked the lady in a tone of voice which suggested that he might as well have been a road sweeper or a public toilet attendant.

'I was a French teacher,' he replied in a strangulated whisper which he hoped the sweet young things would not hear.

'Ah, a languages teacher!' exclaimed the HP, raising her voice and infusing the words with as much contempt as she could muster. 'They are *always* the worst.'

What was fundamentally wrong with Adam's lesson? 'You talked too much!' stated the High Priestess, a woman in her early thirties called Ms Youleha, or something which sounded similar.

'But I am the *teacher!*' replied Adam feebly.

'Yes, you *are*,' continued the HP. 'But who needs to learn English most - you or the students?' It was obviously a rhetorical question. Thus Adam learnt the first of the **'Thou shalt nots...'** of the EFL teaching world: 'Thou shalt not monopolise the lesson.'

As Adam thought about this over the next few days, he came to the conclusion that there was a large amount of truth in what the HP had so disparagingly declared in front of the whole class. He began the humbling process of revaluating his teaching techniques.

Half way through the course, his tutor, Matthew, who spent his leisure time streaking up and down the Fells in the Lake District, informed him that he might just possibly not fail the course if he avoided making too many errors in the remaining two weeks. 'Great news!' thought Adam ironically.

At this point, he might easily have thrown in the towel, but was saved by a timely interview with an intelligent but eccentric gentleman from Vicenza by the name of Mr Beardsley. John Beardsley happened to own an English language school in that city – half way between Venice and Verona, famous for its Palladian architecture. Adam had sent off his *curriculum vitae* even before the course in Piccadilly had begun. In the turmoil of the first two weeks of his ordeal by humiliation, he had forgotten that he had applied for the post.

The interview was to take place in West Kensington Town Hall during Adam's lunch break. He would miss the first session of the afternoon at the school. He was very condescendingly granted an hour off by the High Priestess and company, who let it be known that they did not approve of their victims absenting themselves for even one minute of the precious and formative time spent in their care. 'Tough!' thought Adam, who then had to consider the awful possibility that his years spent as a French teacher might count for nothing in the eyes of Mr John Beardsley. So he swallowed his pride and thanked the HP profusely for her generosity in allowing him to deprive himself of her words of wisdom for such a protracted period of time. He omitted to point out that she had no jurisdiction over his lunch break, which would account for nearly half of his absence. Neither she nor his tutor, Matthew-the-fell-walker, wished him good luck. But one of the 'sweet young things', an Italian girl called Maria, hoped the interview went well and gave him a rapid *bacio* on his cheek – a gesture for which Adam, of course, felt inordinately grateful.

Mr John Beardsley had a moustache despite what his surname might have suggested. It was reassuring to discover that he was almost exactly the same age as Adam himself. Adam was handed some photocopied sheets taken from an English language text book. John Beardsley advised him to study them in preparation for his interview while he, JB, interviewed another candidate. Adam had the distinct impression that his course had not quite prepared him for the grammar points covered in his interview material. The EFL world into which he had ventured was obviously full of traps and pitfalls for those who dared to assume that it was sufficient to be a native speaker to teach one's own language. He need not have been concerned. He realised later on that JB loved to pontificate and needed to feel that he knew more than his teachers in matters linguistic. Adam's relative ignorance of the intricacies of English grammar worked to his advantage. After an interminable ten minutes of suspense, JB ushered him into the interview room. He found himself in the Council Chamber occupying one seat among thirty empty chairs round a vast oval table. JB conducted the interview on the hoof, walking restlessly round the table munching a Tesco's tuna and mayonnaise sandwich whilst firing a series of unanswerable questions at his luckless candidate. This left Adam with the choice of either swivelling his head round at impossible angles to look politely at his 'interlocutor' (A word which, he had noticed, the High Priestess was very fond of using) or staring straight at the Council Chamber wall opposite him, waiting for JB to come into his line of vision.

Adam drifted back to Piccadilly to complete the afternoon session with ambiguous feelings. Mr John Beardsley's parting words had been: 'Oh, we will probably give you a job,' and 'There's a pub in Vicenza which serves an excellent Theakstons'. Adam decided that, if anything, he ought to feel positive about the outcome of his interview. At the same time, he was beginning to have doubts as to whether teaching in the JB school was a sane course of action in view of the owner's apparently eccentric tendencies.

The Italian sweet young thing came up to Adam at the end of the afternoon session. 'How did your interview go?' she enquired – sweetly.

'Let me buy you a coffee, Maria, and I'll tell you all about it,' suggested Adam. She was amused by the account, which Adam embellished here and there for comic effect. He took pleasure in Maria's laughter. In some obscure way, looking at Maria and chatting to her, led him to believe that accepting JB's offer – if it was made – was the right step to take in his new life. On the strength of his brief acquaintance with this one Italian girl, he came to the conclusion that there was something agreeably natural and appealing about Italian girls in general. Before they went their separate ways, Maria gave him another *bacio*, on each cheek this time. That clinched it for Adam.

The last two weeks of the English course passed rapidly after his interview. Ms Youleha only managed one further act of public humiliation in the aftermath of Adam's now forty-five minute long teaching practice sessions.

'If you, Adam Knight, keep on correcting every tiny error that your students make when they are speaking in public, they will end up not daring to open their mouths at all for fear of being picked upon. Give them a chance, for heaven's sake!' Thus, Adam learnt another of the Ten Thousand Commandments of EFL teaching: 'Thou shalt not correct every syllable that a student gets wrong'. Adam wished that he had done this course years ago, before he had ever begun to teach languages. He was beginning to feel a degree of gratitude towards his tormentors. He was impatient to put his new found knowledge into practice. One of the cleverest demonstrations that the Language School had devised was to make him and his fellow students learn Turkish – a language that nobody except Matthew-the-fell-walker could speak a word of. The mental agony of making sense of such foreign sounding words and then attempting to pronounce them brought vividly home to them the real pain involved in learning a new language. Adam came round to the belief that the four weeks of humiliation had been of positive benefit.

Nevertheless, he was awarded only a grudgingly given Grade C. Maria and many of the other sweet young things came out with a Grade B. Only one student, a good-looking woman in her late twenties who had spent a great deal of her energies impressing Matthew-the-fell-walker, managed to achieve the coveted Grade A.

Adam sought out Maria before leaving. 'Well done, Maria. Best of luck for the future,' he added making as if to kiss her on the cheeks as she had done to him two weeks previously. To his surprise, she pulled away quite abruptly, saying almost sadly: 'You don't understand women, do you, Adam?' And she disappeared from his life for ever before he could think of a suitable reply. It felt to Adam as if she had perceived some flaw in his psychological make-up that he was only dimly aware of. Characteristically, he took the observation to heart and he felt inexplicably saddened. Afterwards, he tried to dismiss her words as those of a naïve twenty-two year old. But a tinge of sadness remained for days afterwards – the shadow of a missed opportunity.

5: How Adam Fails to Impress JB

Adam had to wait for nearly a month before John Beardsley deigned to respond to his frantic enquiries. JB, it transpired, ran three schools dotted around the north of Italy and was deciding which one was most appropriate for Adam to work in. The lack of any certainty in his new teaching career should have forewarned Adam as to what he might expect under JB's management. In the end, JB must have decided that Adam needed to be in Vicenza under his watchful eye.

On a rainy night at the beginning of October, Adam found himself standing outside the railway station in Vicenza. It was past midnight. There was no sign of JB, who had promised to meet him off the midnight train from Venice. Doubts about his own sanity in undertaking this venture surfaced once again as he prepared to wander round a town in which he was a complete stranger in search of somewhere to sleep. At around half past midnight, JB pulled up in an old FIAT Tipo and asked Adam what his name was. It was apparent that JB had no recollection of what the person whom he had appointed looked like. When Adam had been officially identified, JB offered no apology for his lateness but took Adam's suitcase without a word and stowed it in the boot. Judging by his breath and his erratic mode of driving, JB had obviously wiled away the time waiting for Adam to arrive at his favourite pub. Fortunately, there were few other cars on the road.

JB spoke very little, imparting only essential items of information. His avowed intent, it appeared, was to deposit Adam for the night at a flat he owned in Vicenza which was currently housing the *fanciulle*, the 'young maidens', he translated for Adam's benefit. He offered no further explanation. He informed

34

Adam in a tone laden with heavy humour that he had instructed the 'maidens' to lock their bedroom doors that night, for their own safety. Presumably, thought Adam, to protect them from the rampant fifty-year-old who was going to invade their privacy.

'Tomorrow, my wife will take you to your permanent lodgings. This is just for tonight,' added JB.

'How long have you lived in Vicenza, John?' asked Adam in an attempt to kindle a conversation.

'Twenty years,' was the gruff reply. It was as if Adam had asked JB how much he had paid for his house, so grudging was the reply. Despite his twenty years spent in this small town, it became apparent that JB was having difficulty in finding the street in which his flat was located. Adam had to admit the task was difficult since this residential area was divided up into a bewildering system of one way streets. The effect of the Theakstons only made matters worse. They drove down a darkened street whose pavements were lined with a glittering array of Ladies of the Night. '*Le lucciole,*' said JB in a voice tinged with embarrassment. 'They are called *glowworms,*' he explained. 'Because they come out at night,' he added needlessly to a fascinated Adam. When, eventually, JB found the right street, he could not remember the house number and had to walk up and down the street trying the entrance key in all the doors until he found the one which his key fitted. 'This is the one,' he announced with inebriated confidence. Once inside the flat, JB went 'Shhhh!' so loudly that Adam started in alarm. Having shown Adam his room, JB muttered a curt 'goodnight' followed by the injunction that Adam should present himself at the school the following morning at nine o'clock. 'But where is the school?' asked Adam in an urgent whisper.

35

JB replied, saying something that sounded like 'Thomas's sins will take you!' as he stumbled out into the night, leaving Adam with a feeling of being abandoned before he had even started his new life. The following morning, Adam wandered into the kitchen with the aim of finding a coffee maker. Seated at the table and still wearing pyjamas, Adam found a studenty-looking young woman. She wore steel-rimmed spectacles and was unconcernedly sipping tea from a huge mug that looked like a Toby jug. She seemed unperturbed at the sight of Adam prowling around. He greeted her in Italian. She replied in Italian. After five seconds of conversation, it became obvious that neither of them was Italian. John Beardsley had neglected to inform Adam of the fact that this was the English teachers' flat. She introduced herself as Thomasin, thereby explaining JB's parting words.

'That's an unusual name,' commented Adam.

'My parents are fans of Thomas Hardy,' replied Thomasin. At first, Adam failed to see a connection between his comment and her response until she explained that Thomasin was a character from Hardy's novel, *The Return of the Native*. He was afraid that his new colleague was going to be very clever. Thomasin spoke rapidly in a nervous, staccato Yorkshire accent – which sounded, nevertheless, agreeable to the ear. They chatted about their TEFL English courses during which Adam's worst fears were realised. Thomasin had come out of her course with a Grade A. 'Oh heavens! She *is* clever!' Adam decided. She even sounded clever every time she opened her mouth. The humiliation was going to continue, no doubt, at the hands of his new colleague.

After stage one of John Beardsley's special induction course that morning, Adam was driven by Adriana, JB's classy and vivacious wife, to a flat that they had found for Adam - a bus ride's distance from the school. He lasted precisely ten days in his 'permanent' accommodation. He was supposed to share the flat with the owner, a man called Matteo Trevisan. The first disquieting thing that Adam noticed in the living room above the television set was a stone sculpture of an outsized penis. Less obvious, but equally telling, was the lavender and turquoise bathroom. But what worried Adam the most was the fact that Matteo Trevisan slept with his bedroom door invitingly wide open.

On the second evening, Adam stayed out late to have a drink with his new colleagues; a vivacious, good-looking girl called Sarah from Oxford, a strange woman of forty called Sybille whose nationality it was difficult to determine and, of course, Thomasin. When he let himself into the flat at half past eleven, Matteo Trevisan was sitting at the kitchen table with a reproachful look on his face – and an equally reproachful looking bowl of cold pasta in the place that had been laid for Adam. Matteo Trevisan was sulking – there was no other word for it. There was no way that Adam could announce tactfully that this flat was not right for him. Even less could he tell Matteo that he would be unable to provide an outlet for his sexual preferences. So Adam told him outright that he was moving out as soon as he found somewhere else to live. Signor Trevisan looked relieved and told Adam that he had already arranged for a young male student to move in the following weekend. Adam forbore to ask Matteo where he had intended the student should sleep – there were only two bedrooms.

Adam spent the rest of the academic year in a self-contained ground floor flat of a four storey house owned by a middle-aged spinster who collected stray cats. Adam counted seventeen in all.

Some had only one eye or were missing a tail. Others had only three legs. One cat belonged to Cat-Woman. It was a beautiful, sleek, grey animal which Adam assumed must be her 'familiar'.

One day when Cat-Woman was out at work, Adam explored the rest of the house. It stank of cats. Accumulated junk and decomposing clothing were strewn higgledy-piggledy over the unwashed floors. Bowls of half-eaten cat food were growing mouldy in various locations throughout the house. Cat-Woman intimated to him, at a later stage of their acquaintance, that she sometimes shared the cats' food when her pittance of a salary was running out. There was a special cats' room on the ground floor which reminded Adam of a scene from Mervyn Peake's Gormenghast trilogy. The room contained a filthy bunk bed where Cat-Woman sometimes slept. The animals were free to come and go through a window which had several panes of glass missing. What shocked Adam most was that she had put a whole tree trunk with branches in the middle of the bedroom floor. Cats were roaming freely in and out of the garden; a nightmare scene from which Adam fled to the relative normality of his own quarters. At least the rent was cheap.

Thomasin and Sarah represented sanity in contrast to the eccentricities of John Beardsley, the nightmare of Cat-Woman's living conditions and the memories of his brief ordeal *chez* Matteo Trevisan. If one took into account Sybille, the linguistically erratic English teacher, the balance seemed to come down on the side of madness. At one of JB's regular staff meetings, Sybille had announced that she was having trouble with one of her 'students' whom JB had transferred to her class. 'He is a *poisonous gift,* John,' she had stated. Thomasin had doubled up in silent mirth. JB, with great tact, referred to Sybille's troublesome student as a *poisoned chalice* by way of subtle correction. Adam ruined the effect by suggesting that Sybille had simply meant the student was a *poisonous git.* JB had scowled threateningly at Adam.

When Adam told his favourite class about Cat-Woman, they laughed uproariously. When Adam looked taken aback by their reaction, they explained that, traditionally, the people of Vicenza bear the nickname 'Cat-Eaters'. *'Vicentini-mangiagatti',* they chanted. By the end of the year, Adam counted only nine cats. Maybe there was some truth in the tradition.

On the whole, the year passed quickly. Adam believed he had adapted well to teaching English to foreigners. He began to feel more confident as he put into practice the teaching techniques that the High Priestess, his indoctrinator, had bullied him into accepting. He was constantly surprised how well the techniques worked in the classroom. Unfortunately, his relationship with JB went steadily downhill. Quite early on, JB had sworn at Adam and thrown a ball point pen at him as a result for some innocent request for enlightenment.

'I bloody well told you once already, Adam,' he declared.

'Please don't swear at me, John,' Adam said with annoying restraint.

'I'll do what I fucking like!' was JB's blunt retort. So much for an amicable relationship!

Adam had yet again succeeded in upsetting his boss. This time, he was not quite clear as to the reason. At the end of the academic year, he was not asked to return. He felt slighted and, it has to be said, humiliated. Thomasin and Sarah were invited back, but declined of their own free will. Adam joined Sybille in the ranks of the rejected.

'I wouldn't worry, Adam,' said Sarah kindly. 'JB is barking mad anyway.'

Adam was grateful for the crumb of comfort. In an odd way, he had grown quite fond of JB and his eccentric ways. But, alas, a second year in Vicenza was not to be!

On the plane back to England, Adam debated endlessly with himself as to the possible reasons for having alienated JB so completely. Was it that JB loved beer and Adam only drank wine? He had never managed to fulfil the role of drinking companion, which he suspected was what JB had been hoping for. Surely it could not have been the occasion when he had unwisely allowed himself to be seduced by a married, nymphomaniac student from the school – on a piano stool of all things? Or was it the time he had thrown a text book out of the first floor classroom window in frustration at the nonsensical content of the lessons contained in the book? Maybe it was simply that JB did not like him. Adam gave up the fruitless speculation. Back in England, he completed an advanced teaching diploma. He narrowly missed gaining a Distinction and got two percentage points higher than Thomasin, who had done the same examination by distance learning during the school year. Some of his self-esteem was salvaged, at any rate.

* * * * *

And here was Adam listening to his ex-wife pouring scorn on his plan to return to Italy only one year after the Vicenza *débâcle*. Since Adam remained silent before her verbal onslaught, she added:

'Besides, you have just bought a lovely new flat and done it up beautifully. Now you want to go back and make a mess of things all over again. You are mad!' she finished off for good measure.

'Maybe I *am* mad,' he thought. He certainly gave the impression of someone who never learnt from his own mistakes.

'Well, be that as it may,' he said quietly to her, 'I am going to teach in Puglia. But it will only be for six months. I don't suppose you would consider keeping an eye on my flat while I am away?'

'I would certainly not, Adam! This is your idea and you can stick with its consequences,' she replied and stalked off in righteous indignation.

Adam felt that her reaction was justified. He would have felt the same in her shoes.

To make matters worse, Adam's handful of Italian friends – from the north of Italy – warned him of the huge 'culture shock' that he would experience by going so far south.

'Give me an example of what you mean,' he said challenging their assertion.

'Everything, just everything!' they replied with an airy gesture of the hands. They refused to be more specific and wished him *buona fortuna* in an ominous tone of voice, as if they were secretly convinced that wishing him 'good luck' was not a powerful enough injunction to ward off the evil spirits of the place. Adam began to conjure up images of roving mafia gangs on the look-out for defenceless foreigners unwise enough to have strayed out after dark. He tried to convince himself that his Italian friends were suffering from the Northerners' widespread prejudice against their 'distant cousins' from the Deep South. After all, geographically speaking, the south of Puglia was nearer to Africa than to Milan. Quite a sobering thought!

The butterflies were fluttering busily inside his stomach. He was filled with an almost paranormal dread about the step he had rashly taken in accepting this teaching post in this unknown provincial town called Campanula. In vain did he try to convince himself that it was an extreme case of travel nerves. That part of his mind which dealt with premonition, a sense of the unknown, was telling him to prepare himself for a life-changing event. In retrospect, his qualms would prove to be well-founded, but not at all in the manner which he imagined.

And so, Adam, the reluctant hero, set off on a raw winter's day, in the closing moments of December, and headed off into the unknown, wearing a pair of corduroy trousers and a green cardigan with brown leather knobbly buttons – looking just like a typical English teacher.

6: *Gathering Clouds*

'But where are we going to start, Rosy?' asked Martina when the silence had become protracted.

Rosaria looked at her sister with a radiant smile.

'Does the *'we'* mean you really believe me now, Marti?' she said teasingly. Martina nodded after only the briefest of hesitations. Rosaria could read on Martina's face that she desperately wanted to share her convictions. But a vestige of doubt remained before she could logically accept that some terrible fate had befallen their cousin, Diletta. Rosaria urgently needed to do *something* to convince her sister that she was not merely being paranoid. Then she had a flash of inspiration.

'Can you lend me your iPhone for a minute, Marti?' The new gadget had been a present from Marcello, Martina's boyfriend in Rome. Martina tended to use it as if it was a normal cell phone without exploring its range of applications. In Rosaria's hands, the device was put through its paces within minutes.

Martina expressed her puzzlement as she handed the iPhone over to her sister.

'Just wait and see, Marti,' said Rosaria hoping and praying that her plan would work. Rosaria looked round her bedroom as she switched the device into photograph mode. 'Of course!' she thought. She took a shot of the photograph of her sister acting in the TV hospital soap. Another touch of the screen and a greatly relieved Rosaria showed Marti a close-up picture of herself from *Mio padre è medico*.

'There you are, Marti!' exclaimed Rosaria triumphantly. 'You're famous and you didn't even know it!'

'It's scary, Rosy. But how did you...?'

'It's called Google-something-or-other. You take a picture of almost anything and it will compare it with an image already on the Internet.'

'It's amazing, Rosy. But I still don't see how that is going to help us...'

Her words tailed off as she had an inkling of what her sister had in mind.

'It's a long shot, Marti. But it's worth the try. If that scan of twin embryos was a photo taken from the Internet, then it should duplicate itself exactly.

Rosaria took a careful close-up of the blue-coloured scan picture which had accompanied the letter showing the two little indents that represented two tiny human lives. After a few seconds, Rosaria was beaming victoriously at the picture that had appeared on the screen.

'There, Marti! Just look at that!'

'But it's identical!' said Martina.

'No it isn't. Look more carefully, Marti,' said her sister excitedly.

In the top corner of the new image, there was a name. It read Candy Bauman. There was a date and a reference number too. An expectant American mother had put the photo of her future twins on to the Internet for all the world to see.

'You understand what this means, don't you Marti?'

'Yes, Rosy, it means you are right and Diletta is in deep trouble.'

After a pause, Martina added thoughtfully:

'You've convinced me that Diletta might be in danger. But where do we go from here?

It was a beautiful, sunny day and they both felt the urge to be outdoors.

'Let's go to the beach somewhere quiet and draw up a plan of action,' suggested Rosaria.

They found a sandy cove just south of Gravino where the rocks jutting up through the sand provided shelter from the sea breeze. The bright sunshine was warm on the leeward side of the rocks. With towels spread out and obligatory sunglasses in place, they discussed Diletta for more than half an hour. They agreed that the first step must be to share what they had discovered with Diletta's mother, *zia* Flavia. Inevitably, they would then have to put the matter in the hands of the *carabinieri.* Rosaria did not have much faith in the police, especially since they had scant evidence to show that their cousin was in danger.

Rosaria's mobile phone rang. 'Benedetto,' she said trying to ignore the persistent Nokia theme tune. But she knew from bitter experience that Benedetto never relented on these occasions. In the end, she was obliged to rescue the phone from the depths of her copious beach bag.

'He's checking up on you again, Rosy,' said Martina with malicious enjoyment. There was no love lost between Benedetto and Martina, who was unconvinced by her sister's choice of partner. After resisting for as long as possible, Rosaria finally pressed the green key on her mobile. The daily, banal miracle of man's ability to harness the wonders of the physical universe resolved itself, as she had feared, into Benedetto's first predictable words:

'*Why didn't you answer straight away, Rosy?*'

'Because I couldn't find my phone.'

'*Where are you? Who are you with? Will I see you later?*'

'No, it's Martina's last evening before she goes back to Rome,' replied Rosaria, deliberately failing to answer his first two questions. Martina raised a quizzical eyebrow and shook her head in mock despair. She was not intending to return to Rome until the following week.

'I'll phone you back later, Benedetto,' said Rosaria with all the patience she could muster.

'Why don't you ever ask me where I am?' he persisted plaintively.

'Because I *know* where you are, Benedetto - you're at work, aren't you?'

There was a broody silence so Rosaria knew she was correct. Knowing that she would have to mollify him if the pointless conversation was ever to come to an end, she added more kindly:

'I'll phone you later, *cucciolo,* I promise.' With those words she switched off the phone and put it back into her beach bag, avoiding her sister's accusatory stare. As her nine year engagement stretched to ten, Rosaria was clinging to the relationship because there seemed little alternative on the horizon of her life. The passing of the years had added shackles to a commitment, undertaken in her teens, so that it was becoming increasingly difficult, socially and morally, to manoeuvre herself out of the situation. Indeed, the wish to do so was more unconscious than deliberate. To complicate matters, Rosaria's mother doted on Benedetto. She paid more attention to him than Rosaria herself did whenever he came round to the family home.

The interruption had broken their train of thought. As if by mutual accord, Rosaria and Martina packed up their beach gear and walked slowly back across the strand arm in arm, the warm sun resplendent on a sparkling turquoise sea; two dark angels on their way back to reality in Rosaria's distinctive new FIAT *Cinquecento* with its plum-coloured stripe on a cream-coloured body. Rosaria was disconsolate at not having formulated a clearer plan of action, little realising how darker forces were soon to intervene and lead her along paths that she could not possibly have imagined on that balmy afternoon.

As promised, she phoned Benedetto before falling asleep. She told him enthusiastically about the fifth letter from her cousin and how she had revealed the fake ultrasound scan. She was hoping for a compliment or a little encouragement from her intended husband. As usual, he was at pains to minimise anything positive she achieved. She could not expect any help from that quarter – that much was clear.

That night, before sleep overtook her, Rosaria prayed fervently for the light of inspiration to show her a way forward in her quest to save Diletta. Whatever spirits exist beyond the barrier of normal awareness, they were moved to listen to her pleas.

The following morning, Rosaria had just sat down with her mother and father in the kitchen. She was clutching the first reviving cup of coffee when Martina walked in looking ashen.

'What's the matter, Marti?' she asked anxiously. 'Are you ill?'

'No, I'm not ill. But I had the strangest dream that you can imagine - a nightmare really.'

She paused so long, trying to gather the courage to relate what she had experienced that Rosaria cried out in suppressed suspense.

'Come on, Marti! Tell us please!'

'We were all standing outside our country house,' she finally began.

'We were looking out across the meadow – the one with the well in the middle of it. All of us were there, not just the four of us. The whole family - uncles, aunts, cousins – the lot! The sun was setting and everybody was standing stock still looking at the well, as if we were waiting for something to happen. And then, suddenly it was twilight. I don't know what happened exactly, but I felt myself spinning in ever decreasing circles round the field as if I was being dragged downwards. The well was in the centre of my circles but it seemed to be below me so I felt I was falling towards it. And then, I don't know... I had to clutch on to the edge of the stone parapet round the well and I was screaming for someone to stop me falling into the well shaft...'

As Martina neared the end of her terrifying account, it was evident that she was reliving the sequence of events emotionally. Rosaria stood up and put her arm around her sister's shoulder to comfort her.

Gradually, the mood in the family kitchen returned to normality as Rosaria and her father, Umberto, got ready for work. Irene, the mother, got on with clearing away the breakfast things and Martina smiled bravely and announced that she was going to have a shower. Normality returned for a few brief hours.

'Don't forget that Flavia and Liliana are coming for lunch today,' said Irene. 'It's Flavia's birthday,' she added needlessly. Nobody had forgotten, in fact. Diletta's mother and her sister came round twice a week at least – *zia* Flavia driving an ancient FIAT Tipo with her usual reckless faith in her own immunity. Today, there would be a muted birthday lunch. Flavia was, not surprisingly, still trying to absorb the deep hurt that she felt inside. The suspense of not knowing what had befallen her daughter was far harder to bear than any news that something bad had happened to her. 'It's the uncertainty, just not knowing, that is killing me inside,' she would say repeatedly.

When the two aunts arrived at midday, they were subdued. Flavia responded distractedly to the family's birthday greetings and sat down meditatively at the table. Her next words would propel Rosaria and her family into an unfamiliar world destined to destroy the predictability of their ordered lives.

'I had a really strange dream last night,' began Flavia in a strained voice, 'a nightmare really. It was so vivid and frightening that I find it painful to tell you about it.'

'Then *I* will tell *you* what you dreamt, *zia,*' said Martina with a startling flash of intuition. By the time Martina had finished talking, Flavia had turned deathly pale.

'You have described my dream almost exactly, Marti,' she said in hushed tones, 'except for one detail, one terrifying little detail. In *my* dream, I heard Diletta calling out to me...as if she was miles away; a faint, terrified little voice coming from a distant place, like an echo. But, Marti, how in heaven's name did you know...?'

Rosaria's father had said very little about the morning's events. But then, in a dignified voice, he announced that they should assemble the whole family on their land one evening soon.

'This is more than just a coincidence,' he stated. 'Something that we do not understand is happening to us. It is not to be ignored.'

In their close-knit family, steeped in traditions which predated even Christianity nobody present considered his words to be anything other than a simple statement of fact.

7: *The Well*

Two days later, as the sun was setting in a sky already promising a thunder storm from the West, the whole clan was gathered in the orchard near the country house. Not just on the Miccoli side of the family but also the twin brothers on Irene's side of the family – Matteo and Dino. They were alive with anticipation and eagerness to act, even if they had no clear notion as to why the families had been summoned to the country estate. The twins were in their twenties, both engaged to girls from Milan, whence they had migrated without troubling themselves about going to university. Matteo and Dino were discussing whether to walk across the meadow towards the well, which had somehow become the focus of everyone's attention.

The twins were not alone in wondering what the purpose of this gathering was supposed to be. It had been largely Rosaria's infectious and single-minded enthusiasm that had got so many of the family members assembled together. Rosaria was assailed by doubts as she realised that she had no plan of action at all, driven as she had been solely by the passion of her own internal conviction.

The twins, feeling that they should do something to justify being there, publicly declared that they were going to head for the well. They broke away from the group of thirty or so family members and began, almost embarrassed by their gesture, to step beyond the fringes of the orchard. After all, it would be their impulsive cousin, Rosaria, who would look a bit silly when nothing happened, they reasoned.

It was the noise coming from behind them that first alerted everyone that something was wrong. Nobody could identify its source until they realised that it was the sound of rushing air passing through the orchard. Within the space of seconds, the gust of wind struck them with a blow like an invisible express train. Instinctively, they clung on to the trees nearest them, or to each other if there happened to be a member of the family nearer still. Some cried out in fear at this unexpected attack from the elements. The sky had grown dark and the orchard was in shadow.

'What's happening?' shouted some of the younger ones, panic in their voices, which sounded strangely distant through the roar of the wind. Then, as the first shock passed, they remembered the twins, who had stepped out beyond the protection of the trees. The twins were in trouble. The freak tornado which crossed that part of the Salento region from West to East – as they would learn from the local TV station the following day – had caught up the twins in its invisible clutches. They were screaming out in panic, their bodies leaning back at an impossible angle as they attempted to stay on their feet. The black wind carried them forward in what seemed like a spiral towards the well in the centre of the field. They clutched desperately at each other and then, finally, as they were carried forward to the well itself, they were able to cling on to the parapet. They had the sense to lie down on the ground until the tornado passed. The others looked on in horror – Flavia and Martina reliving their nightmare, which had been transformed into terrible reality. As the wind subsided, the group mobilised itself and some of them, Rosaria included, began to run towards the well. There they found two very shaken, white-faced, twins whom they helped to their feet.

Rosaria stared down into the well. 'There is something *down* there!' she stated simply to those around her. The well, Umberto said, was more than twenty metres deep. He explained that the water had not been drawn up since his own parents had lived there and worked the land.

'There is something *wrong* with this well,' reiterated Rosaria with increasing conviction. Nobody sought to contradict her.

The following morning, the family was despondent, unsure about how to react to the shocking event of the previous evening. 'We can't go down there ourselves. It's far too deep and there are no footholds left,' stated Rosaria's father quietly. Nobody dared to express openly the fearful possibility of what they might find at the bottom of the deep well shaft. It was, as ever, Rosaria who summoned up the courage and energy to take the next daunting step – which she took without a word to anyone else in the family.

* * * * *

The *vigili di fuoco* in nearby Gravino were agreeably surprised to see a beautiful young woman stride into the fire depot the following morning and ask to speak to their chief officer about an urgent matter. It had been very quiet on the incendiary front for a couple of weeks and the men were getting bored. One of the young men, marginally older than the rest, waved cheerily at her and announced that his name was Giovanni and that he was in charge.

'How can we help you, *signorina?*' he asked kindly.

'I'm not sure exactly. There's something strange going on with the well on our property. It's too deep and dangerous for us to attempt to go down it. So I've come to you for some expert help.'

There was a note of pleading in her voice which was irresistible for the young men on duty. They would have fallen over each other to help Rosaria, who bestowed a timely, dazzling smile in their direction. They dropped the playing cards on the table where they had been sitting trying to wile away the time.

'Leave your car here, *signorina,*' said one of the men jokingly. 'We'll give you a ride. Then you can show us the way.'

'Follow *my* car, *ragazzi,*' replied Rosaria invitingly. 'Try to keep up with *me!*'

That was sufficient challenge for the group of young men, all of whom would, by now, have driven their fire engine over a cliff to help out this young woman who had been sent by the gods to alleviate the monotony of the last few days. On the drive back to her town, which was a journey of no more than ten kilometres, the firemen jokingly switched on their siren whenever Rosaria's car exceeded eighty kilometres an hour. It was easy to follow her distinctive FIAT *Cinquecento* – like her, the car's appearance was unmistakable.

As they neared her own town, Montenero, Rosaria had a sudden attack of sheer panic as she realised how great her embarrassment would be if mobilising the local fire service on such a flimsy pretext all came to nothing. She regretted not telling anyone at home what she had intended to do.

'No,' she told herself sternly, 'I *know* I am right!' Nevertheless, she picked up her mobile phone from the passenger seat and called the twins in order to persuade them to come back to the family's country house. Despite not slowing down for an instant, Rosaria managed to find the relevant keys on the tiny key-pad almost without taking her eyes off the road. She reminded herself that she had been stopped and fined by the police two weeks previously for driving whilst using her mobile. But she firmly believed that she could not possibly get caught a second time. Rosaria regarded the ban on using mobile phones in the privacy of her own car as a serious infringement of personal liberty. In that respect, at least, she was like the majority of her fellow countrymen.

The twins, as soon as they heard Rosaria's voice, were quick to detect her anxiety. Driven as much by curiosity as by family loyalty, they assured her that they would be there in fifteen minutes. Rosaria had not dared to tell them that she had called out the fire brigade.

The firemen were highly efficient. Within fifteen minutes of drawing the vehicle up to the stony parapet of the well, they had erected a sturdy scaffolding over the shaft. The apparatus was equipped with a rack-and-pinion pulley attached to a harness that was driven by a motor on the fire engine. The men joked all the time, putting on a show for Rosaria's benefit, pretending they were all too scared to be lowered down the well shaft and inviting Rosaria to make the descent in their place. By now, Rosaria's nerves had almost got the better of her. She smiled a wild smile that betrayed her extreme anxiety. She was very relieved when Matteo and Dino arrived a few seconds later. They were open-mouthed in disbelief at the sight that greeted them.

'Rosy! What have you done?' they exclaimed in unison.

'I don't know. Let's wait and see,' she replied. She could feel her heart pounding already. She was not sure whether it was because of what she feared the men might find or because of the acute humiliation she would have exposed herself to if the manoeuvre proved to be pointless. With a rarely seen act of grace and understanding, Giovanni, the chief fireman came up and put a friendly arm round Rosaria's shoulder.

'Don't be concerned, *signorina*. If there is nothing untoward going on down there, then at least you will have put your mind at rest.'

She wanted to hug him but she was afraid he would notice the tremors that had begun to run up and down her body. She smiled gratefully at him.

'That smile alone makes it all worthwhile,' he said kindly.

It seemed like an eternity before the man who had been winched down the dark well shaft called out, telling the others to bring him up. His voice echoed eerily from the depths below.

'Just as in Flavia's dream,' Rosaria thought with grim foreboding. Rosaria was standing between her twin cousins, who had their arms round her holding her tightly. They could feel her whole body shaking with nerves. The man emerged from the well shaft and was helped over the parapet. He took his chief to one side and spoke to him briefly. 'Giovanni,' he began, but turned away so that Rosaria lost his words. Giovanni walked over to the group of three looking very serious.

'You knew there was something wrong, didn't you?' he said to Rosaria gently. 'I'm so sorry to have to break the news to you, but there's a young woman's body down there.'

The shiver that went down their spines could be felt like an electric shock by all three of the family members.

'I knew it!' wailed Rosaria on the verge of tears mixed with emotions too strong to control.

'But...may I ask you how you knew?' continued the chief fireman, Giovanni, with such concern and sympathy that the three of them felt compelled to tell him.

The twins began telling him about their missing cousin and the dream which two separate members of the family had experienced simultaneously. Rosaria joined in at the twins' insistence, and with a great effort, overcame the onset of tears. She took up the story of how they had all been gathered in the field the previous evening. She spoke rapidly as if to get all the details off her chest as quickly as possible.

'That is the weirdest thing that I have heard in a long time,' said Giovanni. Then, after a pause, he continued softly. 'I'm sorry. I shall have to contact the *carabinieri*. I'm sure you understand.'

The three of them nodded. The twins led their cousin away, knowing full well that she would soon be suffering from an overwhelming reaction to the news they had just heard. Neither Dino nor Matteo thought to offer Rosaria crumbs of false comfort. They too were convinced that this shocking discovery would explain all too poignantly the mystery of their missing cousin, Diletta. Matteo offered to drive Rosaria's car home for her whilst Dino gave her a lift in his car.

And so, tragically, but not unexpectedly, the *carabinieri* identified the body of the girl taken from the depths of the family well as that of Diletta. Rosaria and her family were spared the pain of having to identify the body. Dental records were sufficient to confirm what they knew already. Informally, Rosaria identified a white gold locket and chain that she had given her cousin on her twenty-first birthday. After an interview with the *capitano* from the local *carabinieri* in Campanula, Rosaria was given the handbag that had also been found next to Diletta's body. The identity documents, including driving license, credit cards and tax code card had all been removed by her killer – for it was self-evident that this tragedy had been no accident.

Rosaria had no doubts as to the identity of the killer. Amidst the family's mourning – Flavia had finally been able to give vent to her pent up grief – Rosaria felt a cold, mounting anger rising within her at the crime that had destroyed the life of her closest friend and had brought so much suffering to her family.

'I'm not letting this go,' she had announced to her family a few days after the grim discovery. 'The police will pass this on to Interpol and all that will happen is that *that* Calabrian monster who pretended to love Diletta, will disappear into the crowd in London and go unpunished. We keep what we know to ourselves. Agreed?'

Rosaria's anger was so compelling that she remained unchallenged by all present. Only Martina was filled with secret dread, knowing that her sister would never let the matter rest. Avenging her friend's death would become her next obsession.

During a subsequent interview with the uniformed *capitano*, she had told him briefly about Enrico, the husband from Calabria, who had married Diletta. There was no point at all in concealing what was public knowledge. But she said nothing about the letters she had received from London, purportedly from her cousin, nor about Enrico's inexplicable departure that morning long ago.

But the *capitano* was a shrewd judge of people and situations and he suspected that Rosaria was holding something back.

'What do you think, *signorina,* about the fact that your cousin's ID documents were missing? What implications lie behind this theft, in your opinion?'

After some seconds' careful consideration, Rosaria looked at him and said thoughtfully: 'It probably means that someone is walking round London claiming to be Diletta Miccoli, *capitano.*'

'You are a very smart person, *Signorina* Miccoli – Rosaria,' he added, deciding that she would relax a bit if he used her first name. 'We could do with the likes of you in the *carabinieri.*'

At this point, Rosaria took the risky step of proposing to this senior police officer that the official enquiry should not be 'accelerated' for now. Rosaria argued cogently that any official enquiry in London would run the risk of driving the Calabrian into hiding or effect an identity change. An initial private enquiry could find out the whereabouts of the fake Diletta very much more discretely, and that would lead to locating Enrico without alerting him, Rosaria had argued. She did not say in as many words what her intentions were. Indeed, she had no clearly formulated plan at that point of time.

The captain of police looked at her astutely before replying.

'Well, Rosaria, you can hardly ask me to commit an act of dereliction of duty, can you! But, I imagine that it will be several months before a proper investigation gets underway. After all, from an international point of view, your family tragedy is just a local crime in an obscure little town in Italy – where such crimes are, sadly, all too common.'

'Thank you, *capitano,* for your advice,' said Rosaria. She had the impression that he had understood clearly that she was deeply and personally involved in this affair and its implications. The police officer's next words confirmed her impression.

'Take care, Rosaria. I suspect strongly that it might well turn out that the Calabrian mafia has had a hand in this crime. You are too young and beautiful to fall foul of the *'ndrangheta.'*

One of the most dreaded words in the Italian language had been pronounced, bringing into the open for the first time the secret fear which Rosaria had always entertained.

'I shall take great care whom I have dealings with,' Rosaria said as she took her leave, shaking the proffered hand which held hers for several seconds longer than the occasion demanded. She did not appear to object and did not withdraw her hand from his.

Back home, she related what had happened to her family and intimated that she intended to take steps to pursue her 'investigations' further. Benedetto was there too. He was, as ever, in awe of her determination and annoyed that she always acted without consulting him first. Wounded male pride was all too often his habitual reaction to Rosaria's initiatives.

Rosaria had already decided that she would have to go to London, although she had not said so to her family in so many words. She had never been outside Salento except occasionally to visit Martina in Rome. Nor had she ever flown in an aeroplane. This venture would be a serious challenge to her resolve. Martina had her first inkling of what was going through her sister's mind as soon as Rosaria uttered her next words.

'I think I need to learn English properly,' she said out of the blue. Benedetto had reacted instantly.

'Why should you want to learn English now?' he asked. 'We will never be going to live in England when we are married.'

'I just love English,' she replied. I always *have* loved English. But I want to learn everyday English instead of the literary English that the nuns taught us at school.'

'Well,' said Benedetto reluctantly. 'They are running English courses at my company at the moment. Family members can attend too. I can get you enrolled – if that is what you *really* want to do. But do you really *have* to learn English so soon before our marriage?' he added petulantly.

So it was that Rosaria put the first part of her plan into action, motivated by her deep-seated anger at the callous manner in which her cousin had been despatched into the next world. At night time, often sleepless, she conjured up nightmare images of the terror of Diletta's last few moments alive. She recalled the utter fear on her cousin's face on the last occasion she had seen her. What had Diletta known that was so frightening that she was too scared to tell even her closest friend?

Driven by her sense of outrage, Rosaria attended her first English lesson for years. The teacher was a nicely spoken blond English girl called Susan, who announced, at the end of Rosaria's first lesson that she would have to return to England for family reasons. But, she said, they were to be taught by a 'very experienced teacher' who would replace her. He had just arrived in Campanula, she added. Rosaria felt a twinge of disappointment. It had taken a lot of determination to attend this lesson, only to find that she would have to get used to a different teacher when she had barely begun to feel comfortable with this one – Rosaria's first ever contact with a native speaker.

Furthermore, Susan's successor was to be a *man!*

8: *Adam Meets His Match*

The man in question was sitting in the office of his new school in the small industrial town of Campanula, situated fifty kilometres south of the beautiful baroque city of Lecce. In Campanula, they manufacture shoes, socks and clothing. But, Adam had been told, the town was desperately trying to avert a crisis as these products, vital to the region's economy, were showing signs of emigrating to Romania or the Far East.

'The English Academy of Salento', as the school was over-gloriously named, occupied the first floor of a newly constructed building immediately above the local branch of the Banca Popolare Salentina. The functional building stood in stark contrast to the ancient, cobbled *piazza* with its statue of Campanula's patron saint, San Giovanni, standing majestically on top of his broad stone plinth, his right hand raised in permanent blessing on all who passed below. San Giovanni had been venerated by the townsfolk since the time he had saved them from the plague, Adam had learnt almost as soon as he arrived.

He had travelled to Lecce from Bologna by train. He had been met by his new boss, Daniele, who looked too young to be running an ice-cream parlour let alone a whole language school with three branches dotted around the Salento region, including the one in Campanula. This branch had only opened the previous September. Adam had attended the inevitable induction course in Lecce, where he had been put up in a nearby hotel – all at Daniele's expense. Lecce looked unreal and so different to any other Italian city that Adam had been to. The facades of the myriad churches were all ornately crafted baroque masterpieces, made of the warm, yellowish Lecce stone. Adam spent his free hours walking round and round the city centre marvelling at its architecture. He had fallen in love with an old flagstone courtyard belonging to a former monastery. It had an ancient well in the centre of the courtyard, flanked by lemon trees ripe with early January fruit. The courtyard was reached through massive wooden doors which led directly off the *Piazza del Duomo,* dominated by the cathedral's lofty *campanile* rising majestically up to the heavens. The sun was shining and the temperature was an amazing 18 degrees Celsius. Adam's earlier fears about this venture were beginning to seem fanciful. After the induction course, Daniele drove Adam down to Campanula, one hand on the steering wheel and the other clutching a mobile phone to his ear. Adam sat tensed up throughout the fifty kilometre journey – over, it seemed to him, in a matter of minutes.

And here he was preparing for his first lesson, which was due to start at 7 o'clock that evening. The school secretary was in the office with Adam. She was talking to the boss, Daniele, trying to impress him by sounding business-like and super-efficient. Her name was, confusingly, Daniela. She was about twenty-five, not unattractive but, as Adam could hardly have failed to notice, suffered from a bad case of halitosis. In the end, Adam had to leave the office and continue his preparation in an empty classroom to avoid the noxious fumes in such a confined space. 'A pity,' thought Adam. 'Apart from the Bad Breath problem, she is really quite attractive.'

Obviously, his only other colleague, Glenda, had already encountered the Bad Breath problem and had learnt that the school office was out-of-bounds without breathing apparatus. Glenda was in her early thirties and Adam had taken an immediate liking to her. He found her in her own classroom studiously pinning up all kinds of visual aids on to the walls with an endless supply of Blu-Tak. Adam, therefore, saw it as his duty to interrupt her labours by suggesting a coffee break.

'Not just yet, dear,' she said. 'Give me another thirty minutes.'

Glenda laced her conversations with 'dears' and 'ducks' in great profusion, Adam noticed, with the 'ducks' delivered in a fake northern accent. Naturally, he had already commented on this. Glenda had merely chuckled and replied: 'Sorry, Adam. If you don't like the way I talk, just ignore it...duck!' He had gone through an elaborate mime of lowering his head as if to avoid a low flying bird. It raised the hint of a smile, but Glenda went on 'dearing' and 'ducking' regardless, for the duration of the school year and beyond. Adam sat down at the desk in his classroom desperately trying to concentrate on his lesson preparation. He felt inexplicably restless as if waiting for something unusual to happen. He had just conveniently decided that he would improvise his lesson that evening, which would eliminate the necessity of preparing anything, when he heard, coming from the street below, a brass band playing. As the sound was coming ever closer, he assumed it must be a procession. Glenda waltzed into his classroom and said: 'Here Adam. Come and look! I bet you will never have seen anything like *this* before!' As she was standing looking out of the window, he assumed she must be referring to the band. 'I've seen brass bands before,' he said lazily.

'No, Adam! Come and look, please! You'll see what I mean,' Glenda insisted. Adam stood up and walked reluctantly over to the window. His mouth fell open in amazement at what he saw in the street below.

The musicians were all dressed up in purple uniforms. They were leading a funeral procession. The coffin was on a horse drawn carriage covered with so many flowers that the effect was dazzling. Adam was amazed to see what must have been nearly one hundred people behind the coffin, all wearing black and walking in solemn procession. But what riveted his attention was the sight of two young women walking arm in arm immediately behind the carriage. He could not recall ever seeing two more beautiful women, even in his wildest fantasies. 'They must be sisters,' he thought. One of them, maybe the younger of the two, had jet black hair. She was clutching a handkerchief in a tightly clenched fist. The second girl was striding behind the coffin, dry eyed, but with a look of such passionate concentration on her face that Adam could almost feel it radiating from her, even standing spellbound one storey above street level.

On the coffin, draped with a purple cloth, Adam could make out the word DILETTA spelt out in yellow flowers.

'What does DILETTA mean?' Adam asked Glenda ingenuously.

'It's the girl's name, you wally!' replied his colleague – who also liked using derogatory epithets out of the ark. Adam had never come across this unusual Italian name before.

'Diletta deleted,' he said reverentially under his breath.

'That's not so funny,' said Glenda seriously. 'Rumour has it that she was found murdered. She was only in her twenties, you know.'

Adam looked at her aghast. 'What do you mean, 'rumoured'?'

'It's been kept strangely quiet. The details have not really been made public.'

'So how do *you* know?' probed Adam.

'The students told me. It's a local family from Campanula.'

'But where is the procession going, Glenda?' asked Adam, curious.

'To the Conad supermarket! Where do you think they're going, Adam? To the cemetery, of course! She'll be buried with her family.'

Adam remained very thoughtful. He had a host of questions in his mind that it would seem irreverent to ask at that moment. Deeply affected by what he had witnessed, so unlike anything he had seen before, he sat down again at his desk only after the last family member had disappeared from sight. It was impossible to concentrate on lesson preparation. He retained the image of the girl with dark brown hair who had been striding along behind the carriage as if she was on a pilgrimage. There was some element that he could not define; some reaction to her presence that left him breathless and disturbed. 'She was so beautiful,' was all he could think of saying under his breath to sum up the whole experience.

At seven o'clock, Adam's first class arrived; seven young men of variegated appearance and three not unattractive women. One of the seven men informed Adam that he was the school secretary's *fidanzato.* His name was Claudio. He took it upon himself to fulfil the role of 'pack leader'. He considered it to be his responsibility to lighten the tone of the proceedings throughout the two hour lesson, 'with cigarette break please, teacher!' said Claudio in English. He himself did not smoke but wanted to stamp his authority on proceedings.

'I would rather you didn't call me 'teacher' for the next six months. It makes you sound like a bunch of seven-year-olds,' protested the teacher half way through the lesson, after it had become obvious that this was how they believed he should be addressed. 'My name is Adam.'

There was a significant pause while they digested Adam's words. 'We should call you *professore,*' they almost pleaded.

It was apparent that his students were suffering from the native obsession with titles. But Adam was having none of it. 'We English believe in equality,' he told them. One at a time, they reluctantly addressed him by his first name – which inevitably came out with the stress on the wrong syllable. So, he came to be called A-damn'. 'I don't give a...!' thought the teacher amusedly. Very few of the students had ever managed to pronounce his name correctly by the end of the school year.

Half way through the lesson, the odour in the classroom was overpowering. It had become obvious that all the male students in this group suffered from Bad Breath syndrome – Claudio being among the worst offenders. 'At least he and Daniela are well matched!' Adam could not help thinking. While they were out smoking or drinking their coffees, Adam opened all the classroom windows as wide as they would go. Instantly, the classroom was invaded with the noise and stench of the traffic from the street below. Since most of the population of Campanula drove around in cars that were at least fifteen years old, European exhaust emission laws had had very little effect on the quality of the atmosphere.

Adam mentioned the BB problem to Glenda during the coffee break. She merely laughed. 'Ah you know why that is, don't you Adam?' He was tempted to answer: 'No, that's why I'm asking *you!*' But he waited patiently for her to formulate her explanation in her own good time. 'It's because dentists in Italy charge such a fortune that only the well-off can afford to go regularly. They only visit a dentist when there is absolutely no other solution.'

'By *other solution*, you mean like a length of string attached to a door handle followed by a smart tug?' suggested Adam.

Glenda smiled: 'Yes, that sort of thing, dear.'

After the coffee break, Adam realised that he would have to continue teaching with the windows shut since the noise of the traffic made it impossible to be heard. 'Quite a dilemma!' he thought as he continued to teach the second half of his lesson striving to breathe through his mouth at the same time as talking.

'Plenty of pair-work for this group,' he decided taking a deep breath of air as he stepped momentarily out of the classroom. But as soon as he tried this technique, it was obvious that the temptation to talk in Italian was too strong, especially, Adam realised, as this was almost certainly the first time in their lives they had been asked to *speak* in English. At school, they would have sat listening to a non-native teacher talking to them in bad English without having to contribute verbally at all. Adam's relief from the noxious fumes was, therefore, short lived.

'Cultural difference number one,' he thought ironically as he closed the lesson at nine o'clock. The students streamed out of the classroom chatting animatedly. All of them, with the exception of Claudio, thanked Adam for an interesting lesson and wished him a cheerful *'buona sera'* as they left. Claudio obviously did not consider that it befitted his image as 'union leader' to deign to thank the teacher.

* * * * *

Adam walked back to his rented apartment which was reached by climbing a steep staircase to the first storey. It was even more basic than his flat in Vicenza had been. At least, it did not smell of cats. The bathroom and bedroom brought to mind scenes from a concentration camp. His bed was a single iron frame affair with a few rusty springs holding up a thin, sagging mattress. He nostalgically thought of his cosy flat in England. He made a mental note that he must telephone Daniele and ask him to supply a double bed. He was too tired not to sleep that night. When he woke up in the morning, he discovered that he could reach the flat roof up a second steep flight of stairs. He found himself on a terrace with a view over the surrounding countryside. The early January sunshine was warm on his face. There was some compensation for living in this bleak house.

He spent a few disagreeable minutes under the shower. The ancient immersion heater spat and gurgled in protest before delivering a trickle of tepid water through an old metal shower-head that looked like the spout of a watering can. Adam had half expected the apparatus to deliver a dose of lethal gas, so he was thankful for small mercies. After completing his ablutions, he went in search of a life-saving espresso coffee and a cream-filled *cornetto* in town. He soon identified the bars where they made the best coffee. The suspicious looks that he got as a foreigner in the first few days quickly became grudgingly bestowed nods of the head as the locals realised that he did not pose a threat. Lessons hardly ever began until three o'clock in the afternoon.

Lunch with Glenda at the *Antica Isolata* became the routine. This eating place was run by one, Fernando with help from his family - who had been dragooned into active service. The food was good and cheap. The restaurant was in the basement and had a beautifully restored, stone vaulted ceiling. Fernando spoke good

English and was very attentive to his first two customers of the day. As soon as there were more than six diners at the tables, he went automatically into 'frantic mode', rushing around quite unnecessarily from table to table or table to serving hatch, shouting up to the cook (his brother-in-law), his waitresses (who never survived the ordeal for more than three weeks), and his wife who was cashier (until she became pregnant).

'And yet he seemed busier than he was!' said Adam quoting the only bit of Chaucer that he could remember. Glenda had been a regular customer since September and knew all about Fernando and his family.

'You seem to know an awful lot about *everything,* Glenda,' said Adam somewhat petulantly to his new colleague.

'Oh yes, *Know-it-all-Glenda* my friends call me,' she replied proudly.

'Fine, as you know everything, perhaps you can tell me how I am supposed to get to my lesson at the bank in Montenero this evening.'

'Oh, you'll be picked up at 5 o'clock by Danilo, I expect. That's what happened to Susan,'

'And who might Danilo be?'

'He's Daniele's driver. He brings the other teachers down from Lecce and leaves them at the bank's head office and then comes and fetches you. He's from Naples, by the way.'

'Is the fact that he is from Naples in any way significant?' asked Adam sarcastically.

Glenda laughed in her 'know-it-all' manner and added: 'It's the way he drives.' Annoyingly, she refused to elaborate. 'You'll see, Adam!' was all she deigned to add with malicious glee.

'What did you do before you became an English teacher, Glenda? Were you a police informer?'

'No,' she replied, amused by the fact that she had succeeded in tantalising Adam. 'I was an NHS sexual health care adviser. So any problems you might have while you're here...'

'There won't be,' Adam stated categorically. 'I am decidedly *not* getting emotionally involved in the next few months. Of that I am sure!'

'You never know,' said Miss Know-it-all.

'So what made you become an English teacher in such an out-of-the-way place as this?'

'Oh, I felt like a career change,' was the airy reply.

But she had said this in an unconvincing manner, like an excuse she had used a dozen times before. Weeks afterwards, in a moment of frustration at the way in which Daniela dealt with the school's admin problems, Glenda said without reflection: 'It's enough to drive one back to England!" Adam realised she might inadvertently have supplied the answer to his question - that something must have happened back home to make her want to put a distance between herself and her past life.

* * * * *

Five o'clock saw Adam waiting outside the school entrance on the lookout for anything resembling a school minibus. It arrived as he was blinking. On focusing his glance, he saw a swarthy young man of about twenty frantically beckoning him over to where an army green minibus was parked with engine revving impatiently.

'Danilo,' said Danilo holding out his hand without a smile on his face.

'Adam,' replied Adam with what he hoped was a sympathetic smile.

'Do you like Heavy Metal, A-damn?' asked Danilo as he wrenched the lever into first gear.

'Love it!' lied Adam as he tried to fasten his seatbelt. That was the end of the conversation as, not only was he deafened by the music, but the minibus took off with such speed that Adam felt himself being pressed hard against the back of the seat. The two kilometres to the bank were covered while he was still trying to buckle the seatbelt.

'*Ciao*, A-damn. Nice to meet you! See you later.'

'Thanks for the lift, Danilo,' said Adam mouthing the words over the heaviest metal he had ever heard as he climbed back down on to *terra firma*.

Inside the bank, in a cramped committee room, the group was awaiting their new teacher. No bad breath problem here, noted Adam with relief. This bore out Glenda's diagnosis – those with a steady, well paid, life-long guaranteed job in a bank could afford to go to a dentist regularly. The girls all looked beautiful and the three men seemed motivated.

'Is everyone here?' asked Adam.

'We are just waiting for one person – Rosaria.'

'She'll be here any moment,' said a striking-looking young woman called Federica who, Adam noticed with curiosity, had well-formed breasts on a petite body. A fascinating combination, Adam thought. 'She's *desperate* to learn English,' added Federica with a certain gleam in her eye.

When the last student arrived, the look of shock on Adam's face must have been apparent to all – except Rosaria herself, who sat down between Federica and a girl called Sonia without a glance in the direction of the teacher. It was the girl who had been following the coffin. Adam's initial jolt of recognition was immediately replaced by a deeper sense of awareness. It was as if he had been *expecting* her to arrive, he analysed later on that evening. It was not, he reasoned, merely a retrospective interpretation of events but reflected the prescient conviction of impending change that had assailed him before he had left England. 'A glimpse into the *Future Present*,' thought Adam as if he had invented a new verb tense and thereby added another dimension to his existence.

Adam managed to drag his mind back to the present and made some vague excuse which he hoped would explain the look of shock on his face when Rosaria had come into the room. He completed the lesson like an actor totally familiar with his script. Rosaria had only spoken a few words to Adam during the ninety minute session, but he had been struck by the natural manner in which she had pronounced the few English words she had spoken. During the first part of the lesson, Rosaria had appeared to be brooding darkly and beautifully, wedged between the two other girls. He had the uncomfortable impression that Rosaria was trying to form an opinion of him. What was more alarming was that Adam had to acknowledge the fact that her approval mattered to him in some obscure way.

'No!' he shouted silently to his own brain. 'Don't even consider it for a minute! Besides, you must be nearly twice her age.'

But, after the lesson, Rosaria was just in front of him going up the stairs to the exit. He could not help looking at her ascending figure with a twinge of excitement.

Danilo was waiting impatiently for Adam in the minibus. He apologised but pointed out that he had to run Adam back to the school before returning to pick up the other teachers - who had to get back to Lecce for their late evening lessons. 'What an insane arrangement,' thought Adam. Danilo managed to break his previous land speed record on the way back to Campanula. Adam decided that he would at least spare Danilo the return trip after every lesson.

* * * * *

Adam had looked forward eagerly to his next lesson at the BPS – and Rosaria. At least, the girl in the funeral procession had a name now. As he was going up the steps to the bank, he realised with something akin to panic that the person climbing the steps by his side was Rosaria.

'Hello, Rosaria,' he said smiling. She actually smiled back at him – a radiant smile showing a dazzling display of white teeth, which caused Adam to miss his footing on the top step. Gaining access to the bank was through a double set of security doors with barely enough standing room for two people. His courage nearly deserted him, but Rosaria gestured to him to step through the door with her. Her close physical proximity was unnerving but Adam managed to ask a couple of cheerfully banal questions as they walked together into the classroom. Their entrance was greeted with wry smiles on a couple of faces, notably Federica's. Adam made a deprecatory gesture which was supposed to convey that their arrival together was purely fortuitous.

At the end of another lively lesson, Adam put in his request for a lift back to Campanula from anybody in the group who might be heading that way. There followed a lot of apologies and a catalogue of reasons as to why everyone had various other commitments. Rosaria said nothing. When they were outside, she came quietly up to Adam and said: 'I'll take you back. I go and see my Auntie Flavia in Campanula every Tuesday and Thursday.'

Adam felt a secret thrill at the prospect of being in the presence of this woman. It was as if an invisible hand had just made a determining move in a cosmic game of chess. After his initial surprise, it occurred to him that a preordained piece of his life had fallen into place. 'Don't be so fanciful!' the rational part of his brain said accusingly. He ignored it.

'This is my car,' he heard Rosaria saying as she led him to her cream-with-a-red stripe coloured *Cinquecento*. 'No, I shall do the driving,' she smiled as Adam, out of habit, had opened the door where he expected the passenger seat to be.

'Sorry,' he laughed. 'I still think I'm in England.'

'Ah, but you are not,' said Rosaria. 'Believe me!' She had managed to instil some concealed meaning into those everyday words which Adam noted without discerning what the implication was supposed to be. He suspected that she might be intelligent as well as beautiful.

Rosaria drove fast but not with the same frenetic haste as Danilo. 'I hope my driving doesn't scare you as much as Danilo's,' she said. 'We were very amused by your description, by the way.'

'Were you?' said Adam surprised. '*You* never smiled once as far as I remember - especially not during the first lesson. You looked quite judgemental, in fact, Rosaria.'

'I was wondering why an Englishman was so far from home. I was also asking myself how someone like you could possibly wear such awful trousers and that disgusting green cardigan, if you really want to know,' said Rosaria, laughing.

'So you don't approve of the way I dress?' Adam was startled by such unexpectedly direct criticism.

'It could do with a rethink, my teacher. You are in Italy now, you know. Your image needs to change,' said Rosaria, with the clear message that she was the one to do it.

Adam looked thoughtful. He was astonished – and a little alarmed – at how quickly a feeling of ease had developed between them, in the space of only one kilometre.

'Aren't we going back to Campanula a different way, Rosaria?' He had just become aware of the fact that they were driving down a country road lined with olive groves. Her answer surprised him.

'Yes, otherwise I have to drive past my father's house and my fiancé's house,' she explained. 'They might not approve of me giving a lift to a strange man.' She had spoken without a smile, with even a hint of anxiety in her voice.

'I don't want to get you into any trouble,' said Adam nobly. Privately, he suspected that he had not spoken out of any wish to be gallant.

'Oh, I wanted to speak to you. In any case, I really am going to see my Auntie Flavia. She needs consoling. You see, she's just lost her...' began Rosaria. Adam understood in an instant what she had been about to say. The connection with Diletta fell into place. He said nothing, however.

'One day I want to tell you all about my family,' said Rosaria instead.

There was a promise in those words which did not escape Adam's notice. Already, his defences were being eroded. His undertaking to himself – and Glenda – to remain unattached was under threat. All too quickly, they arrived outside the school.

'I'll see you soon, Adam,' she said simply.

An electric shock went up Adam's spine. *'She called me by my name!'*

'You are one of the few people here who pronounce my name properly, Rosaria. You could speak English very well, you know.'

'I *need* to speak English very well, Adam,' she replied with an urgency in her voice that took Adam by surprise. There was no time to ask her why. He was already late for his next lesson with the BB group. Adam raised the flat of his hand and Rosaria gripped it in hers for a brief second – an instant of time that would be measured in eternity. She drove off quickly without a backward glance.

9: *Adam's Metamorphosis*

Adam fell asleep that night on his rickety iron bedstead and sunken mattress, endlessly going over in his mind the exchange of words and looks that had passed between himself and Rosaria. Adam felt no conscious intention of involvement – indeed he would have rejected the notion outright if there had been anyone there to express such a suggestion. But the harbingers of love creep up on us stealthily, like mischievous spirits shrouded by the night, whispering enchanted words in a secret language of their own. Thus, by the time Adam had lived through a further forty-eight hours of his routine life at the school, he was quite unconsciously more receptive to the idea of Rosaria and more familiar with her sultry looks and sudden dazzling smiles.

After the Thursday lesson, Rosaria accompanied Adam back to Campanula to see her *zia* as if giving him a lift was already an established part of their lives.

'How about lunch together tomorrow?' suggested Rosaria with a boldness and naturalness that nobody, least of all a susceptible Adam, could have refused.

'Don't you have to work in Lecce tomorrow?' asked Adam hoping that she had not confused the day.

'Tomorrow, I don't have to go to work, Adam. The Lecce office is having new computers installed. My *papà* and my *fidanzato* don't know this because I haven't told them. So they will think I am in Lecce.'

'May I ask a personal question, Rosaria?' She nodded, looking curiously at Adam, uncertain about what detail he must have picked up on.

'If the two men in your life are so jealous of other men talking to you, are they jealous of each other too?'

The perception of his question caught her off her guard. But the frown which furrowed her brow for a second was quickly replaced by a radiant smile. Rosaria laid a hand on Adam's sleeve which sent an electric spasm of pleasure along his arm.

'You are very intelligent – for an Englishman, that is,' she added saucily in order to mitigate the compliment. 'My father cannot abide Benedetto coming into the house. If Benedetto is in my bedroom, it drives *papà* to distraction. Once he followed us into the bedroom without knocking and pretended to be inspecting the double glazing. That will give you some idea.'

'Incredible!' said Adam as he mentally put a second tick in the 'cultural differences' box. Was he to be the third man, forming a disparate trinity of competing males? Any distant warning bells in his brain were quickly silenced.

They agreed to meet outside the school at midday the following day. Adam shot off, late again for his BB lesson, after a brief touch of fingertips, which sent the electric currents flowing up the length of his arm again.

At the appointed time, just as the church bells were ringing out the angelus all over this town, deep in the Catholic South of Italy, Adam arrived outside the school entrance, wielding a tightly wrapped umbrella. It had looked as if they were due for a thunder storm when he left his flat and he had not wanted to appear to be wanting on his first date with Rosaria. But the menacing clouds had dispersed and the umbrella, he felt, had become an unnecessary encumbrance. He stood there for five minutes experiencing a feeling of mounting nerves with every second that ticked by. He imagined that he was the only man in the world to feel this way before what risked becoming a romantic involvement. He cursed his lack of confidence in the face of an encounter with undoubtedly the most beautiful woman he had ever met. 'What a wimp I must be!' he thought, judging himself far too severely.

Then he heard his name being called. The voice seemed to come from above and around him. 'Adam!' It was remarkable, he thought, how Rosaria managed to pronounce his name in such perfect, unaccented English. But he still could not identify where she was calling him from. 'A celestial voice!' he thought foolishly. 'Adam!' said the voice again more persistently. 'I'm up here you plonker!' He looked up at the school windows. It was Glenda. 'Are you waiting to take me to lunch, dear?' she said teasingly.

'Damn!' thought Adam. 'No, I can't today, Glenda. I'm...'

'I'll be down in a minute,' said his colleague.

'How on Earth am I going to put her off?' he wondered desperately. 'I suppose I shall have to invite her along too.' Even as this charitable alternative presented itself, the unbidden thought came to him that, without a shadow of doubt, what he desired more than anything else was a chance to be alone with Rosaria.

At that minute, Rosaria's *Cinquecento* drew up beside him. He leapt inside the car and said to Rosaria: 'Let's go!' Rosaria was never one to hang about. They shot off just as Adam saw Glenda appear at street level, looking around mystified at the inexplicable disappearance of her lunchtime companion whose neatly folded umbrella was propped up in the angle of the doorway.

'Strange,' thought Glenda as she sloped off to have her first solitary lunch for some days.

'What's all the hurry?' asked Rosaria curiously.

Adam explained that he was escaping from Glenda. Poor Adam had still to learn about 'cultural difference number three'; where another woman is involved, it is the duty of every self-respecting southern Italian girl to put on a display of jealousy and possessiveness to mark out her territory beyond a shadow of doubt – even if the need for such a display is self-evidently absent.

'Who is Glenda?' asked Rosaria in Italian. 'You've never mentioned *her* before!'

'She's the other teacher at the school,' explained Adam, blissfully unaware of the pitfalls of being honest and direct. Hopes of redemption faded to nothing.

'And why would you want to escape from her?'

'Because we usually have lunch together,' replied Adam digging a deeper pit for himself. There was a stony silence, intense enough to be sensed physically. Adam could feel the silent waves of passion emanating from his companion. Then it was as if a swarm of angry bees had been let loose. He was stung by a series of irate questions and accusations that seemed to come from every direction at once. He defended himself as best he could. Since he knew that there was nothing sexual between himself and his colleague, he could not understand the intensity of Rosaria's reactions. At least, it revealed to him in a moment of clarity that this beautiful woman had, for reasons beyond his powers of comprehension, appropriated him to herself.

'Rosaria,' he managed to say firmly enough to stem her passionate tirade. 'I just wanted the chance to be alone with you.'

The swarm of bees withdrew as suddenly as they had arrived and a ray of sunshine emerged from behind the clouds. Rosaria was smiling happily and apologising for her outburst. He took her free hand, which should have been on the steering wheel, and kissed it lightly; an impulsive gesture that seemed to provoke no reaction, positive or negative. He wondered if he had shocked or embarrassed her. Two minutes later, they pulled up outside an out of town shopping centre.

'I thought we were going to have lunch,' said Adam, taken aback.

'We are, Adam. But first of all, you are going to buy some decent clothes. I refuse to be seen out with a man who dresses like you do.'

Adam's protests were utterly ignored. He had to be forced into a changing cubicle clutching a pair of jeans. 'I have never worn jeans *in my whole life.* It's too late to begin now,' he protested in vain. Fifteen minutes later, he came out of the shop clutching one pair of jeans and the other on his legs. He was also wearing a new white shirt and a casual jacket. He had a broad smile on his face and was attempting to catch sight of his reflection in the plate glass windows. Rosaria was carrying a large bag containing Adam's green cardigan, his corduroy trousers, a burgundy blazer which he had treasured up to that singular moment of his life. To his initial horror, Rosaria opened the lid of a large, foot-operated refuse bin and unceremoniously dumped the bag inside it. He felt a surge of annoyance which was instantly replaced by a desire to laugh. Instead, he shook his head in mock disapproval.

'*Ecco fatto!* Now you can begin your new life. You look ten years younger and...*proprio elegante!'* said Rosaria with the dazzling smile much in evidence. 'Next time, we will sort out the shoes,' she added.

Adam looked down at his feet. In fact, his traditional black, lace-up shoes did not quite go with the new image, he admitted.

'Alright, Rosaria,' he declared with the smug grin still on his face. 'Now, I'm hungry and I want to buy you lunch.'

* * * * *

Rosaria drove rapidly to Gravino, past the fire station where, a short while ago, she had walked resolutely up to the group of men who would help her settle the issue of her cousin's tragic fate. One of the firemen waved at her, recognising her car. Adam looked quizzically at Rosaria, who did not react. The restaurant was in the old part of the town, high above the water on the promontory that jutted out into the Ionian Sea. The restaurant was called *La Scolgliera*. It was supposed to be the best sea-food restaurant in the town, explained Rosaria.

The sun was warm. There was no breeze that day and the water in the bay below them was a calm turquoise blue. The rocks below the surface of the water formed a pattern of shifting darker colours that appeared to be floating like huge black fish. They stood for a while and looked over the bay before going in to have lunch. Rosaria ordered a mixed seafood dish with a local pasta whose name Adam had never heard of. In the course of the next hour, Adam learnt that Rosaria did not drink anything but water, not because she was driving but because she simply did not drink alcohol. Accordingly, Adam felt obliged to reduce his intake of wine to a quarter of a litre so as not to betray the fact that he was a bit too partial to wine. Obviously, if there was to be a relationship with her, his health was going to improve.

'I'm guessing you don't smoke either,' said Adam.

'Never,' she said. 'I tried a cigarette once and vowed it would be the last.'

'Thus the perfect white teeth, I suppose.'

'I don't have a single filling either, Adam,' she said proudly displaying two rows of gritted teeth for his inspection.

'What perfection, Rosaria! You have beautiful...teeth,' he said drawing back from the brink and telling her that it was her whole face that he found beautiful.

A silence fell between them; not uncomfortable, but more of a pregnant pause because they both knew that whatever the next words spoken might be, they would mark a shift in the relationship, a tentative step into unknown territory – or a possible withdrawal from the front line. It was Adam who broke the silence, which had become protracted, while he tried to wind the *linguine*-like pasta ribbons round his fork without splashing the sauce down his new white shirt.

'When you walked into the first lesson at the bank,' he said cautiously, 'I had already seen you a day or so beforehand, walking behind your cousin, Diletta.'

'She was my dearest friend too.' said Rosaria. Her eyes had watered as two large tears ran down her cheeks. Adam looked at her keenly. He put down his pasta-laden fork and reached across the table for her hand. 'I'm sorry,' he said simply.

'I promise to tell you everything that happened very soon, Adam. I must tell you, because that's the reason why I have to learn English.' She provided no further enlightenment. Adam failed to see the remotest connection between the tragic loss of her cousin and the need to learn English. He would just have to wait until Rosaria told him in her own time.

He found himself looking into Rosaria's wide open, brown eyes, appealing to him in some way which he could not fathom. He spoke without thinking, launching the boat into unknown waters.

'You are truly beautiful, Rosaria. If I had been five minutes younger, you would be saying farewell to Benedetto.'

With a few more weeks' exposure to the new love of his life, Adam might have realised that the irony expressed by English understatement is inevitably lost on most Italians. He was afraid that he had made his first move too soon. Thus, he failed to interpret the brief look of disappointment that crossed Rosaria's face. Days later, she explained to him that his subtly phrased declaration of flowering love had been interpreted literally. She had taken it to mean that she was too young for him.

They left the restaurant. Adam's plate had been licked clean, so to speak. Rosaria had left half of her pasta on her plate. 'I don't have a big appetite,' she explained. But she had stopped eating as soon as he had made his clumsy declaration of love, he noticed. The journey back to Campanula was made in almost total silence. Adam was anxious that he had scuppered his chances after those few, well-intentioned words. He was also painfully aware that his time in Rosaria's company was coming to an end. He was about to ask her, with a lump which had suddenly manifested itself in his throat, when they would see each other again. Before he managed to utter the words, however, Rosaria turned to him and said with her beautiful smile: 'Adam. Show me where you live! I want to be able to picture you when I am not with you.'

It was uncanny, thought Adam. She was throwing him a lifeline. Adam, at the tender age of fifty-two – thanks to a recent, unheralded birthday – had still to come to the realisation that women too, suffered from the same pangs of emotion, the same pains of new born love. In vain did he attempt to throw off the encroaching feelings of attachment to this young woman, who was so different to anyone with whom he had shared intimacy so far. 'You are still a free man. It isn't too late!' the other part of his brain told him. The unbidden thought came to him that his 'freedom' from attachment was the last thing that he needed or wanted at this crucial moment in his life. He felt, nevertheless, that he was duty bound to mention the age difference between them.

'Rosaria...' he began hesitantly.

'Please call me Rosy,' she interrupted. 'My sister always calls me Rosy.'

'And what about Benedetto?'

'Yes,' she answered, surprised by the obvious yet challenging question. 'Sometimes he does. It depends whether he's angry with me or not.'

Adam smiled secretly at the skilful way in which she had side-stepped the issue and deflected the full force of his question.

'You are very good with words,' he said holding her gaze. Rosaria looked at him shrewdly, perhaps realising that her verbal dexterity, which was a match for most people, would be challenged by this Englishman.

'But I really do want to see where you live, Adam,' she said, returning to the previously captured mood. 'Why not indeed?' thought Adam, conveniently shelving any awkward questions about their respective ages.

'I am a little ashamed to show *anyone* this place, Rosy. I wouldn't even offer this flat to an immigrant if I was its landlord.'

'It surely can't be *that* bad, Adam.'

The main double doors were painted green and opened up directly on to the pavement. Adam led the way up the flight of steep stone steps, which ascended into the gathering darkness of the stairwell, despite the single bare light bulb at the top of the landing. Another set of green doors led into the first room, a kind of anti-chamber which was cheerless and devoid of even a stick of furniture. The small kitchen had a table and chairs, a rudimentary cooker and sink, a fridge and an ancient television which sat perched precariously on the window sill. Rosaria took one look at it and said: 'It *can* be that bad, Adam!'

'I told you. Don't look in the bedroom. That is even worse.'

And so, of course, Rosaria being Rosaria, immediately stepped into the bedroom, saw the sagging, single bed standing alone in this bare, vacuum of a room. The arched ceiling high above the floor came to a point in its centre, like a star, in the traditional style of Salentino architecture. 'I like the *soffitto a stella,*' commented Rosaria ironically as she looked upwards.

She came back into the bare room next to the kitchen and stood facing Adam, a sympathetic expression on her face. She was perhaps ten centimetres shorter than him. Adam kissed her because her mouth was there, waiting. His hands went instinctively to her waist and then moved upwards to a point just below her breasts. She felt soft, warm, exciting and gentle. Time stood still for a brief instant. He drew back slowly in order to see her face. Her eyes were wide and held his gaze steadily. Finally, they stood apart again, reluctantly, aware that temporal reality had returned once more.

'I must go,' she whispered. 'Thank you for today. *A presto,* Adam. See you soon.'

* * * * *

Fifteen minutes later, Adam was plodding up the stairs to the school. He greeted Daniela distractedly, noting that she had a sour expression on her face. Since there was nothing unusual about this, he did not give it much thought.

'You left these on my desk, A-damn.' Adam looked. Daniela handed him a folder of, as yet, uncorrected essays written by her fiancé's group. 'I have read Claudio's essay,' she said moodily. 'I wanted to see how his English is progressing.' This last sentence was clearly meant to be an accusation.

'Good for you, Daniela!' said Adam cheerfully. 'I was just going to correct them.'

'After your next class which is waiting for you,' said Daniela in a tetchy voice.

'What class?' asked Adam in bewilderment.

'There are five new girls in your classroom, A-damn. They have been waiting since four o'clock. I told you about this class yesterday.'

'I don't believe you did, Daniela,' he replied. Whatever Adam's shortcomings in his private life, he was meticulous about his professional life. 'In fact,' he continued, 'I am quite positive you didn't tell me.'

Daniela, he knew, was trying to cover up her own omission. She had not wanted to lose face, which, for Italians, is the worst fate that can befall them. 'Ah well, not to worry, Daniela,' he said airily. 'It's only ten past four. 'I'll give them extra time at the end of the lesson.'

He went into the classroom and was faced by a group of young women, younger than Rosaria, all of whom had jet black hair, beautiful brown eyes, olive skins and smiling faces. Adam apologised for his lateness, saying that he had lost track of time –

which was certainly true. He resisted the temptation to say that the school secretary had forgotten to tell him about the new class.

'I hope we shall get on well together,' he added.

'Oh yes!' they assured him with renewed smiles.

At the end of the ninety minute lesson – without cigarette break – Adam ran into Glenda.

'Ah, Adam,' she said in a tetchy voice. Not another one, thought Adam. 'I suppose you will be wanting your umbrella back?'

'Oh, Glenda, I am so sorry!' He had completely forgotten about his act of desertion at lunchtime. I'll explain what happened when we next have lunch together.'

'There had better be a woman involved,' she said. Glenda's good nature had reasserted itself immediately – unlike the school secretary who continued to scowl darkly at him.

'What's eating Daniela?' he asked Glenda.

'Oh, you mean you don't know? Haven't you read Claudio's essay yet?'

Adam explained that he was about to do so. 'Well, go on then!' said Glenda, obviously maliciously enjoying the situation. Since she annoyingly refused to explain what was amusing her, Adam had no alternative but to sit down and correct the group's essays.

He had set a simple essay to be written in the closing twenty minutes of the last lesson with the BB group in order to allow him to escape outside and get a breath of fresh air. 'Write a few words about how you see your future,' he had instructed them. Now, overwhelmed by curiosity, Adam rifled through the sheets of notepaper until he found Claudio's literary offering, written in blue ink and small neat handwriting.

Esteemed teacher

My name is Claudio. I have 38 years. I work for a syndicate called CGIL. I am engaged to my girl called Daniela who work in this school. She is secretary. My biggest wish is to meet a beautiful blond Sweden girl with large brest who will make love with me all day and night. She do not need to be rich because I will be principle director of big italian company that export Salento's wine and oil of olive in America.

Signed Claudio.

Adam was choking with laughter while he read the essay. No wonder Daniela had looked at him accusingly – as if he was entirely to blame for Claudio writing such scurrilous material. Later, as he made a photocopy of Claudio's essay for the sake of posterity, he thought he should pour a little oil on troubled waters. Adam marked the remaining essays, which were mundane by comparison. The other members of the group merely wanted safe, permanent jobs – largely a pipe dream in southern Italy – and to be married and have two or three beautiful children. None of them, thought Adam sadly, wished to be cured of the Bad Breath problem, which, in his opinion, may well have paved the way to success in achieving their other ambitions. Adam was not looking forward to facing Claudio and telling him that his masterpiece had been discovered by his beloved *fidanzata.* Later on that day, he only had to take one look at Claudio's face to understand that war had already broken out.

'I'm sorry, Claudio,' Adam said in Italian. 'Daniela read it without asking me. But I shouldn't have left the folder lying about.' It was plain that a deflated Claudio was not holding Adam responsible.

'Your English is really quite good,' he said with a smile – which was not reciprocated.

At lunchtime, the following day, Adam and Glenda were having lunch chez Fernando and joking about Claudio's essay. 'I think that we can conclude from the text that Claudio is not getting it on a regular basis,' said Glenda mischievously. After the main course, Adam apologised for leaving Glenda in the lurch the day before.

'Oh, there's no need to apologise, Adam. I can see there's a woman in your life and I'm happy for you. And...' she added, 'I was right. You will be needing my professional help after all.' Adam was piqued that she had arrived so self-assuredly at the correct conclusion, and furthermore, that she was taking so much pleasure in being right.

'How can you jump to such wild conclusions?' he said defensively. 'I might have had a dental appointment for all you know.'

'Well,' replied Miss-Know-it-All, 'in the first place, no Italian dentist would work over lunchtime and siesta time. And secondly, the transformation of your image from corduroy trousers, green cardigan and that awful maroon blazer to jeans and casual jacket clearly indicates the hand of a woman. You look *very* nice, by the way, Adam.'

Adam conceded with good grace that she was right on all counts, but he took his revenge by refusing point blank to divulge any details. He took some small pleasure in the look of thwarted curiosity on her face as she cut up her meat balls in tomato sauce.

'Are you *with* anyone, Glenda?'

'Yes, I suppose I am. He's called Antonio. We aren't married.'

'What does he do?'

'Sometimes he digs holes with a mechanical digger. At the moment, he's playing at being a fisherman on his cousin's boat. He's out most nights and thinks he's supporting me when he brings back a sea bass or something.'

'So you don't see him much or...' Adam left unsaid what he was about to say. He was thinking of the shortcomings in Claudio's intimate life.

'Which suits me just *fine!*' she added decidedly.

In future conversations, Glenda's partner was usually referred to as Pedro or 'The Big A'.

After the meal, Adam felt more like a siesta than teaching. He had been very busy that morning. Not only had he bought a pair of casual shoes but he had also overcome his reluctance to buy his first mobile phone, at Rosaria's insistence. He had to ask a student for help in sending a text message to Rosaria, giving her his number.

At five o'clock, he was teaching at the bank. Rosaria was not there. Inside, he felt the onset of panic.

'Where's Rosaria?' he asked in what he hoped was a casual voice. Evidently, it fooled nobody.

'Don't worry, A-damn,' said Federica in a reassuring voice. 'She's probably been held up at work.'

'Or she's met her *fidanzato*,' suggested one of the others in all innocence.

'Oh, I'm not worried,' Adam lied with the certain conviction that Federica had understood everything. She had already confided in Rosaria that Adam looked at her with that *occhio speciale* – 'that special look'.

One of the men took Adam back to Campanula that evening. He wanted to invite Adam round for coffee there and then. Adam excused himself saying that he had to teach but that he would certainly accept the invitation with pleasure another time.

Adam taught his evening class and walked back to the bleak house where he ate a slice of heated up pizza. He had the awful sensation that he had been abandoned. The next day was Friday - a normal day of food shopping, lunch with Glenda and teaching the afternoon and evening classes with little prospect of seeing Rosaria.

He went to bed for want of anything better to do, a feeling of encroaching loneliness stealing up on him. He was dozing off when an unaccustomed series of twin beeps brought him back to consciousness. His new mobile phone, he realised. The gadget informed him that there was a text message waiting for him. After some fumbling with the tiny, unfamiliar keys, he succeeded in revealing the message. It was all in capital letters with no punctuation. It read: ADAM I AM OUTSIDE YOUR FRONT DOOR ROSY

10: Extracurricular Activities

Adam's reaction to Rosaria's unexpected text message might have been comical had it not been also life threatening. He hopped around the bedroom trying to get his legs into a pair of jeans without removing the pyjamas he was already wearing. There then followed a wild, arm-waving performance as if he was sending frantic semaphore messages as he attempted simultaneously to do up his trousers, take off his pyjama top and put on a shirt, whose tiny buttons were too great a challenge for his fumbling fingers. The hasty descent down the steep, stone staircase in semi-darkness, shoes unlaced, could easily have pitched him down to the bottom of the stairwell, thus ending his short career as an English teacher and latter-day Casanova in one fell swoop.

Oddly enough, even amidst his headlong dash to catch the new love of his life before she gave up and drove off into the night, the part of his brain still capable of exercising rational judgement was questioning whether anyone was worth risking life and limb for in this undignified manner. 'And why did you not just send her a text message telling her to hang on a minute?' Adam even had time to find an answer to that challenge, namely that it would have taken him longer to have fiddled with the tiny keys than simply getting dressed. 'So why didn't you call her?' persisted the other part of his brain. 'Ah!' he replied, 'why didn't I think of that?'

He made it safely down to the bottom of the stairs and flung open the door just in time to see Rosaria crossing the road towards her car. 'Rosy!' he shouted desperately into the almost deserted night-time street. She turned round and started to cross back towards the flat. The expression on her face appeared to be one of disapproval, which registered painfully in the pit of his stomach.

Dancing to the Pizzica

An over-sensitive Adam had still to understand that it was not disapproval but total mental and physical stress at the risk involved of being identified by someone she knew, driving past, who might witness her entering a stranger's house at that time of the evening. Adam had no concept of the scandal that such an act would provoke in this small town where half the population was related to her. Even later on, when he had begun to grasp what was at stake, his Anglo-Saxon mind-set rejected the notion that a twenty-nine year old woman was not free to act in any way she saw fit.

'Rosy,' he began, still breathless after his exertions and the secret thrill of this unexpected twilight visit. She pushed him into the darkened doorway before grasping him in her arms, her lips seeking his in a warm kiss.

'Shall we go upstairs?' he asked needlessly. As he led the way, Adam felt the gust of wind that blew through the house and stairwell just an instant before he knew that the door to the apartment was about to slam shut. Of course, in his haste, he had left the keys in the lock on the inside of the door. He had visions of having to sit on the landing all night and then seek help in the morning, half-dressed, with no money, no passport and no mobile phone. Rosaria seemed more amused than alarmed. Afterwards, she told him that she would have found somewhere for him to sleep. He felt his panic attack to be unmanly, but he could not overcome the insidious fear of being homeless in a strange town. There was only one solution as far as Adam was concerned and, propelled by a mixture of frustration and anger at the living conditions foisted on him by Daniela, he aimed a vicious kick at the double doors, which yielded with a crack as the latch was forced apart from its housing. Amazingly, there was no lasting damage done. He felt irrationally jubilant – as one does when fear is banished to reveal banal reality to be, after all, something to be treasured. He took Rosaria by the hand and led her into the house with a feeling of profound excitement at her nocturnal visit. They stood in the tiny kitchen and kissed again, more confidently now that they were safely inside the house.

'Where have you been, Rosy? I was beginning to wonder if I would ever see you again.' She made no attempt to reply. Instead, he felt her warm tongue pushing against his while she was propelling him backwards on to the waiting kitchen chair.

'You are being seduced,' he thought with a rational clarity that impressed him. 'By a woman little more than half your age,' added the still functioning part of his brain accusingly. But Adam had been leading a celibate life for a staggering four years – apart from his single transgression in Vicenza. Thus, he had no more chance of overcoming his physical desire than a man jumping from an aeroplane without a parachute has of avoiding being dashed to pieces on the earth below. 'An apt metaphor,' added his brain in a timely warning which he simply ignored.

He felt the back of his knees being pushed up against the seat of the chair, forcing him to sit down. Rosaria sat astride him high up on his lap, revealing to Adam the apex formed by her bare legs and the black material of her panties curving smoothly round her inviting thighs. She was wearing the most intense expression that he had ever seen on a woman's face. He could feel the soft warmth of her flesh transferring its warmth and softness to him as he felt the swell of the rising tide. Her mouth kissed his mouth. 'Now you're finished!' said the small voice that was still feebly resisting the temptation to give in. Adam marvelled at the physical mechanism by which the coming together of two people's bodies in the sacred act of making love had been designed by nature to be so irresistible and inevitable.

'*Facciamo l'amore,*' whispered Rosaria's voice in his ear as his final attempt at resistance collapsed. He just had time to register that these were the first words that she had uttered since her arrival. They made love for the first time with passionate intensity on the narrow bed which sagged even lower under the weight of their two bodies. It had not lasted more than a few immeasurable minutes. Adam explained that it was the first time for ages that he had made love. The look on her face showed a mixture of mild disbelief accompanied by a hint of relief that she was not just one woman in a rapid succession of lovers. 'I'm sorry if I came a bit too...' he began. She kissed him all over his face and smiled with an imperceptible shake of her head. They curled up in a close embrace, made almost essential if one of them were not to be pitched over the edge of the bed. Their faces were only inches apart. How strange that they could look into each other's eyes without averting their gaze, thought Adam, thinking that this had never happened to him before.

'But why choose me, Rosy?' Adam asked when, finally, the tides of passion had retreated. 'You are young and very beautiful. You could have the whole world courting you, if you wanted. Besides, I must be as old as your father,' he said expressing this doubt in full for the first time.

'Slightly older,' admitted Rosaria with a smile. 'But it doesn't matter, Adam. I don't think of you as older than me. You are brave because you are so far from home. I wish I had that level of courage. You are independent. I want to share that independence with you. You are lovely. I love the shape of your legs and your shoulders. You are not like any fifty-year-old *I* have ever known. I don't care about your age. I was so afraid, in the restaurant, that you were telling me I was too young for you. I want you the way you are – for ever.'

They began to kiss again, slowly, enjoying the new sensation at a more measured pace. After a time, Adam became aware of the sound of a yapping dog. It was a constant noise that was becoming an irritant. The noise came from an animal that was kept permanently on its owner's flat rooftop. The sound kept him awake for hours on end as he lay on the uncomfortable bed in the small hours of the morning. Rosaria could see that it bothered her new lover.

'I can arrange for the problem to be solved, Adam,' she said in all seriousness. He looked askance at her. 'What *do* you mean?' he asked. 'Oh, I know people who can take care of any problems,' she answered. 'It would cost you in some way – money, or returned favours. It would depend on the terms they set.' The matter-of-fact manner in which Rosaria had delivered this statement sounded sinister. He wanted to seek further enlightenment but she pre-empted any further questions by curling her body tightly round his. Her breasts, pressed up against his chest, were an irresistible distraction. 'I want to tell you about my cousin, Diletta, too, but not now, not tonight Adam. I just want to enjoy our first...'

Whatever Rosaria was about to say was interrupted by the ringing of her mobile phone somewhere in the vast space of the bedroom. The spell was broken in a trice. She broke free from the embrace with a look of near panic in her eyes as she rifled feverishly through her handbag. She looked at the screen and then at Adam. 'It's *mamma!*' she said putting her forefinger to her lips, signalling to Adam not to betray his presence. The rapid conversation with her mother, whose raucous cigarette smoker's voice Adam could clearly hear, was yet another cultural revelation.

'But *mamma,* why are you so anxious?'

'It's nearly half past eleven, Rosy. Where are you?'

'I'm in Gravino with Anna,' Rosaria lied smoothly. 'I didn't realise it was so late. I'm on my way home now.'

Then he heard the mother's voice saying something that he could not quite catch. Rosaria's face had turned white. She rang off and said to Adam: *'Papà* is out in his car driving around looking for me. He is about to call the *carabinieri.* I have to go *now,* Adam.'

She had hardly begun to get dressed whilst collecting her scattered belongings when the phone rang again. 'Benedetto!' she exclaimed in irritation. 'Inevitable, I suppose,' she added as if talking to herself. Once again, she pleaded for silence while she took the call. Adam was, in any case, too shocked to say anything, feeling distinctly that he was a mere spectator in this family drama unfolding before his eyes. Benedetto was dismissed in a peremptory manner. 'I'll see you tomorrow,' she added by way of grudging consolation.

'Now you understand why I couldn't come and see you before tonight, Adam,' she said closing the gap between them and kissing him hurriedly on the mouth. She pulled away quickly before the inevitable parting became harder. 'I have to cope with all of this,' she added waving a hand at empty space. They both went down the stairs as far as the front door. 'Don't come out in the street, Adam, just in case my *papà* is in the vicinity. I'll see you as soon as I can. I promise.' She planted a fleeting kiss on his lips and she was gone without a backward glance, nervously looking to the right and left as she crossed the road towards her car.

'Incredible!' thought Adam as he plodded up the steep steps once again, this time clutching the keys tightly in his balled fist. The usually miserable flat seemed filled with her presence, the perfume of her skin and the sound of her melodious voice. Adam felt a mixture of contentment that he had made love to Rosaria, tempered with only a touch of guilt that he had poached the forbidden fruit – even though reason told him that he had been invited into the whole orchard. Above all, he no longer felt alone. He lay down on the bed, once again reminding himself to phone Daniele the following morning and ask him to send a double bed down from Lecce. The dog on the roof began its endless yapping – or maybe it had never ceased barking and he had simply not noticed it. Adam thought again about the ominous offer of 'help' that Rosaria had proposed. He was deeply curious as to what she had meant. In the end, he drifted into a dreamless sleep sometime after one o'clock. The dog had grown momentarily tired of its rooftop protest. Adam's final thought before sleep overtook him was that it should be the owner rather than the hapless dog that needed eliminating. As he drifted into sleep, he wondered what price would have to be paid to achieve such a drastic outcome.

* * * * *

The following day – a Thursday – started off like any normal day for Adam, in as much as any day in this period of his life could be called 'normal'. He was sitting in the *Antica Isolata* waiting for Glenda to arrive for their usual lunchtime tryst. She duly appeared after a few minutes with a broad grin on her face. Adam had the distinct impression that her smile seemed to be directed at the world in general rather than specifically at her colleague. Never mind, he was feeling magnanimous today and as she sat down opposite him, he commented wryly:

'You're looking perky today, Glenda. Is something right in your life for a change?'

She laughed as she sat down but, as usual, was not going to enlighten him – at least not without keeping him guessing for as long as possible. Today, Adam decided to play along with her game.

'Is it the Big A?' he asked. 'Has he managed to get a job demolishing the centre of Lecce? Did he catch a whole tuna last night?'

'He's certainly managed to achieve *something* at last!' she exclaimed with elation in her voice. 'I'm pregnant,' she declared. Adam showered his colleague with delighted noises of congratulations. He proposed a toast with their two glasses filled with mineral water. She had already told him repeatedly that having babies was the main reason for staying with Pedro.

'Just one or two more to go,' she said seriously, 'and I can leave him.'

This, Adam decided, was the remarkable thing about Glenda. Most other women whom he had come across wanted to have children as part of an economically and emotionally stable family life. Glenda just wanted to have children for the sake of being a mother. It was noble of her in some crazy kind of way, he considered. She had set aside any dream of future prosperity, being quite content to survive from week to week.

'Anyway, Adam,' commented Glenda with a twinkle in her eyes. 'You're looking a bit perky yourself today!' Adam was astonished –

and mildly irritated – that she had been so perceptive. 'Oh well, you know,' he replied in his usual unconvincing attempt at sounding casual, 'I'm beginning to feel a lot more relaxed about life down here.'

'Oh,' said Glenda sarcastically, 'you mean it's nothing to do with that beautiful girl who drops you off outside the school after every lesson you have at the BPS?' Adam's surprise was impossible to conceal. He had the strong desire to tip his plate of spaghetti and tomato sauce over her just to see the smug expression on her face disappear for a minute. But his sense of humour got the better of him and he admitted defeat gracefully.

'Are there any secrets in my life that I *can* keep from you?' he said with mock annoyance.

'None at all, Adam,' she said delightedly. 'I have seen you on several occasions getting out of that *Cinquecento* – you can hardly fail to notice her car! She is *very* beautiful, by the way.'

'That, at least, I cannot dispute,' he conceded willingly.

'Have you already...?' she began with ill-suppressed curiosity.

'Oh yes, Glenda, I'm sorry. I've already ordered pork steak in tomato sauce – with *patate al forno.'*

Seeing the look of mild frustration on Glenda's face was very satisfying.

'You be careful, Adam!' Glenda added, taking Adam's evasive answer to her intended question as an affirmative.

A bit late for caution, thought Adam, with a twinge of apprehension.

* * * * *

Later on that day, Adam was waiting for Danilo outside the school. He had arrived earlier than usual and seemed even more under pressure than usual. 'There's a bed and a mattress in the back for you,' he declared impatiently. 'Daniele says he's sorry but the school doesn't provide double beds for teachers. He says will another single one do?' Adam took the news philosophically. The fate of all EFL teachers was to live out their lives in celibate poverty like medieval monks and nuns. They took the bed frame and mattress round to Adam's flat and Danilo helped him upstairs with them. They were only five minutes late for the lesson. Danilo, his underlying Neapolitan good humour restored, held out his hand and shook it warmly.

'Congratulations, A-damn,' he said. 'I hope it helps!'

Apparently, Adam had no hope at all in this country of keeping his personal life a secret from those around him. *'Viva l'Italia!'* he muttered under his breath. As he was going up the stairs to the bank, his mobile phone gave a double beep. A message from Rosaria – he had not yet given his number to anyone else. She was delayed at work, she said, but would do her best to meet him outside the bank after the lesson. Adam felt a strange mixture of disappointment and relief; disappointment because he was unsure whether he would see her that day, yet relief because he would not have to pretend to treat her like the rest of the class. He had already told her off once for speaking in Italian instead of English, which had not gone down well. He was greeted warmly by the group. Federica announced with a teasing smile that Rosaria did not appear to be present. 'Ah well, she has probably been delayed at work,' he said in the most unconcerned voice he could muster. Federica merely waved her mobile phone from side to side in a conspiratorial gesture which clearly told Adam that *she* was not to be fooled. For a brief instant, Adam entertained the treacherous thought that, had it not been for Rosaria, he might have pursued this petite, lovely, lively woman. He was instantly appalled by the ease with which this thought had popped up unbidden and smothered it immediately. *'Men!'* he thought ironically and began teaching.

At the end of the lesson, he was offered a lift by one of the other girls in the group. He declined the offer, making some excuse that Danilo had to return to the school to collect some documents. 'Adam, you are besotted,' he told himself in no uncertain terms. If Rosaria had not made it in time, he would be forced to walk the two kilometres back to Campanula and be really late for his last lesson. Adam walked down the steps looking out for Rosaria's car in the approaching dusk. His faith in Rosaria was vindicated; he could see her car at the far end of the parking area, standing out like a beacon amidst all the old grey and dark blue-coloured cars favoured by most of the drivers in Salento.

He almost failed to register the presence of the old, dark blue FIAT parked just in front of the steps outside the bank. A man of about thirty, whose head and shoulders were visible above the door sill of the car, was scrutinising intensely every person who was leaving the building. 'I wouldn't like to run into *him* on a dark night,' thought Adam. There was something disturbing about the expression on his face – like a hawk eying up its prey. Adam felt that he was being singled out for special scrutiny in the few seconds that it took him to walk past the car and its occupant. But a brief glance back at the car confirmed that he was still checking everyone as they came down the steps. The impression that Adam had received in the split second of eye contact with the man was one of suspicion and fear rather than threat. And yet, Adam had felt a hint of menace. He had the impression that he should have drawn some conclusion from the presence of this individual, which was eluding him.

He got into Rosaria's car and leant over to kiss her. 'Not here!' she hissed. He suspected that he had deliberately made this gesture to be provocative and to put their new intimacy to the test. Evidently, it was premature.

It is, Adam had read somewhere, a sign of intelligence in a person that they will make logical connections that the less intelligent do not. He had noticed that Rosaria often surprised him with comments displaying a perspicacity that was obvious once the thought had been expressed. Adam assumed, wrongly perhaps, that he was not overburdened with intelligence. However, he did occasionally display the gift of intuitive insight. He had such a flash of inspiration at that moment, sitting next to Rosaria in her car.

'Does Benedetto drive an old dark blue *Cinquecento* with the letters KP in the registration number?'

'Yes,' she replied. 'How did you know?'

'Because he's sitting in his car over there, looking at everyone coming out of the bank,' stated Adam.

The effect on Rosaria was electric. She turned pale, as the blood drained from her face. She accelerated the car out on to the road already becoming congested with cars being driven home in the growing twilight.

'*Oh Dio!*' she said looking desperately in the rear view mirror. The fear on her face was too obvious to ignore. 'Let me get out quickly here,' offered Adam.

'No, it's too late. He must have spotted my car, leaving. He is already following us five or six cars behind. Adam, PLEASE,' she pleaded, 'I don't want him to find out this way. Will you hide on the floor of the car while I lose him. I'm sorry. He mustn't see I've got a passenger with me. There will be an hour-long interrogation. He's so jealous and suspicious of *everybody!*

Adam was about to protest, but the look on Rosaria's face was compelling. He slid the seat back as far as it would go and crouched uncomfortably on the floor with his knees almost touching his nose. He was so impressed by *her* fear that he had no room for fear himself. He had an entirely novel view of his new lover looking up at her from below and he found the situation exciting. He attempted humour but Rosaria was too terrified to appreciate anything but the immediate threat of exposure. Adam was flung around as she took unexpected turns. Judging by the hoots from other cars, he guessed that she had cut in front of a few irate drivers. The car came to a sudden halt. Rosaria said: 'Stay there a bit longer Adam – please! I'm so sorry about this. I'll phone you later. Give me a couple of minutes to get clear.' She got out of the car and walked down the street without locking it. A few seconds later, he heard her voice talking to someone whom he presumed must be Benedetto. He heard the rough, local accent of a male voice saying something he could not catch. The voices moved away. Adam counted up to fifty before extricating himself from the car. This manoeuvre was trickier than he had anticipated. He had to get out on to the pavement feet first while his bottom was still on the floor of the car. He got a very strange look from a woman pushing a pram along. 'Dropped my keys,' he said with a stupid grin on his face as he righted himself and took stock of his surroundings. He did not recognise where he was but thought he should head off in the opposite direction to where Rosaria had gone. After a five minute walk, he found himself back in the main square. He ran up upstairs and arrived out of breath in order to impress Daniela. He was treated to a disapproving scowl as he passed her office. He felt disinclined to grace her with an explanation for his lateness. It was obvious that she was still nettled by Claudio's fantasy blond Swedish girl 'with large brest'.

Adam was developing a liking for the Bad Breath group – despite their obvious shortcoming. Most of the group were surprisingly serious about learning English. Like many southern Italians, they saw English as a kind of exit visa to other parts of the world, where they imagined that the economic climate was as favourable as their own meteorological climate in Puglia.

That evening, after a drink with the BB group in the bar opposite the school, Adam went home. He had decided he should remonstrate with Rosaria next time she phoned, so that they could avoid any repetition of the incident earlier that evening. Adam was nearly asleep again when the sound of his mobile phone trilling out some version of a Chopin piece echoed through the empty house.

'Adam,' her voice whispered in his ear. 'I'm so sorry about this afternoon. Are you angry with me? I panicked a bit. I'm so ashamed.'

'Don't be silly, Rosaria,' he said magnanimously, inexplicably forgetting to remonstrate. 'I panicked too when I thought I had locked myself out of the house. Remember? Besides which you drove like a champion.'

'Grazie, Adam. Senti, ci vediamo sabato. D'accordo?'

'Saturday sounds great to me, Rosy. See you then.' He was pleased that the time spent without seeing her had a term to it.

'*Ti amo. A presto, Adam,*' said Rosaria and rang off before he could react. 'She just said she loves me,' said Adam as a feeling of warmth spread over his body. 'You pathetic romantic!' said the other part of his brain which, Adam noticed, was becoming increasingly persistent.

Adam's sleep, however, was upset by dreams of being chased around the dimly lit streets of some alien city by shadowy figures wearing hoods. He woke up to the yapping of the dog. After two hours of sleeplessness, he began to think seriously about Rosaria's offer of contacting 'the people who could solve any problems'. But what if Benedetto knew these nebulous problem solvers too? Perhaps Adam himself might become the victim of some efficient, invisible eliminating agent. In the end, the dog got tired and Adam's fears subsided, allowing him to fall asleep for three more hours.

The morning dawned warm and sunny and the inhabitants of Campanula began to go about their early morning business – the refuse collectors did their daily round at the crack of dawn. Adam's night time fears receded like the early morning mists. Life felt reassuringly normal again. He started to compose a text message to Rosaria saying...what, exactly? He contemplated sending her the words: 'I love you too', but felt it would be a copy-cat reaction. He wanted to savour the thrilling sensation of hearing those words from her for the first time. And then he would choose *his* moment when he would say the same words to her spontaneously. For now, he contented himself by saying simply: 'I can't wait to see you again, Rosy.' He walked happily into the town centre for his first *espresso* of the day – the magic dose that would dispel the lingering images of his nocturnal dreams.

11: In Which Adam Learns an Awful Lot

The town centre of Campanula was undergoing some drastic transformation. Men, with the agility of monkeys, were climbing up vertical ladders which were attached to trolleys some ten metres below them. These trolleys were being held steady by two other men to prevent them free-wheeling down the street. Nobody was wearing safety helmets or harnesses. In England, Adam mused, the streets would be awash with Health and Safety inspectors busily preparing their civil case notes. The men at the top of the ladders were manoeuvring white wooden arches into position, attaching them by any available means possible to buildings or street lights either side of the narrow streets. The arches were studded with different coloured light bulbs, like jewels in a crown. Other men were unloading a lorry, stacked high with arches, as the vehicle proceeded at a steady pace up the road towards the main piazza. Adam felt he was observing the progress of some wild, arbitrary circus act.

'What's going on?' he asked the barman in his favourite bar.

'*La festa!*' replied the barman in a tone of voice that suggested it was blatantly obvious. '*La festa di San Giovanni* – it's on Sunday,' he added seeing Adam's uncomprehending expression. Adam thanked the barman and ordered a *cornetto* and another espresso. Know-it-all-Glenda would be able to fill in the details at lunchtime.

On this bright, sunny morning, it was difficult to imagine what the effect of all these coloured lights would be when nightfall descended on the town. In the main *piazza, San Giovanni* towered above the proceedings, his hand still raised in blessing on all the frenzied activity going on beneath him – in his honour. A large stage mounted on scaffolding with batteries of loudspeakers all around was being erected at the foot of *San Giovanni's* plinth. Adam was amazed at the transformation being wrought by just a handful of men working like bees. It would never happen like this in England, he thought. The whole procedure had an air of spontaneity about it that marked it out from anything he had witnessed in his own country.

Glenda added further interesting details over lunch. He learnt, for instance, that a group of singers and musicians from Sannicola, the village where she lived, would be performing live on Sunday evening, singing and dancing the *pizzica*.

'Sounds more like something you eat,' muttered Adam.

'You must come and see for yourself, Adam. It's really quite spectacular in a unique southern Italian kind of way. People flock here from all the surrounding villages. You can't move for the crowds – or their cars.'

'Of course I'll come, Glenda. I hope Rosaria will be there too,' he muttered to himself without thinking.

The Glenda ears were twitching.

'Rosaria?' she said. 'Adam, I think you have just let a small cat out of the bag!'

Adam swore quietly to himself. He had spoken without thinking. Know-it-All Glenda had gleaned another fragment of information to add to her store of knowledge. Adam was obliged to confirm to Glenda that Rosaria was a member of the group he was teaching at the BPS. As a result of talking about teaching at the bank, Glenda added details about Danilo, the driver, telling Adam that Danilo had got into some kind of trouble with his local *Camorra* clan in Naples.

'Danilo is virtually in hiding down here,' she explained. Adam digested this piece of information thoughtfully. Something that Danilo had told Adam about Naples being 'too hot for him' now made a lot more sense.

* * * * *

It was Saturday morning. Rosaria would be arriving at some unspecified time of the day – or night. This time, Adam resolved to be ready for her and to avoid the undignified haste occasioned by her previous visit. He could no longer deny the role that this singular woman was playing in his life. The gradual process of getting to know her – emotionally and physically – was like discovering a new, unchartered country. He was an explorer braving an unknown land in search of that ultimate treasure – true happiness. 'Fanciful nonsense!' exclaimed other brain. But Adam was happy to be carried along on the tide of events and quickly relegated any rational objections to the outposts of his mind.

Adam busied himself erecting the spare bed that Daniele had supplied. Comically, he improvised with the complete lack of suitable materials in his possession. He found some string and Sellotape and bound the two single beds together by their iron frames to make something resembling a double bed. But the mattress which Daniele had supplied was of a different thickness to the existing one and left a lumpy ridge down the middle. As good luck would have it, he heard a vendor's lorry in the street below. Such vendors passed every day, he had noticed, selling everything from pots and pans, fruit and vegetables and, of more immediate interest, bedding and mattresses. He could just make out the words for 'duvets' and 'mattresses' announced by the vendor over the loudspeakers attached to the lorry. He ran downstairs, keys in hand, just in time to see the lorry driving off and turning up a side street. Minutes later, Adam and the vendor were humping a double mattress up the steep stairway. He also bought fitted sheets, a duvet and new pillows, parting with a quarter of his monthly wages in the process. A small price to pay, he considered, to render the remaining months of his stay more bearable. Now, all he had to do was to wait for Rosaria to arrive.

This took most of the remaining daylight hours. Not only was Rosaria fearful about being seen going into a stranger's house, but Saturday mornings, he soon learnt, were taken up by scheduled visits from her hairdresser or her beautician, a compulsory family lunch with whichever aunties, uncles or cousins came along, a siesta to recover from the rigours of ensuring that one continued to look beautiful during the week to come, a hair-wash and, finally, a trip with *papà* to his shop to sort out some tax issue.

Being ignorant of how onerous Rosaria's responsibilities were, Adam became progressively anxious about her non-appearance. All his latent insecurities prompted him to believe that she must have had a change of heart. The other part of his brain suggested to him that he should consider the possibility that he was just a middle-aged man sliding down the slippery slope of infatuation. It took Adam a little more time to subdue this unwanted message. Just as he was about to concede that 'other brain' had a good point, Rosaria arrived. She had parked some way down the road that descended to the station and had walked up the hill texting him at the same moment. All the shadows of doubt mysteriously vanished as soon as she was standing in front of him smiling and happy. She was wearing some dark blue lacy garment that allowed a glimpse of warm, tanned breasts beneath the shifting strands of material.

'Other brain' gave up in despair. Adam felt the comfortable stirring of warmth in his loins, a manifestation which seemed not to have escaped Rosaria's notice. She headed directly for the bedroom and stared in astonishment at the changes that had been wrought.

'How strange, Adam,' she said with an entirely serious expression on her face. 'It appears that our bed has doubled in size too.'

'I suspect the bed's change of dimensions will be longer-lasting,' he commented.ironically.

It had become a natural linguistic response to being of different nationalities for Rosaria to speak in Italian while Adam replied in English. Rosaria was fond of mimicking Adam's accent when he spoke Italian, even though Adam, the teacher, regularly complimented her on her English accent. But in the end, the purposes of communication were better served by talking in their respective languages.

Words became redundant after their brief exchange about the size of the bed. Adam still felt nervous about making love to a woman so much younger than he was, even though she was showing no signs of embarrassment herself – quite the contrary.

Adam had suspected that his past lovers, though willing and compliant enough, had not reached a climax. He had tried to increase his powers of endurance but had usually surrendered to the inevitable before his partners had reached that explosive moment of release.

With Rosaria, he wanted making love to be different. He was not sure what was prompting this shift away from mere sexual self-indulgence. His motives were complex. Adam was convinced that his relationship with Rosaria was going to be something special;

that she had been the reason why fate had played a hand in his coming to this place so far from home. He had the intuitive belief that she was to be the last great gift from the abundant store of treasures that life can bestow so unexpectedly.

Rosaria did not seem to need a long period of foreplay. She gasped with pleasure as Adam entered her slowly and deeply. He tried to distract himself from that initial surge of pleasure. He had recently watched a comedy on TV about a man who underwent a course designed to increase his sexual staying power. He had visited the same prostitute three times a week for a month. She had devoted herself whole-heartedly to her task and her 'patient' had improved visit by visit until she had become so sexually satisfied that she had waived the payment. To his credit, Adam had never watched porn movies. He failed to understand how people were turned on by watching the parody of love-making as portrayed so mockingly in porn movies. It degraded the act of love. It should be a mental experience, Adam believed. As he made love, Adam felt as if he was deep inside a grotto, bathed in warm water that was drawing him down to the depths below. Then there would be that wonderful, timeless moment when all the images exploded inside his head like a rainbow fragmenting into a shower of tiny particles of coloured stars before he became aware that the clock had started ticking again.

With Rosaria, he was swimming deep inside his grotto. But now he had to face the practical problem of delaying the climax of such powerful sensations. He began to plan what he would eat for lunch the next day. He kept up the physical motions of making love, placing his hands around her buttocks and holding them tightly. She had fallen silent, however. He was afraid she was getting bored. He was becoming more and more excited. He desperately resorted to counting mentally the number of times he moved inside her body. He began, very optimistically at fifty-one, fifty-two, fifty-three... Rosaria's silence protracted out to an interminable fifteen seconds more. He was about to let go. Then the miracle happened. He heard those enchanted sounds coming from inside her as she gasped out her long cries of pleasure. He could let go at last.

He stayed inside her but raised himself up on straightened arms, so he could look down into her eyes, glazed with pleasure, seeing what his perseverance had achieved. This was to be a turning point in his life. Not even 'other brain' could contradict him this time.

'*Grazie amore. Sei stato magnifico!* I knew I was right to choose you,' said Rosaria finally. The irony of the situation amused Adam. 'If only you knew, Rosy,' he thought.

'So were you, Rosy. Magnificent! Now I can stop looking.'

It was doubtful if Rosaria had understood the significance of Adam's last sentence. But *he* knew what he meant. With Rosaria, he was ready to keep those empty promises made so long ago at the altar – promises so shamefully broken. His search was over; that is what he had meant.

After a minute of gazing intensely at her new lover, Rosaria said: 'I need a coffee, Adam.' He would get used to this ritual and would always have the *moka* pot primed and ready on top of the cooker. Adam's post love-making fix consisted of eating cheese, which he could not readily explain. Happily, this was a craving that could easily be satisfied in this land of plenty. Rosaria stayed in bed with the duvet wrapped round her, while Adam brought the tiny cups of scalding black liquid back to bed. Then there followed the best part of love-making; the hugs, the cuddles, the relaxed caresses and the quietly expressed words of comfort and affection. And afterwards, it was time to talk, or rather, in Adam's case, to listen. After Rosaria's period of reluctance to broach the painful subject of her murdered cousin, at Adam's prompting, the words came tumbling out. He was impressed and amused that, before launching into the events surrounding Diletta's death, Rosaria felt it necessary to get half-dressed again – out of respect for the fact that, in her mind's eye, her whole family were gathered together in the room as well. Her account was vivid and compelling as she conjured up images of her sister, Martina, the twins, her aunties Flavia and Liliana, her own parents and the eventual discovery of Diletta's body. Adam wanted to ask her questions, but there was barely a pause in Rosaria's narrative.

By the time she had finished talking, night time was once again falling outside. There was no question of Adam doubting the veracity of this incredible account. Rosaria had tears in her eyes and her deep involvement in these tragic events was all too apparent.

When she had finally come to the end of her narrative, there was a prolonged silence. Adam had so many questions to ask that he could not decide which one to ask first, So he began with one aspect that puzzled him most of all. 'But what possible reason could Enrico have had for murdering his wife? Why go through with the wedding at all?'

'I don't know. I lie awake at night trying to find an explanation that makes sense. I believe Diletta must have found something out about Enrico. Maybe she told him that she did not want to marry him. Maybe he was frightened of being exposed for what he is –

almost certainly part of a Calabrian mafia clan. He is an evil, ruthless man, Adam. I could sense it as soon as I met him. He knew that I did not like or trust him. He *knew* I had seen through him.'

'Are you *certain* it was Enrico who killed Diletta?'

'Yes, absolutely certain - I could see that she was upset before the wedding and rigid with fear as soon as she was married. I know her, Adam. She is my oldest friend as well as my cousin. And don't forget, Enrico left for London suddenly that morning without allowing Diletta's own mother to say goodbye to her daughter. He pretended she was still alive.'

'Yes, Rosy, you are right, of course. That is quite conclusive. Another thing,' asked Adam pensively. 'How come you managed to convince a captain of the *carabinieri* not to proceed with the investigation or pass on the information to Interpol in London?'

Rosaria was once again struck by Adam's perspicacity. 'In fact,' she answered, 'I suspect that I have only managed to stall an official investigation for a short period of time – maybe no more than a couple of months at most.'

'But surely the captain runs the risk of losing his job – or at least being disciplined in some way.'

Rosaria smiled a wistful smile as if wishing she too could share Adam's naïvety about her country. 'Oh Adam, you really don't know much about how our country works, I'm afraid. I'm not surprised. England must be so *uncomplicated*. The captain had a bit of pressure put on him to delay the investigation.'

'Pressure? Who put pressure on him, exactly? Apart from *you* I would imagine!' added Adam, knowing how persuasive she could be.

Rosaria became embarrassed, as if she had been caught out hiding a guilty secret. Adam had the impression that she had coloured slightly, although in the evening light it was difficult to be sure.

She took a deep breath before continuing: 'Adam, can I trust you *absolutely?* You must promise to tell *nobody* – especially not your colleague... What's her name? Glinda.'

'Glenda,' he corrected. He assured her that it would give him the greatest pleasure imaginable to know something that she did not. 'Besides,' he added, seeing that Rosaria had not appreciated his attempt at English irony, 'I would never do or say *anything* that might harm you.'

'You must also promise not to be shocked,' continued Rosaria. 'Even if you are, please don't make a hasty judgement about what I did.'

Adam was intrigued and not a little alarmed at what he was going to learn about his new lover. But he took her hand solemnly and said: 'I promise.'

Rosaria took a deep breath and began talking again. In the gathering gloom, she could not see Adam's mouth slowly opening in shocked surprise as her account unfolded.

'You remember, don't you Adam, I told you there are people who can solve your problems for you? Well, I know someone who is the *boss* of such an organisation. I went to convent school with his daughter, who is about my age. We were friends at school. We still are, I suppose, but not so close now. She lives in my home town too.' Rosaria paused and looked at Adam. 'Do you know what I'm talking about, Adam?'

'The mafia,' stated Adam in awe.

'*La mafia* is a generic term. In Puglia, it's called *La Sacra Corona Unita.*'

'The Sacred United Crown,' translated Adam for his own benefit. 'It sounds almost...*religious.*'

'It is, Adam. It's meant to sound religious. We call the *bosses* 'Don' so-and-so, as if they were priests.'

'That is scary!' said Adam.

'*La Sacra Corona Unita*' isn't as well-known as the *Cosa Nostra* in Sicily or the *Camorra* in Naples. Or...' she added with a look of fear and hatred on her face, 'the *'ndrangheta,* which is the name of the Calabrian mafia that Enrico is part of. 'And would you credit it - the word *'ndrangheta* is derived from two Greek words meaning *Virtue* and *Heroism!*'

'How bitterly ironic!' commented Adam.

'Our home-grown mafia is still tightly controlled by different families operating in their own territories. Our local boss operates mainly in and around Gravino. Did you notice the other day, when we drove through the new part of the town, how many jewellers' shops there were? Did you see that all the shop doors were wide open? They are operated by our local mafia. The owners all pay their protection money – the *pizzo* – and they know that no small time crook would dare to try and rob them. They would be found floating out to sea the following day. Did you see on the news yesterday that a shop in Lecce has been bombed? That was some shopkeeper who had refused to pay his *pizzo.*'

Adam was trying to assimilate all these words that he had come across recently; *pizza, pizzo, piazza, pizzica* – all sounding almost identical and yet each word meaning something quite unconnected to the other words. He was feeling very 'foreign', an outsider in a culture that sounded alien to his middle-class English way of thinking about society.

'You make it sound as if these mafia clans uphold law and order,' suggested Adam.

'They do, in one way, I suppose. There is very little petty crime because the clans punish it ruthlessly. The police know that it makes their life easier in some ways. But police action against the clans has become a great deal more rigorous recently. But the negative effects of the mafia in our everyday lives far outweigh the positive aspects. The mafia bosses never pay taxes to the State, which loses us, the citizens, billions of potential revenue each year. It has been estimated that the *'ndrangheta's* annual turnover represents 3% of Italy's GDP! Can you believe it? And too many of our politicians have connections with their local clans or are financed by them. This country is in a *terrible* mess, Adam. And the clans are stretching out their tentacles to the north of Italy...and even abroad.'

'It's hard enough for me to grasp all this as it is, Rosy, but you were about to tell me something else. I think I had better know everything, don't you?' said Adam, fearful as to what he might hear from the lips he had so recently kissed.

Once again, there was a long thoughtful pause while Rosaria summoned up the courage to talk about matters that she feared might change Adam's opinion of her.

'After I had spoken to the *capitano*, I just wanted a bit of back-up to make sure he would not initiate an investigation too soon. If Enrico found out that we knew what he had done to Diletta, he would just disappear. He would be protected by his clan and go into hiding. Many mafiosi go into hiding and are not discovered until they are old men. I want Enrico to be held to account immediately,' she concluded passionately.

'You really *are* convinced it was Enrico, aren't you Rosy?'

'It was him alright, Adam. It could not have been anyone else. Diletta must have found out somehow what she was getting involved in. Perhaps she overheard a telephone conversation. Maybe she told him that she would not marry him. His ego would never allow him to lose face in front of everybody – especially not his own clan. *'What?' they would say. 'You are telling us that a WOMAN has turned you down?'* Taking ruthless action like that is typical of his kind when they believe the occasion demands it. They are always grimly charming on the surface, but beneath the veneer, they are *evil*. They are like Jekyll and Hyde.'

Adam nodded, finally totally convinced. 'So, what happened next?'

'I got in touch with the local *boss* through his daughter, my school friend. I was picked up outside my house one morning in a black Lancia Delta with tinted windows – that's the car which many senior politicians use too! Don P... I can't mention his name,' interjected Rosaria out of a deeply ingrained habit of silence on matters involving the mafia, '...was sitting in the back seat. I was petrified, Adam. Have you ever been close, physically close, I mean, to a man who knows he is powerful?' In the shadows, Adam shook his head imperceptibly. 'Their power radiates from them like a dark force. He just said to me: *'How can we help you, signorina?'* in a way which meant, *'I can do anything.'* I stammered out my story to him and told him about my conversation with the *capitano*. On the way to his house, one of his houses, we passed a big, old country house. *'I would like to buy that place,'* he said to his chauffeur as if it had been a nice pair of shoes. *'You already own it, signore,'* the chauffeur replied coolly. His own house was enormous, with a swimming pool as large as a football pitch. He just wanted me to be impressed by his power. He informed me that he wasn't married. This made me feel very vulnerable in his presence. I am convinced it was said on purpose just so he could enjoy my discomfort; there were three beautiful Brazilian...prostitutes sitting round his swimming pool. His harem, I supposed. When he was sure that I felt sufficiently overwhelmed by his power and wealth, he dismissed me. *'Don't worry, signorina,'* he said. *'I will settle the matter with the carabinieri. Let me know when you have found this evil man, Enrico.'* Can you believe the hypocrisy, Adam? He gave me a number on which I could contact him and then his chauffeur drove me home in silence.'

Adam was speechless. He wanted to ask questions about this 'Don P's' wealth, but supposed it was all from the usual mafia sources of drugs, prostitution, building contracts, waste disposal and protection rackets – all laundered through investments in legal businesses. Instead, he asked Rosaria about the aspect of her account which was worrying him above all else.

'But now, Rosy, *you* will be beholden to this man and his organisation. What price will *you* have to pay?'

'He told me that he would do me this as a favour – because I am a friend of his daughter. Don't worry, Adam. I'm not in any danger.'

'Not yet, at any rate,' added Adam with a touch of prescience. 'And what happens next, my incorrigible Rosaria?'

'We must go to London, Adam, and find this murderer who killed my beautiful friend, Diletta. You *will* help me, Adam, won't you? I can't possibly do this on my own.' She came up close to him and held him tightly in her arms. The look of appeal was irresistible, the smell of her skin as bewitching as the scent of oleander carried on the evening breeze. 'Other brain' was busy at work thinking of countless objections and pitfalls to the scheme which Rosaria had just hinted at. He could sense danger.

'Well, Rosy,' he began, 'I would love to take you to London. But...'

'Oh thank you, Adam. *Grazie infinite!*' I knew you would help me, *amore.*' The relief in her voice and the elation on her face were so evident that Adam did not have the heart to disappoint her.

'But you've got nothing to go on, Rosy. Do you *realise* how many millions of people there are in London?'

'We do have something to go on, Adam. I haven't told you about the letters yet.'

'What letters?' he asked fearful that his arguments about not undertaking this venture were about to be undermined. But before she could elucidate further, her mobile phone rang. It was Benedetto again, with his usual barrage of questions. Rosaria looked crestfallen at the sound of his voice. But the spell had been broken. 'I had better go, Adam,' she said reluctantly. 'Thank you for a wonderful afternoon – and evening. I just loved the way you...' But she did want to spoil the memory of their love making by putting her thoughts into crudely expressed words. Adam understood. He looked at his watch and was amazed to see how late it was. No wonder he felt the need for cheese.

'I'll see you tomorrow, Adam, at the *festa*. You are coming, aren't you? You must come. I'll find you wherever you are.' With that, she hugged him tightly again, kissing him on the mouth. She left him to ponder on all that he had learnt during the last few hours.

12: *Dancing to the Pizzica*

Adam spent his Sunday morning walking out of the town centre in search of a new church. Sundays had, so far, proved to be a battle against solitude. Since the sanctity of Sundays was still rigidly observed in the south of Italy, there were no shops open, only bars until midday – and churches, of course. He had been going to mass just to relieve the tedium. It was a new cultural experience to hear the familiar ritual spoken in a foreign tongue - quite Pentecostal, in fact. The sermons proved to be a linguistic challenge, since they were usually delivered from a lofty pulpit high above the congregation, so that the words of the priest echoed round ancient stone walls before reaching the ears of the Earth-bound listeners. Adam had even contemplated going to confession but baulked at the idea of confessing any wayward sexual fantasies he might have entertained recently in a language that he was still trying to master.

He trusted that God looked reasonably indulgently on his flights of carnal imagination. After all, Adam reasoned, it was God who had created sexual desire in the first place. He tended to believe that the Creator had gone overboard in his desire to see the human race prosper on the face of the Earth. Thus, it would be kinder to spare some seventy-year-old priest the embarrassment of having to listen to a catalogue of his more lurid thoughts in badly expressed Italian.

He had attended different churches in Campanula every Sunday – including the town's oldest and holiest little church, normally known simply as *Il Casaranello.* Its origins went back one thousand years and more. It was the first church in Christendom to be dedicated to Mary the mother of Jesus – thus its proper title: *La*

Chiesa della Santa Maria della Croce. Adam's hunt for new churches had become almost as exciting as his crusade to try out new restaurants. It had got him through those difficult hours leading up to lunchtime. Furthermore, *Il Casaranello* was a mere stone's throw away from his house, providing a sanctuary, ornate yet welcoming, when he wanted to escape the relative squalor of his accommodation. On this particular, post-Rosaria Sunday, Adam did not feel lonely at all. He had noticed a little church perched on a hilltop above the town and resolved to go and seek it out. The church was much further away than it had looked and it took him the best part of an hour's vigorous walking uphill to reach it. He took many wrong turnings because the church was no longer visible the closer he came to the spot where he assumed it must be. In the end, he asked an elderly lady dressed in widows' black. His first problem was that he did not know what the church was called, so his closest description was just 'that old church on the hill'. In the second place, the old lady only spoke dialect. Adam had difficulty deciphering what this impressive, toothless old lady was saying. But she still had a flinty sparkle in her eyes set in a weather-beaten face. Adam could make out her gestures as she pointed out a road about 100 metres in front of him. He touched her lightly on the arm and thanked her as she stumbled off on her purposeful, dominical mission, with only a curt nod in Adam's direction. When, breathless, he reached the top of the hill, it was to discover that there was no mass on that particular Sunday. Due to a shortage of priests, they did the rounds of all the churches, saying mass in different places each Sunday. But the door to this little church, so simple and solidly eternal to look at from the outside, stood open. It was called *La Madonna della Campana.* Later on, he learnt from Rosaria that the church had been built on that site to replace a much older, Byzantine chapel. Legend has it that an ox began to excavate the land on which it is built with its hoof. The animal had refused to move from the spot until construction had begun. Whatever the truth of its origins might be, the church became a place of refuge for the townsfolk in times of trouble.

The instant he crossed the threshold, he was enveloped by its unique atmosphere of tranquillity and holiness; a refuge from the hustle and bustle of industrial and commercial life in the town below. Adam stood looking in wonder at the imposing, baroque altar which seemed to fill the whole church. The space for the congregation was filled with a handful of wooden chairs, not fixed to the stone floor. It was a reminder that, when the church had been built, the population of Campanula must have been a fraction of what it is in the present day. Two high windows, situated either side of the altar, allowed beams of sunlight to bathe the little church in heavenly splendour. Adam walked around touching the stone colonnades which felt cool and reassuring against the palm of his hand. As he walked back down the aisle towards the portal that led back to the 21st century, his footsteps echoed on the flagstones. He went outside to send a text message to Rosaria telling her where he was. She sent a message back saying simply: 'Say a prayer for you and me, Adam'. Adam was drawn back inside the church and he sat down on one of the wooden chairs. He said his prayer for Rosaria and himself. A sense of calm descended on him. He thought about the host of Christians who must have passed through here over the ages, bearing problems far graver than any he was facing now. He experienced a momentary flash of comprehension as to what Rosaria must be feeling so intensely;

the risk of exposure that she ran whenever she came to see him. The revelation might have been fleeting but it left an indelible mark on his conscious mind.

Adam just went on sitting there staring at every intricate detail of the altar and the statues that adorned the tiny church. There were intimations of eternity in the very stones and the rays of light streaming through the windows above the altar. Another five minutes, he decided. He heard footsteps entering the church - a woman's shoes clip-clopping up the aisle. She was quite young. Adam watched the figure going up the aisle in her Sunday-best to light a candle by the altar. She made the sign of the cross and turned round to go out. It was Daniela, the school secretary. Adam gazed meditatively at the altar as she walked down the aisle. She had not noticed him. What a relief! But then he experienced a tenuous bond of kinship with the school secretary accompanied by a pang of guilt. He resolved to try and build a bridge of friendship with Daniela next time he saw her in the school.

Five minutes later, Adam left the church, promising that he would return one day with Rosaria, just to be able to sit side by side with her for a few quiet moments of contemplation together. Adam walked back downhill to the town, thinking deeply about the striking contrast between the diverse elements that played a part in shaping the lives of those who lived out their years in this extraordinary and contradictory part of the world.

The rest of the day passed quickly enough. He had a simple lunch and fell into a light sleep, tired and relaxed after his eight kilometre walk up to the church and back down again. A phone call from Rosaria woke him up at about four o'clock. She asked him if he had remembered to say a prayer for them both. 'Of course,' he replied. Her voice was guarded. 'Where are you, Rosy? Why are you whispering?'

She informed him that she was sitting on the toilet seat in her bathroom and that she was talking quietly because her family were all around the house. Adam was disturbed to discover that the image conjured up in his mind's eye was vaguely exciting. He laughed as if to himself and Rosaria added quickly that she had retired to the toilet merely to have a moment's privacy. A raucous female voice called out her name. No peace when the family were around, obviously.

'I'll see you tonight, Adam. Look out for me, won't you?' They exchanged rapid endearments and she rang off to the sound of the toilet flushing. She obviously wanted to make her visit to the toilet seem realistic, Adam supposed.

'How romantic!' he said sardonically as he ended the call.

* * * * *

Night time fell on the town of Campanula. Adam became aware that the *festa* must be about to begin because someone was shouting 'Testing, testing, one, two three,' into a microphone. The loudspeakers boomed out his magnified voice around the town. It was not going to be a quiet night, he thought, remembering the tranquillity of the little church that morning. He set off from his house closing the door behind him. He had brought a chain that attached to his belt so that he would not run the risk of forgetting the keys again – a necessary precaution, he had discovered, since not even the landlord had a duplicate key. He gasped in wonder as he turned the corner into the main street which led to the *Piazza San Giovanni*. The transformation from daytime reality to night time magic was startling. The effect of all the coloured lights arching up from shoulder level to a point high above the street was to create a rainbow tunnel which wound through the narrow streets to the main square. People of all ages thronged the main *piazza*, talking animatedly to nobody in particular and everyone in general. Italians seemed to be able to hold a conversation simultaneously with at least three people and still make sense of what was being said, Adam thought. The effect of all the coloured lights in the *piazza* was intensified by the brightly lit market stalls that had sprung up, selling toys, baubles, crêpes, nuts and sweets whose colours matched the lights above. From time to time, Adam was greeted by cheery calls of *'Ciao, professore,'* from students whom he taught, a note of surprise in their voices as if astonished to discover that any teacher led a life outside the classroom.

The musicians arrived and unfurled a banner which had the word *SCHIATTACORE* written across it in bold letters. Adam worked out that it must mean *Heartbreak* – a striking name for a group of local musicians. There was a brief round of applause as they stepped up on to the stage holding their instruments. The group consisted of five men of various ages and a girl who looked about sixteen. They had an array of simple instruments between them – an accordion, a violin, guitars, a mandolin, a flute and percussion instruments. The group, talking and laughing amongst themselves, seemed in no particular hurry to begin entertaining the crowd. Then, amid an amplified shaking of tambourines, the older man stepped up to the microphone and announced the first number. The anticipation in the crowds nearest the podium was tangible. They played a catchy song with a simple rhythm. To Adam's surprise it was the sixteen-year-old girl who took centre stage. She was petite, dark-skinned and wore glasses. Her voice was strong and natural with a good vocal range. Adam could not understand a word she was singing. 'Is she singing in Italian?' he asked somebody standing next to him. 'No, she's singing in dialect,' was the reply. '*Our* dialect,' he added proudly. During instrumental passages, she played her violin instead of singing.

Adam was fascinated by it all. Here was a manifestation of local folk music being played, not for tourists, but for the inhabitants of Salento. What a far cry from Britain, he thought disloyally, where, if you were unlucky, you might come across a group of Morris dancers skipping around knocking sticks together. In this small town, he was witnessing something heartfelt which had risen out of the dust of the grey cobbled streets. Even the crippled car park attendant who stuck tickets on windscreens in the *piazza* during the daytime was there, enthusiastically beating time to the music with his crutch. The character of the music changed with each song, encouraging people, young and old, to begin dancing in the space in front of the stage.

The older man stepped forward to the microphone and was given a round of applause. He introduced himself and the members of the band one by one. The girl was his daughter who, he announced, had just begun her studies in the Faculty of Music at Lecce University; applause from the crowd. She must be eighteen then. The other members of the group consisted of his son, a cousin and a friend of the family who shared an enthusiasm for Salento folk music. Adam was feeling, perhaps for the first time, that he belonged in this part of the world. An old aunt of his, who had died at the age of ninety-five, claimed to have traced the Knight family tree back to the early nineteenth century. 'Ah, you're a Grimaldi,' she would say to her nephew whenever he showed signs of eccentricity or 'foreignness'. Grimaldi, he had discovered, was a very common surname in these parts. 'Maybe I really *do* belong here genetically,' he reasoned. 'Maybe I really *am* meant to be here.' He expected to hear the usual objections from 'other brain', but there was a strange silence from that quarter on this occasion.

Francesco Giafredda, as he had introduced himself, announced that the next number would be the much awaited *pizzica*. There was a cheer from the crowd and more people detached themselves from family groups ready to take part in their best known dance.

If Adam had been impressed so far, he was about to reach new levels of emotional involvement as the music got under way. The dance opened with the rhythmic beating of tambourines, one strong beat and one weak beat, the strong beat accentuated by the players smartly tapping the drum skin of the tambourines. The guitar began to play the melody. The girl, Ylenia, began singing accompanied by the accordion in a clear, strident voice. The infectious, insistent rhythm, magnified by the loudspeakers, held the crowd in its sway. It was impossible not to move in time with the music. Adam had never heard music quite like it in his life. The sounds sprang from some antique, deep-rooted pagan culture, far removed from the trappings of modernity. The music's hidden message pulsated in every beat. Adam watched the dancers in the centre of the town square. Elderly couples were doing their best to keep up with the fast rhythm. Children, too young to have mastered the skipping steps danced around in each other's company inventing their own choreography as they became caught up in the tempo of the dance.

But Adam's attention was drawn to the group of dancers nearest the stage, mainly young women in their twenties in the company of the more energetic young men. One girl in particular fascinated Adam. She was wearing a loose-fitting, lacy skirt and a white blouse. Her whole body moved in time with the rhythm of the dance, captivated by the lilting melody. Her shapely legs followed the complex prancing movement of the dance, her feet hardly seeming to touch the ground. Her hair was tied up above her head and the intense expression on her face was mesmerising. She appeared to be releasing a lifetime of accumulated passion. Adam had never seen anyone who moved in such perfect harmony. It was uncanny – almost as if the girl herself was creating the music as she danced. It was only when the music came to its frenetic conclusion and she stopped dancing that Adam, with a profound shock, realised that it was Rosaria. She must have been only twenty paces away from where he was standing, yet he had not recognised her. Adam looked at her in awe, amazed that a woman with whom he had been in such intimate contact could be transformed into such a whirlwind of passionate movement.

In that instant of time, Adam experienced his own very particular kind of transformation. Later, when he attempted to put it into words for Rosaria's benefit, he could only say that he felt like a blind man who suddenly, miraculously, has had his sight restored. When he tried, for the sake of accuracy, to substitute the word 'blind' for 'partially sighted', he felt that he had somehow diminished the impact of what had happened. He no longer wanted to spend the rest of his time on this planet standing like a spectator in the outer ring of life's circle watching everybody else dancing to a different tune. He felt an overwhelming urge to embrace his new life fully instead of living it as if it was just another transitory step on the road to old age.

He woke up from this powerful inner vision to see Rosaria frantically trying to catch his attention. She had broken free from her group of friends, which included a man who could well have been Benedetto. Rosaria was walking uphill towards the far end of the *piazza* where the streets were less well lit and the crowds had thinned out. When he reached her, he led her down a dimly lit side street.

He gripped her arms tightly and spoke the words which sealed their fate. Looking directly into her eyes, he said: 'Rosy, I love you. We will go together to London and find the man who killed Diletta.' The die was cast. The look on her face was radiant. Instead of kissing him, as he had expected, she whirled him round and round in a tight circle, as if they had been dancing a duet version of the *pizzica*, chanting: *'Grazie! Grazie! Grazie!'* And that was how Benedetto found them.

'Cazzo Rosaria! Che diavolo stai facendo con quell'uomo? Chi è lui?' Adam instantly identified Hawk Eye from the brief encounter outside the bank. He did not need a translation of Benedetto's crude expression of displeasure at seeing *his* fiancée cavorting round with a strange man. Rosaria had frozen in fear at this unwanted and premature revelation. Maybe even a day ago, Adam, too, would have been fearful of such an encounter, especially as Benedetto was a good ten centimetres taller than he was. But buoyed up by his new found purpose in life, he had the presence of mind to bluff his way out of the predicament. He stepped confidently up to Benedetto with right hand extended in greeting. 'Ah, you must be Benedetto, Rosy's fiancé!' he exclaimed (in

Italian). 'I'm Rosaria's English teacher from your bank.' He remembered to drop the familiar form of her name the second time he mentioned it, in the hope that Benedetto would not notice the slip. Benedetto would have looked churlish to have refused a stranger's hand so he had no choice but to reciprocate. Adam had to prevent himself wincing at the firmness of the grip. 'Rosaria was trying to get me to dance the *pizzica*,' continued Adam without a break in the flow of his eloquence. 'But I guess it's too late at my age. You dance very well, Benedetto.'

'Alright, Adam!' he said to himself. 'Don't overdo it!' Why had Rosaria chosen this man, he wondered. The man in question felt the need to assert his proprietorial rights. 'Come on, Rosy,' he said gruffly. 'The others are waiting for us.' Adam was hoping that Benedetto would not ask why he had found them together so far away from the crowded *piazza*. Right on cue, Benedetto asked Rosaria precisely that question.

'Ah, that was my fault, Benedetto,' piped up Adam, inwardly cursing the man's pertinacity. 'I couldn't hear what Rosaria was saying to me because of the noise. Sorry! *Buona sera*,' he added as Benedetto led Rosaria away by the arm, leaving Adam standing under the glow of a rather dim street light. Rosaria looked round over her shoulder as she was led away, a brief glance which expressed a mixture of emotions. '*Scusami Adam!*' she mouthed the words silently in his direction.

Adam remained standing where he was under the street lamp, trying to work out how he was feeling after his brief encounter with Benedetto. He was alarmed by the ease with which Benedetto had apparently reasserted his hold over his *fidanzata*. It occurred to Adam that, during the few minutes that this drama had been enacted, Benedetto had not spoken a single word to him. He had hardly needed to; the look on his face was far more expressive than a tirade of words. But Adam accurately interpreted Benedetto's reaction at finding them together as being born of the fear of losing his prized possession rather than a naked display of male domination. Either way, his behaviour towards Rosaria was unjustified.

Adam made his way thoughtfully back to the *piazza*. In his great new scheme of things, he would have to do something far more decisive if he was to change the course of his – and Rosaria's – life. The days when other people and extraneous events determined the course of his life were supposed to be over, weren't they! He was meditating on this theme when he reached the main square again. The musicians were taking a break. Unexpectedly, he found himself looking directly at a man's shirt pocket. The initials MM were sown on to the top left hand corner of the pocket.

'How strange!' thought Adam as his gaze travelled up from the pocket until, by straining his neck somewhat, he recognised the face of his only 'one-to-one' student, Massimo. In this part of Italy where most men were actually shorter than average-sized Adam, Massimo was unusually tall. Since his lesson with this relative giant was always conducted sitting down, Adam had not realised just how tall the lawyer was.

'Good evening, Massimo. What a pleasant surprise!'

'*Buona sera, professore,*' replied the lawyer looking down at Adam from what seemed to be the height of *San Giovanni* on his plinth. 'May I introduce you to my *fidanzata*, Mirella?'

Adam was able to adjust the angle of his neck to a marginally more comfortable position. Mirella was a beautiful blond with blue eyes, quite unusual for these parts. Had Adam lowered his neck to its normal position, he was sure he would have been staring at her cleavage.

'*Piacere signora,*' said Adam.

'Mirella,' she corrected with a smile. 'I come from the north of Italy,' she explained accurately interpreting Adam's puzzled expression. 'And my father is Swedish,' she added.

'I believe you teach my cousin, too, Adam,' the lawyer was saying from somewhere up in the stratosphere.

'Do I?' said Adam, curious.

'Yes, she's called Rosaria Miccoli.'

'She would be!' replied Adam in English ignoring the lawyer's enquiring expression.

He managed to complete the conversation with Massimo and Mirella in a socially acceptable manner, during which he learnt that the initials MM stood for the couple's first names, and not Massimo's name and surname – a feature of Massimo's shirt which had been puzzling Adam.

'A nice romantic touch, Massimo,' he said complimenting the lawyer's good taste. The lawyer checked the time on his Rolex-look-alike watch and the couple took their leave with smiles and handshakes. Adam was finally able to readjust the angle of his neck back to normal. The musicians were back on the podium. Francesco Giafredda explained that the next number had been composed by his daughter. The crowd nearest the stage applauded and the music began again with a beautiful, lilting ballad.

Adam was quite prepared to enjoy the rest of the evening getting used to the notion that this was his home for the foreseeable future and that he was finally in control of his own destiny. But in the next few seconds, he found himself being propelled, protesting feebly, into the centre of the circle of dancers. He had felt a tap on his shoulder and turned round to find one of his 'afternoon girls', Silvia, asking him why he wasn't joining in the dancing. She was pretty, petite and quite forceful. She refused to listen to his protests and led him towards the swaying figures dancing the lilting melody. At first, Adam felt a bit like a puppet whose puppet-master had been imbibing the local wine. His movements felt wooden and unnatural. But as he realised that nobody was taking any particular notice, he began to relax and to fall into the rhythm of the song. The dance came to an end and he was slightly out of breath. Silvia was not going to risk a second round and she led him back to her group of friends, whom Adam recognised as the other members of the class. *'Bravo, A-damn! Sei proprio bravissimo!'* they complimented him quite convincingly.

He felt another tap on his shoulder. 'Oh, not again!' he thought. It was Rosaria this time and she was looking like thunder. 'Rosy!' he exclaimed with pleasure. She scowled at him, grabbed hold of him and pulled him once again towards the dancers by the stage. 'Who was that *girl?*' she asked in a furious whisper. Adam should have remembered how she reacted when he had first brought up the subject of Glenda. 'It's alright, Rosy,' he tried to assure her. 'She's just one of my students.'

'Why did you ask *HER* to dance and not *ME*, Adam?'

'I didn't ask her. She asked *me!* And I didn't want to get you into trouble with Benedetto again.'

'Adam, I don't care if I get into trouble with Benedetto. *You* are my man now. Haven't you realised that yet?'

'Really?' beamed Adam. 'Am I truly *your* man now?' he asked unnecessarily.

Her only answer was to hold him tight and to make him dance at twice the speed that he had danced with Silvia. It sounded like another *pizzica*. He felt the suppleness and firmness of her body as she moved in time with the music, turning him, twisting him and springing round and round in a breathless frenzy of movement before breaking free and dancing separately as the *pizzica* should be danced. It was a more traditional version of the dance – one which got faster and faster during the closing bars.

When the music finished, Rosaria was smiling again. 'There, *mio amore!* Now you have been truly initiated into our way of life. And that means you are *mine!*' Adam was trying to catch his breath as he spoke.

'I never doubted it for a second, Rosy. But neither should *you!*'

Benedetto was on the scene in a trice, looking daggers in Adam's direction. 'I don't ever want to see you with my *fidanzata* again! *Chiaro?*'

'Quite clear, Benedetto,' said Adam standing his ground, although still being short of breath made it difficult to assert any moral authority. 'But it is really *not* up to either you *or* me, for that matter, to decide who Rosaria talks to. I hope *that* is clear to *you!*'

Benedetto glared in hostile fury at Adam and tried to persuade Rosaria to dance with him. Adam was pleased to see that she refused and headed back towards her group of friends. 'Ciao, Adam,' she said provocatively. 'See you soon. We're going for a pizza now. Would you like to join us?'

Adam thought not, on balance, even though the idea of eating a pizza made him realise how hungry he had become after all his exertions. He shrugged his shoulders and mouthed a secret 'good night' in her direction. *'Ricordati!'* was Benedetto's parting shot directed pointedly at Adam.

'I'm not likely to forget,' he thought as he headed for his flat – and a cheese sandwich.

He sat at the kitchen table and meditated on the extraordinary events of that tumultuous evening. 'No backing out now!' he told himself as he bit into a *provolone* sandwich, washed down with several reviving gulps of red wine.

13: A Sixth Letter from 'Diletta'

Adam was too exhausted not to sleep a seamless, dreamless sleep that night. The following morning, the first one in his 'new life', he reminded himself, Adam took a cup of coffee up onto the flat roof above the house. The sun shone down from a clear blue Mediterranean sky. Two straggling palm trees, whose brittle leaves rattled in the breeze, just managed to reach up above the level of the roof top terrace where he was sitting. He exchanged a series of text messages with Rosaria, who was primarily concerned that he had not changed his mind about their expedition to London. With a brief stab of anxiety, quickly repressed, he reassured her that there had been no change of heart. Almost immediately after the first message, came one which pleaded with him never to leave her.

'I will promise on bended knee if you want,' Adam replied.

Adam should have known by now that any irony with which his words were often laced would be taken quite literally by Rosaria.

'Yes, please. I'll keep you to that promise,' came the instant reply.

At midday, he wandered happily into town clutching his text books and a garish yellow and purple A4 folder covered with quotes from Oscar Wilde, translated into Italian, on the inside of the cover. The men were dismantling the wooden arches with the same dexterity and speed with which they had been erected two days beforehand. Campanula's everyday working face, without its gaudy, festive make-up, was rapidly being restored.

Lunch with Glenda at one o'clock; she breezed in smiling happily, talking to Fernando and the waitress on her way over to their table where Adam was busily devouring their ration of bread. Glenda spoke Italian fluently but had decided from the outset that it was preferable to let everybody know that she was English, and therefore, 'different'. She deliberately cultivated an awful English accent and intonation with the sole purpose of asserting her Britishness; the verbal equivalent of waving a Union Jack in everybody's face, Adam had pedantically informed her. She had laughed at this image, pleased that she had achieved the desired effect.

'Good afternoon, dear,' she said as she sat down at the table and asked Fernando to replenish the bread basket. 'Congratulations, Adam!' she continued with that familiar smug expression on her face which meant she was about to impart some little piece of gleaned information that she hoped would needle her colleague.

Adam just continued to look at her, expressionless, wishing to deny her the pleasure of feeling too self-satisfied.

'It's not every Englishman who comes down here who gets to dance the *pizzica* – even if he does look a bit like an out-of-sync Pinocchio!' Funny that Glenda should use the same puppet image that he had thought of himself.

'At least, I tried!' he said huffily, wondering why he had not spotted Glenda in the crowd.

'You did very well – for a man of fifty-three, Adam,' she said rubbing a grain of salt in the wound.

'Fifty-two!' corrected Adam uppishly. 'Is it preferable, in your opinion, dear Glenda,' continued Adam in an attempt to defend his honour, 'to make a minor spectacle of oneself or to stand on the touch-line making cynical observations about ones friends? Besides which, I was practically coerced!'

'So I noticed, Adam. Twice, if I am not mistaken,' she laughed.

Adam told Glenda about his first encounter with Benedetto. To his surprise, Adam had felt more than a vestige of guilt about

Benedetto. He had entertained some doubts as to whether it was morally correct to poach Rosaria from under his nose. He mentioned this to Glenda. Her next comment surprised him greatly and went a long way to assuaging any sense of guilt that he might have been harbouring.

'I think that – what's her name – Rosaria is much better off with *you*, Adam.'

'Do you really think so, Glenda?' he said, taken aback by the sincerity and seriousness with which she had endorsed his new relationship, quite unlike the usual teasingly cynical tone that she enjoyed indulging in most of the time.

'With *him,* she would be committing herself to a lifetime of misery and servitude. So many girls down here are dominated by their fathers up to the age of twenty-eight or so. They get married thinking they are going to be free at last and then find that all they have done is exchange one dictator for another. I've seen it happening so often, Adam. Believe me. It's frightening!'

Adam remained pensive for so long that Glenda added:

'No Adam, if you really love her, then I wouldn't hesitate. Go for it!'

'Thank you, Glenda,' he said simply. He wanted to ask her whether she fell into the same category in her relationship with Antonio. But Glenda pre-empted any enquiries.

'That's why I won't marry the Big A,' she replied, which went some way to satisfying his curiosity.

Back at the school, Daniela was in her office looking self-important again. Adam, mindful of his resolve to be more charitable towards her, greeted her with a guarded smile and said he hoped she had had a good weekend. To his amazement, Daniela gave him her version of a friendly smile, which, as far as Adam could interpret it, involved parting her lips and showing her teeth – in need of some whitener – whilst her cheek muscles were still considering whether it was all worth the effort. Still, Adam reckoned, it was an improvement. He was just walking out of the office to prepare for the arrival of his 'afternoon girls' when Daniela announced: 'You've got a new class starting immediately after this one, A-damn.'

Adam looked at her and thought: 'Being nice to you, Daniela, is nothing but an invitation to allowing oneself to be exploited.'

'And, by the way,' she continued, 'there's a new student in your three o'clock group, too. His name is Leonardo. He's a musician.'

'Thank you, Daniela. As usual, you have managed to give me a generous five minutes' advanced warning of any changes; ample time to prepare myself.'

Needless to say, his sarcasm was wasted. Daniela's cheek muscles won the battle over her lips, which snapped shut in a *moue* of displeasure. 'Congenitally miserable, that woman,' Adam reckoned. Obviously, her clandestine act of piety in the little church had only had a transitory effect on lifting her spirits.

Leonardo, the tall musician, appeared on first acquaintance to be gauche and excessively nervous. His contributions to Adam's lesson were hesitant or even inept. The girls went out of their way to make him feel wanted and paid him so much attention that Adam felt quite put out that he was no longer, according to a beautiful Italian expression that he had just learnt, 'the only cockerel in the henhouse'. Adam, following the example of the girls, was rewarded for his perseverance by discovering that Leonardo was a gifted pianist who was possessed of an unusually dry sense of self-deprecating humour. By the end of the course, Leonardo was able to expound in good English on a variety of music-related topics.

On concluding the lesson with his new student, Adam deliberately went down to the bar to have a coffee, just to get his own back on Daniela for foisting a new class on him without even a five minute break. When Adam returned a few minutes late, he found a class of lively eight-year- olds sitting at the tables looking expectantly at him. In the following weeks, Adam exacted retribution on Daniela by ensuring that every activity they did in the classroom was as boisterous as possible. They played bingo, charades, hangman, 'I Spy' and Simon Says. They sang songs in English, listened to the Beatles and acted out little plays. Even Glenda complained that it disturbed her teaching in the next classroom. Daniela fumed in her office and became even more morose when the parents collecting their offspring told her how much the children enjoyed coming to their lessons.

The Easter break was approaching – when Adam and Rosaria had planned to fly to London on their 'mission' of retribution. In the meantime, Adam and Glenda continued to go to lunch *chez* Fernando. It was during one such occasion that Glenda decided that it was high time Adam's technical skills caught up with his new sartorial elegance. 'It's time you had an e-mail account,' she told him. Adam tried to resist.

'Even my dad's got an e-mail address,' Glenda told him, 'and he still wears corduroy trousers and a green cardigan.' That was a sufficiently strong argument to sway Adam. He allowed himself to be led to the altar of modernity without resistance.

* * * * *

Any minor annoyances on the teaching front were more than compensated for by the blossoming, but still clandestine, relationship between Adam and Rosaria. Shortly after the *festa*, Rosaria was transferred to the local town hall in her own commune, thereby saving her a ninety kilometre round trip every day. This left her free some mornings. February had given way to March and a warm, sea-scented air pervaded the countryside.

'Come on, Adam,' she said one morning. 'I want to show you how beautiful our Salento really is. And we have so much to talk about.'

That was true. Indeed, Adam thought, there was so much ground still to be covered before they went to London on their mission of vendetta that he did not know where to begin. A part of Adam still hoped that this perilous cup that he was about to drink from would be taken from him by the hand of some deity. He contented himself by asking the most obvious question that sprang to mind.

'Where are we going?' he enquired as Rosaria drove off purposefully in the most noticeable car in town and headed south out of Campanula.

'*Finis Mundi,*' she replied enigmatically in Latin. 'Wait and see!'

'The end of the world!' exclaimed Adam. 'That sounds suitably doom laden for us.'

'Don't say things like that!' pleaded Rosaria, revealing a streak of superstition that Adam noted with quiet surprise. Adam placed his left hand on her lap to reassure her, intending to remove it immediately, since she was driving along the straight *superstrada* at something over 100 km per hour. But, to his silent horror, she took one hand off the steering wheel and placed it over Adam's to keep it where it was. Instead, Adam looked out of the window and concentrated on the scenery. Vineyards planted next to groves of olive trees flashed by. Occasionally, they would pass by white-washed little towns or ancient stone chapels by the roadside. Beneath the gnarled old olive trees, shepherds from a bygone era were tending flocks of sheep that looked more like scraggy goats. Atop the gentle hillsides, old grey farm houses called *masserie* stood where they had been for centuries, defying the passage of time. Strains of the *pizzica* went through his mind, the music seeming to be so much a part of this landscape. It was as if the strains of the music echoed off the old stone walls like ghosts from a forgotten age.

'How many women did you have before me, Adam?' asked Rosaria abruptly breaking into his reveries. He was so taken aback that he withdrew his hand from her lap whilst he considered what his reply should be. Certainly not the truth, he decided wisely - not whilst travelling at this speed.

'Well, let me see, Rosy,' he replied teasingly, performing a charade of counting off imaginary beads on a rosary. She hit him smartly on the thigh with the hand that was not steering the car. 'Only three,' he said while surreptitiously crossing the first two fingers of his right hand out of sight of the driver. 'The most recent was four years ago. But, if I had known that I was going to meet you, I would willingly have abstained for much longer. Only now I realise that I have been waiting for you all my life,' Adam concluded smoothly. It was not difficult to instil sincerity into his voice. He genuinely wished that his words did represent the literal truth.

'That's so beautiful, Adam,' she said sweetly with only an edge of menace in her voice. Adam was metaphorically wiping the sweat from his brow when she added: 'Even if I don't believe a word of what you have just said.'

'And *I* have a question for *you,* Rosy,' he said thinking it was time to change the subject.

'Only Tomaso and Benedetto,' she said guiltily.

'That is *not* what I was about to ask you, *amore.* As far as I am concerned, your past lovers are your business, not mine. I am fortunate enough to have you now. That is all that matters. I was going to ask you about the letters you received from London.'

Rosaria laughed, a little embarrassed that she had been wrong-footed.

'They are in my handbag on the back seat, Adam. Have a look at them and tell me what you think. I want you to keep them safe for me until we go to London. I am terrible at organising myself.'

Adam carefully removed the letters and their envelopes and meticulously smoothed them out.

'I kept the envelopes for their postmarks. They may tell us more than the letters. Look Adam! We are nearly there.'

'Santa Maria di Leuca,' he read as they entered the small town. He remarked on the fact that the roads had recently been resurfaced – unlike the rutted, pot-holed roads of Campanula.

'That's because the pope is coming here next month, Adam. The central government has magically been able to supply the necessary funds to mend the roads in Leuca. Normally, the south of Italy has to wait years until money becomes available for such projects. Lecce waited for twenty years for its ring-road to be completed.'

Adam tucked the letters carefully into the capacious, zipped inner pocket of his jacket until such time as they were sitting down for a mid-morning drink. Rosaria drove uphill to the promontory where a lighthouse stood sentinel over the waters below and the relatively new church of Santa Maria, perched on the very edge of the Puglian coastline; 'World's End', or so it must have appeared to the early settlers staring over the immense stretch of sea beneath them.

They walked to the western parapet overlooking the marina below them. Adam admired the mixture of expensive yachts and little old fishing boats in need of a coat of paint, their chugging diesel engines sounding as if they had been nursed into life over the decades to ensure that their owners could continue to eke out a living fishing ever further out to sea as fish stocks dwindled.

'This is the Ionian Sea, Adam,' explained Rosaria. 'And...' she said taking him by the hand as they walked across the broad *piazza* towards the eastern parapet, '...this is the Adriatic Sea. This is where the two seas meet,' she added waving her free arm vaguely in a southerly direction beyond the lighthouse. There were very few people about – a few couples with little children skipping across the square which formed the courtyard in front of the church and a handful of tourists taking photographs or filming their children's freedom against the airy vistas beyond them.

The Adriatic side was in sharp contrast to the Ionian coast. They looked down over steep cliffs falling to the sea below, sparkling in the early spring sunlight. 'What a lovely end to the world!' exclaimed Adam.

'Just look along the coastline, Adam,' replied Rosaria pointing northwards to the sheer cliffs that wound around deep bays, turning blue in the distance. 'We shall drive up there after we've looked inside the church. There's another place I want to show you.'

'You are so much more relaxed than you are back home, Rosy,' Adam observed.

She wrapped herself in his arms. 'Yes, I know. I feel freer when I've put fifty kilometres between me and Campanula. Besides which, here I can see the approach of the enemy,' she said indicating the expanse of the *piazza.*

'By enemy, I suppose you mean Benedetto?'

'Yes, along with an army of uncles, aunts and cousins too,' she added.

'But it's good to have family around you, Rosy. My nearest relatives live in Australia,' replied Adam, always struck by this positive aspect of local culture.

'Yes, I feel protected. But there is no *privacy.*'

Adam remarked on the fact that Italians had adopted the English word 'privacy' – albeit said with an American pronunciation. Apparently there was no native word to express this concept, he commented dryly. Rosaria shrugged. 'Languages are *your* special field, *amore.* I just speak them.' A typical Rosaria response, thought Adam, hugging her.

They stood in silence for several minutes. Adam was leaning out over the parapet when he noticed the pink roof tiles of a stone building below them barely above the reach of the blue waters. 'There's a house down there, Rosy,' he remarked in surprise. She looked down to where Adam had pointed.

'Of course! I read about it in the newspaper. It's a disco-restaurant that has just opened. You can only reach it by boat.'

'So, only for the rich,' said Adam.

'Yes, I expect so. And it's *abusivo*,' she explained. 'It's been illegally built without proper authority. I saw a report on the local TV station too. It's a huge problem all around the Italian coast,' she went on. 'People pay out large bribes to local councillors to turn a blind eye to planning regulations. It happens all the time – not just in Puglia.'

'That's so corrupt...and sad,' said Adam shocked.

Rosaria nodded in agreement. 'They say that this disco-restaurant was built by that man I know,' she added in an awed whisper.

'You mean by the *Sacra Corona...*' He never completed the sentence. Rosaria was looking fearfully and furtively around her. She put a stern finger on Adam's lips and said 'Shhh' fiercely. 'We never say those words out loud in public.'

The darker side of Italy had impinged on their joy at being free and alone together.

'Come on, Adam. Let's look inside the church. It's actually designated a *santuario.'*

'A sanctuary - what a lovely word, isn't it? For all us refugees seeking protection from the evils of the world,' he said thinking about their half-finished conversation.

* * * * *

Half an hour later, they were driving northwards towards Otranto, stopping well short of that town at a place called Ciolo. They crossed a ravine over an arched, concrete bridge. They drew up in front of a little log cabin style café and sat down overlooking the sea below having ordered their drinks. There was nothing but an expanse of turquoise water, rugged cliffs and the scent of wild thyme carried on a gentle breeze. Paradise restored.

Adam took the letters out of pocket and read them one by one, eyebrows raised in astonishment.

'No wonder you are suspicious, Rosy. These letters have to be the most blatant – and clumsy – attempt at a cover-up that one could imagine.' Rosaria nodded in agreement. He placed a heavy, glass ashtray on top of the letters to prevent them being whisked away by the breeze. He looked at the postmarks shaking his head mournfully.

'There's precious little to go on here, Rosy, I'm sorry to say. They only show where the main sorting offices are. Three of them were posted south of the River Thames – south-east London, in fact. The other two were sorted at Mount Pleasant, which is the main sorting-office for north London.'

Not for the first time, Adam had an inkling of the huge task involved as a result of his rash offer of help. However, it was too late to be negative and no time for misgivings. Rosaria looked at him dejectedly. But it was one of her positive characteristics that she never remained discouraged for long. Her face brightened up as she said:

'Don't forget that Diletta told me that she met Enrico at the Italian Embassy. She told me that he works there. In any case, they will have a record of every Italian citizen who has visited the embassy in the last year or so. Do you know where the Italian Embassy is, Adam?'

'Yes, more or less. It's near Oxford Street. It overlooks one of those beautiful green squares that are dotted all over the centre of London. I forget which one for the moment. Do you intend to stand guard outside until we see Enrico coming out?'

'Oh, I'll find a way of persuading someone there to divulge something. Don't forget there is probably a girl with Diletta's identity card masquerading as my cousin.' Her confidence and optimism were infectious.

'Maybe we should go together to that little church above Campanula and pray for guidance from above,' said Adam half in jest. To his surprise, Rosaria's eyes lit up. 'Yes please, Adam. Let's go this week,' she said enthusiastically.

'What inspiring optimism!' Adam thought ironically. But, with Rosaria, he could never be sure. The whole of his life seemed to have been taken over by forces that he had not reckoned with before. A visit to the little church on the hilltop might well be merely the next step along their predestined path towards...Adam was not at all sure where this path would lead them.

'Come on, Adam!' she said brightly, all the clouds dispersed. 'Let's go down to the bay.'

They had to cross back over the bridge which spanned the ravine to reach the steps cut out of the rock that led down to sea level.

'In the summer, Adam, the teenage boys jump off this bridge.'

'What? Suicide?' exclaimed Adam in genuine horror.

'No,' she laughed. 'It's a game of dare. They dive from the bridge into the sea below.'

The look on Adam's face was one of total disbelief. 'You're joking, aren't you, Rosy? It must be a thirty metre drop.'

'We'll come back in the summer, Adam, and you can see for yourself.'

'If we live to see the summer after our trip to London,' he thought, quickly banishing the negative image from his mind.

They ran down the steps to the 'beach', which turned out to be slabs of stone rather than sand. They were the only mortal souls present, standing between the cliffs towering up on either side of them, stretching back to form a steep gully behind them.

'Now we can do it, Adam,' Rosaria said mischievously. Surely she couldn't possibly mean what he thought she meant.

'What?' he said with a note of alarm in his voice. But she was enjoying teasing him and continued to flirt with him, playing on his embarrassment. After a while, she relented.

'Down on your knees, Adam. You promised eternal allegiance to me a few days ago. Remember? Now is the time to fulfil that promise.'

Adam was so relieved that he laughed at the proposal and went solemnly through the little ceremony as the waters of the Adriatic lapped on the shoreline near his feet. To his surprise, he felt quite moved with emotion. The words that he uttered were binding, set in the granite stone of the soaring cliff walls on either side. They drove back to Campanula in a happy frame of mind, chatting about any subject that occurred to them. At one point, Rosaria realised that she had got lost due to the sudden disappearance of all sign posts. Rosaria asked an old lady the way to Campanula. The elderly citizen looked bewildered and muttered some words in dialect which Adam could not comprehend.

'She told me that she has never left the village in her whole life,' Rosaria translated. It was yet another moment of revelation for Adam, astonished that, in modern Europe, you could still find people who had never moved beyond the confines of their place of birth. It was comforting yet disturbing in the same instance. When they eventually chanced upon an isolated road sign that enabled them to escape the time warp, Adam noticed that the fuel tank was on empty.

'Oh, there's enough fuel left to get us home, Adam,' she declared dismissively. She never went to a petrol station until the gauge was on the zero mark and, when she did, never put more than ten euros worth of fuel in the tank, so the gauge hovered permanently round the empty mark. He was torn between amusement at her quirkiness and irritation at her lack of forethought. She herself had no idea why she acted this way. 'Because I'm Rosaria, I suppose,' was the only explanation on offer. It was the same when it came to putting credit on her mobile phone.

'There seems to be a kind of 'future gene' missing from your mind, Rosy. You never believe you're going to run out of fuel until the very last moment when the inevitable finally catches up with you.'

Rosaria was silent for several minutes before she said in all seriousness: 'Adam, I have never really thought about myself in that way before. I think you may be right. I think you understand me better than *anyone* I have ever known. Maybe,' she added after another pause, 'that is why I cannot break off my engagement with Benedetto. I don't really believe the marriage will ever happen.'

'Until it is too late. Going to the altar is not quite the same as stopping off at a petrol station.' She smiled and held Adam's hand all the way back to Campanula with only her left hand on the steering wheel. 'Point proven', thought Adam. He became increasingly of the opinion that the hunt for Enrico must fall into the same philosophical category. He was unsure whether this boded well or not for their imminent mission to London.

There were many similar, joyous trips to explore the jewels of Salento over the next couple of weeks. Adam's favourite excursion was the hour spent in Otranto. It was old. Older than almost any place he had ever visited. Rosaria took him to the cathedral and showed him the ancient mosaics on the floor and the extraordinary memorial to the Martyrs of Otranto. The skeletons of the town's inhabitants, who had been ruthlessly slaughtered by the Turks for their refusal to renounce their Christian faith, were displayed behind huge glass screens. It looked like some macabre work of art exposed to view lest anyone dare to forget the ravished past of the inhabitants of Otranto. Adam had noticed, all around the coastline of Salento, the presence of huge granite watch-towers looking out to sea to give the vulnerable inhabitants a last minute warning of the next wave of invaders.

They made love some evenings. Adam was no longer concerned about the outcome. He had grown familiar with Rosy's strange lapses into silence, which were the precursor to her almost inevitable climax. Making love was reassuring, comforting, mutually satisfying and helped them survive the times when they were apart. She had taken to switching off her mobile phone when they were together, for as long as she dared, in order to gain an hour or so's peace from its insistent intrusion. Mobile phones, Adam decided, had sounded the death knell for infidelity. Even if the wretched devices were switched off, one still revealed that one's privacy was more important than the caller's demanding attempts to monopolise ones attention. The caller could always wonder suspiciously why you had not bothered to answer.

And so life continued for two long weeks. They went, as promised, to visit the little church on the hilltop and sat side by side in meditative silence, asking for guidance, inspiration and, above all, the courage that would be required for their next step. But they heard only the echoes of their own meditations reverberating round the ancient walls.

Until, one evening, out of the blue, Rosaria arrived breathless, clutching another letter from London. 'She's sent a sixth letter, Adam. This one is so different,' she said excitedly. 'Just read what it says! It's our breakthrough, *amore mio.*'

14: Rosaria's Case Unlocked

Rosaria spread the letter flat on the table, scarcely able to contain her triumph. Adam looked at the postmark – South London again. He turned his attention to the letter itself. It appeared to have been written in haste, as if the writer had been possessed by a deep sense of urgency. The layout of the letter was very unusual too. Rosaria had her arm round Adam's shoulder and was breathing excitedly into his ear.

'What do you think, Adam?' she asked impatiently.

'It looks intriguing, Rosy. Give me a chance to read it first,' he said, amused but distracted by her impatience. 'Let me concentrate.'

He began to study the letter. As he read it, he instantly realised why Rosaria had attached so much importance to it. The tone and the text were far removed from the previous five letters and the layout *was* distinctly odd.

Ciao Rosy

At last

I can tell

U where

To find me

A Londra

Maybe you could come over and meet me? PLEASE

I work in the market near the big cathedral in South

Devo andare! LUI sta arrivando. Ho paura.

BOR

Sofía

Adam read the incomplete missive again, looking at the strangely formed signature scribbled in haste at the bottom of the page.

'Look at the signature, Adam. What does it look like to you?'

'It seems to spell *SOFIA* – as in Sofia Loren. But the *s* looks more like an *f*. Or maybe the *f* looks more like an *s* with a line through it. You could read it either way. It's odd – as if she is trying to send us some hidden message.'

Adam had meant to say 'send *you* some hidden message' but he felt so involved that the 'us' had come out without thinking.

'It's not all that hidden, Adam.'

'Ah, I see, Rosy. Your powers of deduction have already been at work.'

He had spoken without sarcasm. He understood instantly why she seemed to be brimming over with excitement; she had spotted something which Adam was missing.

'I'm sorry to be so slow, Rosy. I am merely Watson to your Sherlock Holmes.'

'No, Adam. You're not slow at all. It's because the 'hidden messages', as you called them, are in Italian – even if most of the words are written in English. Just look at that signature!'

'Maybe it reads SOS', he exclaimed hopefully - 'Help!'

'Maybe, Adam,' she said containing her impatience at his obtrusiveness. 'But if you take the whole signature as if it is spelt with an *S* followed by a second *S*, it reads *SOSIA*. Don't you see?'

Adam did not see – largely because he had never come across the word *sosia* before.

'I can't help being English,' he said defensively. 'You'll have to tell me.'

'Oh, I'm sorry, *amore*. But I can't believe how clever she has been. I would guess that her real name really is *Sofia*, but the word *sosia* means a 'double' in Italian – an identical person. Don't you see? She's telling me that she is the one with Diletta's identity.'

Adam felt a frisson of excitement run up his spine at this revelation. It *was* clever, if true, and it changed the whole character of their mission to London.

'But that's brilliant! *You're* brilliant!' he added in admiration. 'What do you make of the rest of the letter? Is there anything else – apart from the interesting point that she calls you *Rosy* for the first time instead of *Rosaria?*'

'Yes, I noticed that immediately. But that's not all, Adam. In my opinion, she has been forced to write the other letters under duress and she began to realise that something was very wrong. She's scared of him, isn't she? Look what she says at the end: 'He's coming! I'm frightened!' before she tries to finish the letter.'

'But what do you make of the fact that she has split the sentences, beginning a new line after every couple of words?'

'That is where she has been really ingenious too, Adam. Look at the initial letter of every line and read downwards.'

Adam took the letter and did just as Rosaria had said. The second shock was as great as the first. The initial letters clearly spelt the words *AIUTAMI* – Help me!

'That's amazing, Rosy,' he said in awe. 'We are in business, I believe. What a pity she could not complete the end of the letter!

We know that she works in a market near a cathedral in South London. But I can't think why she wrote the letters *BOR.'*

Adam turned silent. A warning signal had sounded in his mind. He did not want to dampen Rosaria's enthusiasm, but the obvious had to be stated. 'We shouldn't get too excited, Rosy. It might...it might just be a trap.'

But Rosaria had already followed that train of thought.

'Yes, I considered that possibility, too – obviously. But, don't you see, Adam? Even if it *is* a trap set by Enrico using this girl, it still gives us a lead. It just means we shall have to be doubly *astuti* when we track him down.'

'We shall need to be more than merely crafty,' Adam thought.

'To my mind,' Rosaria continued, 'either the false Diletta has become scared stiff of the situation in which she finds herself – which is what I believe to be the case. Or, Enrico is beginning to panic because he is not convinced that he has got away with his crime. He doesn't want to leave any loose ends. Either way, we have a positive lead - if only you can work out where this cathedral is, Adam.'

The implication was clear; deciphering the rest of the message was his responsibility. He did not want to disappoint her.

'Let me have another look, Rosy,' he said trying his best to sound intelligent. She passed him the precious letter just as all the lights went out.

'This house will be the death of me,' muttered Adam. He fumbled around for matches and a candle that a previous occupant had left on the window sill. The eerie light from the candle cast elongated shadows round the empty room adjoining the kitchen. 'It makes the place look almost cosy. Maybe I should live by candlelight for the next few weeks,' he said half seriously. Rosaria had visions of her lover and accomplice being reduced to ashes whilst asleep and told him not to entertain the idea for a second.

Rosaria excused herself as it was getting late. She hugged him and kissed him full of the passionate energy that she had brought with her that evening. She entrusted the sixth letter to him as if it had been an antique scroll beyond value. Together they groped their way downstairs by the light of the guttering candle. As soon as they opened the front door, it became apparent that it was not just Adam's house that was suffering from the blackout. There were no street lights, nor lights shining in the neighbouring houses. People were calling out in panic to their neighbours asking what had happened. The night sky was resplendent with a panoply of stars normally hidden from view. The Milky Way, just visible, wrapped its smooth sheen of satin around the night sky. Adam felt his usual surge of anger against the complacency of modern society which had allowed light pollution to destroy the beauty of the night.

'It's wonderful!' he said. 'I wish the nights could always be like this.'

Rosaria was far less impressed and was anxious about driving home.

'You still have your car headlights,' he pointed out. 'But send me a text message when you get home.' A final kiss and she was off. At least, tonight, there was no fear of being spotted by a passing relative.

Adam remembered that he had packed a small torch. When he had located it by the light of the candle, he climbed up on to the flat roof. It was obvious that the power cut had affected the whole region. None of the neighbouring towns or villages was visible. Adam was happy to revel in wonder at the spectacle of the night sky but equally glad when Rosaria sent him a message telling him she was safely home. There was no way of knowing the extent of the power cut. After a while, even mobile phones ceased to work. It was not until the following morning that everybody learnt by word of mouth that this unprecedented power failure was nationwide. How vulnerable Italy felt all of a sudden at the realisation that their country depended almost entirely on the Swiss for its electricity supply. In a trice, the dependable sense of civilisation and security had been wiped out. Standing on his rooftop, strains of the *pizzica* echoed in his mind. Unable to identify the reason, he guessed it must be something to do with the preternatural gloom into which they had been precipitously plunged; the trappings of civilisation suddenly withdrawn.

He lay awake for hours under the star-shaped ceiling, shrouded in darkness. The barking dog was silent, undoubtedly shocked by the transformation to its canine world. The wind began to get up and rustled in the palm trees. He was on the point of falling asleep when the solution came to him in a flash of inspiration. He grabbed the torch and padded barefoot into the kitchen. That was it! He felt a thrill akin to that of breaking a secret wartime code. *The cathedral in South...* It wasn't South London at all, but Southwark. And the *BOR...* could only be Borough Market. There were always dozens of Italians working there. It was obvious! How amazing that the solution had just come to him as soon as he had ceased trying to cudgel the answer out of his brain.

He wanted to phone Rosaria whether she was asleep or not but, frustratingly, the network had collapsed. He would have to savour his moment of triumph alone for a few more hours. In point of fact, thirty-six hours would elapse before power was restored to Puglia, by which time, supermarkets and private homes had thrown away tons upon tons of frozen foods, which clogged up the waste disposal systems for days to come. The billionaire prime minister appeared on all the TV channels, which he either owned or controlled, acting out his favourite role of saviour of the nation. He promised that he would build new power stations all over Italy so that 'our beloved country does not have to depend on anyone else for its electricity supplies.' Some of the country's pundits, still free or brave enough to express an opinion, wondered whether their leader intended to construct new power stations with his own vast fortunes rather than expecting the project to be funded by the treasury – implying that the former were in a healthier state than the latter.

On a local level, Daniela panicked about the loss of a day's teaching. There was no lighting or current to operate computers and CD players in the school on the following day. She arranged for lessons to be held the following Saturday, but omitted to consult either of her teachers beforehand. Glenda categorically refused to cooperate. Adam, who didn't really mind, told the secretary that it was high time she stopped considering herself to be more important than the teaching staff. Daniela wore an expression of thwarted rage on her face like Medusa who had just discovered that her serpents were, after all, non-venomous. The boss, Daniele, had to come all the way down from Lecce to pour oil on troubled waters. In the end, the situation was saved by them all agreeing to extend the summer term by one day. Glenda expressed the opinion to Adam afterwards that, by that time, the students would have forgotten to care either way.

* * * * *

When Rosaria appeared briefly in his life late on Saturday evening, her joy that Adam had worked out the final clue in the letter seemed to be tempered by some other preoccupation.

'What's on your mind, Rosy?' he asked concernedly.

'Nothing, Adam,' she replied.

It made no difference at all when he said simply that there obviously *was* something troubling her. All she said was: 'It's not *you*, Adam.'

It was the first time in their relationship so far that she had not been emotionally, physically and mentally focused on him. He was faced with the realisation that he would have to deal with the reality of a complex woman in a complicated emotional situation. It would require reserves of patience and sympathy that had hitherto been untried. He had usually run away from relationships as soon as they had become taxing. With Rosaria, he did not want to make the same mistakes. 'You are my rock, *mio punto di riferimento,*' she had recently told him.

It was apparent to him that, henceforth, he should endeavour to become 'rock-like' in order to live up to her image of him. After a few more months together, he would learn that Rosaria always bottled up her troubles whilst she imposed some internal mental analysis on herself before she could discuss openly whatever was worrying her. Thus it was not until the following day that she decided it was the moment to unburden her troubles on Adam. They had been lying on the bed for some minutes, in a gentle embrace, after making love and drinking strong, black coffee.

'It's Benedetto,' she began. 'I have to go with him to see the priest one evening soon. The Church insists that we follow a preparatory course to make sure we understand our marital obligations before the ceremony. There will be two other couples there too. And my mother and father are beginning to talk about making arrangements for the wedding. Adam, I'm getting scared. It's just like what you were saying about leaving my fuel tank empty until the last moment. This wedding is suddenly a reality that needs to be faced.'

She was on the point of tears and needed to be hugged tightly for a long time before she began to calm down. Her underlying optimism eventually returned, as if the present asserted a more powerful hold over her than a future that she did not want to confront. She was soon talking animatedly about the journey to London and was full of praise that Adam had succeeded in solving the last link in the sixth letter.

'Rosy, we must book tickets for the flight before it's too late. We shall only have about ten days in which to bring about...' He had been going to say 'the demise of Enrico' when the full implications of their undertaking had struck him with full force. Rosaria read his thoughts. 'You don't have to come, Adam, if you don't want to. I shall quite understand.'

The revelation that she was determined to see this venture through gave him back the courage which had nearly deserted him. 'You don't seriously believe that I could stand by and let you go through with this thing on your own, do you, Rosy?' At least, the words sounded brave enough. She hugged him again tightly, giving herself strength too. 'Besides which, I really want to see London,' she added brightly. 'And get over my reluctance to fly for the first time in my life. Above all, I want to see where you live and share a bit of *your* life in England.'

Adam agreed to book the tickets himself until the words 'book online' sent him into a computer panic. They agreed to go to an internet point the following morning. Adam had assumed that they would fly directly to London from Brindisi, but, it appeared, matters were not that simple as far as Rosaria was concerned. She pointed out that her father – or Benedetto – would inevitably insist on taking her to the airport at Brindisi. Then they would know she was flying to London and whom she was travelling with.

'I've worked this out, Adam. I'm going to tell them all that I am going to see Martina in Rome. That way my father will only offer to take me to Lecce station. Then we can meet on the train and we'll be safe together.'

Adam was unconvinced that the word 'safe' applied to any part of this venture, but merely said: 'I hope your sister is in on all this.'

'Oh yes, Adam. I spoke to her yesterday. Of course, she thinks I am mad. But I told her you would be with me all the time.'

There was nothing useful that Adam could add to that. He had to accept that his profoundest aspirations were about to become reality. It would no longer be possible to stand on the fringes of life. He had become involved in events that would dismantle for ever the protective barriers with which he had surrounded himself since childhood. So be it. He was committed. He managed a smile in Rosaria's direction. This relationship might prove to be the death of him, but, at least, he would go out in a blaze of self-respect, if not necessarily glory. Adam was more acutely aware of future possibilities than his companion. He was glad that she was protected from his alarming visions of the ghosts of what might be to come. Let her continue filling up her tank at the last moment. He must love and accept her the way she was. 'Other brain', silent for too long, made a vain attempt to curb the excesses of his mercurial romanticism. But Adam was not listening.

After they had booked the tickets – one way from Rome to London – they felt calmer. They had decided on one way tickets because it was impossible to know how long it would be before they even found Enrico, let alone bringing about his 'demise'. Rosaria must have sensed Adam's underlying fears because, out of the blue, she said to him as they were driving away from the internet point, tickets in hand:

'You needn't be too concerned about what we are doing, *amore*. We will not be acting alone when it comes to the...climax.' Adam raised an eyebrow or two at her enigmatic choice of words. But she refused to be drawn, leaving Adam to guess what she had meant. At that point, he did not realise just how elaborate her scheme was to be – nor whom it would involve.

They found a bar along the sea front in Gravino and sat outside sipping drinks. Rosaria was reading the local newspaper intensely while the familiarity of the surroundings lulled Adam into a sense of security. Adam looked at Rosaria while she was concentrating on the news item. He admitted to himself that he was captivated by her looks, but there were invisible strands that bound them together now on a less worldly plane. Rosaria caught the expression on his face as she raised her eyes from the page she had been reading.

'What are you thinking, *amore?*'

'I don't quite know – maybe that life feels right when we are together, that we were meant for each other despite obvious differences in age and circumstances. I feel comfortable with you. I get the impression that I have always known you, and...' The words petered out as if, by uttering them, he had unravelled the fabric of his inner thoughts. Rosaria reached over for his hand and said: '*Ti amo.*'

'Ah,' said Adam ironically. '*That* must have been what *I* was trying to say.'

'I know. I feel the same.'

They had two weeks left before leaving for London. Two weeks during which they would have to try and concentrate on work. Rosaria dropped Adam off outside the school. 'I'll see you as soon as I can, *amore mio,*'

'Don't forget to tell me about your visit to the priest, will you, Rosy?' She grimaced and nodded. It was going to be a busy time for both of them.

'Just as well,' thought Adam as he headed off towards the *Antica Isolata* for lunch. He found Glenda sitting at their usual table devouring the bread from the little wicker basket as if she had not eaten for days.

'Hello Glenda. Are you hungry by any chance?' he began sarcastically; 'The Big A not supplying you with enough omega 3?'

'Ah well, Adam,' she explained. 'I'm eating for two people now, you know.'

'I can see that, Glenda. But I am quite capable of helping myself – given the chance, of course,' said Adam snatching the last piece of bread.

'Not you, you wally! I meant the baby.'

'Would you rather it was a boy or a girl?' he asked, thinking that it was high time he asked the stock question.

'Adam, I really don't mind *which* sex it is as long as it comes out with two of everything. Where appropriate, of course,' she added to forestall any witticism that he might attempt. But Adam did not feel like making cheap and obvious quips about Glenda's future child. 'I'm sure he or she will be fine,' he said.

Over lunch, they chatted on about the usual things; the school and Daniela, who, Glenda claimed, was trying hard to be nicer to them. 'I think the boss must have had a word with her.' Glenda asked Adam what he was doing over the Easter break. Adam remained suitably vague about his plans. There was no way that he was going to reveal to Glenda any detail about the trip to London. But he did tell Glenda about Rosaria's 'marriage guidance' class with the priest instead.

'That will put her off getting married after one session,' proclaimed Glenda with confidence. Adam had not considered that Rosaria's encounter with Holy Mother Church might have a positive outcome. He allowed himself a glimmer of optimism. Like Adam, Rosaria was nominally a Catholic, but he had not noticed any excessive signs of devotion in her, apart from when they entered a church and she dipped her finger in the holy water stoop to cross herself.

Adam's lesson with the BPS group came round again. He knew that Rosaria would not be there because it coincided with her first *rendez-vous* with the parish priest. To his mild disappointment, neither was the petite Federica present. She had been complaining of feeling tired because she was being kept awake by a barking dog. It seemed that the problem was endemic in this part of the world.

Rosaria met Adam outside the school at nine o'clock and offered to drive him home. She was in a strange mood. Glenda's prediction about the pre-nuptial class with the parish priest turned out to be prophetic. Rosaria had run out of the instruction class while the priest and Benedetto gaped in disbelief at her fleeing figure. Adam felt secretly delighted at the outcome of events but did not want to show his pleasure too obviously.

'But why, Rosy?' he enquired with curiosity. It had, after all, been a very public and drastic step to take.

'The first part of the class was the usual thing about the sanctity of marriage and its main purpose – having children and bringing them up according to the teachings of the Church. But then – and I believe the priest did it as a test of our conviction – he took us into the church and made each couple stand in front of the altar and say the words: *'I will stay with you and be faithful to you until the day I die.'* Adam, we were the last couple to do it and I just couldn't tell a lie. I kept thinking of you and me. I ran off and went straight home. Benedetto followed me home. He was furious with me. Even my *papà* didn't try to interfere. Benedetto threatened to leave me for good if I didn't make up my mind immediately. And the awful thing was, I felt *glad* that he had threatened me. Adam it was *terrible!*'

Adam had become very thoughtful. When she had calmed down a bit, he said: 'It strikes me, Rosy, that you are finding it impossible to break off this engagement because you don't want to hurt him. So, rather than confronting him with the truth, you are hoping that it will be *him* who takes the step for you.'

There followed a protracted silence that became unnerving. Finally, Rosaria just nodded in admission of the truth of Adam's analysis of her situation. She kissed him and he felt the residual wetness of her tears on his cheek.

15: Tracking Down Diletta's 'Double'

The whole London venture was nearly sabotaged at the outset by Rosaria's last minute arrival at Lecce station. Adam had boarded the Intercity train as soon as its doors were open. He had deliberately set off early from Campanula taking the local train to Lecce as dawn was breaking. It was his first journey on Salento's local railway line – *Le Ferrovie del Sud-Est*. It was like stepping back into post Second World War Italy. The train was antiquated. The entire locomotive and carriages had been manufactured in Germany and had obviously become redundant as the modernisation of the railway system had got under way in the prosperous north of Italy. The two carriages chugged along, driven by a noisy, vibrating diesel engine, between olive groves and isolated white farm houses where elderly men and women stooped over vegetable patches or tended small vineyards before the sun's heat made labour impossible. Every single little station, serving the communities that were dotted along the route to Lecce, had its own station master, who dutifully appeared as the train arrived, shepherding the scarce passengers on or off the train and shouting *'Via!'* to the driver to send the train on its way. It was engagingly quaint and revealed yet another secret aspect of this ancient land. To Adam's surprise, there was even a ticket inspector on the train. 'Do I have to change trains?' asked Adam, who had been warned by Glenda about the quirkiness of the journey. 'We don't know yet,' replied the ticket collector in all seriousness. 'I'll tell you when we reach...' He mentioned the name of a station which Adam did not quite catch as the train continued on its time warp journey. They did have to change trains at a picturesque and ancient town called Soleto, seemingly in the middle of nowhere. The whole journey to

Lecce along the single track line took ninety minutes as opposed to the forty-five minutes that it took by car. But the journey had cost him under two euros. Adam decided that it had been well worth the discomfort to appreciate rural Salento in a way that he would never have witnessed travelling by road.

And here was Adam, sitting in their comfortable pre-booked seats, looking anxiously at his watch every ten seconds. Rosaria never wore a watch, he recalled. 'How could she do this?' he thought angrily. The train was due to leave in ten minutes. The most important journey in her life – in both their lives – and she was about to scupper the whole endeavour. He was on the point of abandoning their mission and getting off the train. With little more than a minute to go before departure, he looked desperately out of the window and noticed a man of about his age peering in through the window from the platform. He was good-looking with a neatly trimmed moustache on a swarthy face. He appeared to be waving at Adam. It was an instinctive gesture to wave back at the man who definitely seemed to recognise Adam. He had begun to raise his hand in salute when he heard a furiously hissed whisper from someone standing behind him in the open corridor.

'NO ADAM! That's my father!'

He stopped himself just in time and looked at Rosaria in fury. Rosaria went through the ritual of waving to her father and smiling politely at Adam as if to a fellow passenger, while she said in a more normal voice: 'Wait until we are out of the station, Adam. *Ti prego!*'

Adam took one look at the love of his life as the flat countryside rolled by at a gathering speed. She still looked tense after her last minute rush to board the train. There was, Adam decided, little point in berating her for her lateness even before their journey to London had got under way. 'Rosy,' he said quietly. 'Have you any idea how worried I was when you didn't arrive?'

'Adam,' she said, the tears of frustration shining in the corner of her eyes. 'I'm so sorry, *amore*. It was my father's fault. He refused to drive quickly even though we had started out late. He *knows* I'm up to something. He was trying his best to make sure I missed the train. I really shouted at him in the end. You still have little idea what I have to put up with at home. *Papà's* idea of happiness is to keep me at home every hour of every day.'

Adam recalled Glenda's words about dictators. Yet again, her analysis of social life in Puglia proved to be well-founded.

'Never mind, Rosy, we're here together and we've begun our journey,' he said sympathetically. The train left the flat plains of Puglia and began to wind its way through the deep valleys of the *Appennini,* across swiftly flowing rivers, stopping at only a handful of major towns on its tortuous way across Italy towards the western coast – and Rome. Rosaria relaxed visibly as the journey progressed. She leant across the tiny table that separated them and squeezed his hand tightly as her legs wrapped themselves round his under the table, a discreet public display of love being allowed for only the second time. She looked content with the present moment, the tension caused by her late arrival receding as they drew nearer their destination.

'I suppose you've been to Rome before, haven't you Adam?' she asked.

'Never,' he replied simply. Rosaria shook her head in disbelief.

'We'll visit it properly after all this is over.'

The monumental task before them struck both of them at the same instant. Their sharp intake of breath was simultaneous and comical as they both dissolved into quiet laughter.

'One step at a time,' said Adam. Rosaria nodded in agreement.

'Never fill up your tank until it is empty,' he added under his breath and received a sharp kick under the table.

At one point during the journey, Adam thought of something that he realised he should have mentioned before they set out.

'Photographs!' he said. 'Do we have any pictures of Diletta and Enrico. I might need to know what they look like. At least it would help if I could visualise them.' Rosaria pointed smugly at her suitcase in the rack above their heads and nodded.

When the train drew into *Roma Termini* and they stepped out on to the platform, the change in atmosphere was tangible. There was a buzz in the air that you could not fail to detect. A variety of different sounds and smells infused the air around them.

'Are you ready for a surprise, Adam?' asked Rosaria suddenly as they walked up to the ticket barrier.

'Yes, Rome does feel different, doesn't it?' he said assuming she was referring to the sense of change in ambience which he detected in the air. But Rosaria had a very different kind of surprise in mind.

Adam recognised Martina as soon as she waved cheerily at her sister. The memory of the two of them following Diletta's hearse all those weeks ago came back vividly to his mind.

'Why didn't you tell me, Rosy?' said Adam, delighted that he was finally going to be allowed to meet a member of Rosaria's family in the flesh.

'I wanted it to be a surprise,' she answered. 'And I thought that you would have had time to become nervous if I had told you beforehand.' Rosaria, he had realised, often assumed that his reactions would be similar to hers in any given circumstances.

'It's a lovely surprise,' he said warmly as they approached a smiling Martina. Sisterly hugs, words of mutual joy, exchange and updates of news before, finally, Rosaria introduced Adam to her sister with an apologetic smile.

'I'm pleased to meet you, Adam. Rosy has told me all about you. In fact, she talks about nothing else.' It became quickly apparent that Martina did not speak or understand English. Adam would have to resort to Italian for the next hour or so.

'I hope you haven't grown bored with the topic, Martina,' said Adam, forgetting that Italian brains are not programmed to grasp the irony of English humour – especially when directed against oneself.

'He's being modest in an English sort of way,' Rosaria explained to her sister. 'You get used to it.'

The three of them took the local train to *Fiumicino* airport. Adam was happy to listen to the non-stop exchanges between the two sisters, making only occasional polite contributions to the conversation. Whenever he thought of something interesting to say and had formulated the Italian words in his head, the conversation had progressed beyond the point when his observations were relevant. He contented himself with being fascinated by the sight of these two diversely beautiful women between whom the bond of sisterhood was so strong.

When it came to the moment for them to go their separate ways, Martina turned to Adam and said with urgent appeal in her voice:

'Please look after my sister, won't you Adam? I am so worried about what she is undertaking. But I am truly relieved that you are going with her. I know she would have gone on her own if you hadn't been there.'

Adam uttered some reassuring words – as another wave of minor panic shot through him, quickly suppressed as he remembered to apply his new-found resolution to remain 'rock-like' in the face of all odds.

'It was lovely to meet you, Martina. I hope we shall meet again soon.' To his agreeable surprise, she proffered her cheeks for the customary, affectionate *baci* - a sign that he had been accepted.

Adam and Rosaria went through the habitual, monotonous airport routine. They boarded the aircraft. Rosaria sat holding Adam's hand as her maiden flight got underway. Her grip tightened as the plane began to shudder and bump along the concrete runway at an increasing pace before gliding upwards into the skies above. Adam himself felt only wonder at being inside a vibrating machine weighing several tons that struggled against the forces of nature to leave the solid ground behind. He looked at Rosaria, She smiled bravely as they rose into the air but, at no point during the flight, did she dare to look out of the window, even when Adam pointed out the Alps, whose white fangs seemed to be reaching up to pierce the vulnerable underbelly of the aircraft.

During the flight, they chatted about Martina and what was happening in her life. 'She likes you,' declared Rosaria almost in surprise and certainly in relief. Adam was relieved too; she was an important ally in the enemy camp.

As dusk was falling, they arrived at Adam's flat in the small Buckinghamshire village where he lived. 'This is my village,' said Adam as the taxi drove through the village centre. By the time that a travel weary Rosaria had reacted to what he had said, they had driven through the centre and out the other side. 'What village, Adam? It must be invisible!' she exclaimed in alarm. His flat was cosy and welcoming. Rosaria took to it at once. Adam was amused at how quickly she adopted it as her own – draining the hot water tank with a shower that lasted twenty minutes.

'It's as if you have always lived here, Rosy,' he said with a touch of sarcasm.

'It's nice. It's *you*, Adam. And so it feels like mine too.' Adam was happy that she felt that way, even if he determined to have his morning shower before she did.

Then it was bed and sleep. Tomorrow, there would be no time to spare for sightseeing. They had decided to set off for London early the next day to begin the search for Diletta's 'double'.

'Goodnight, Rosy,' he said revelling in the feeling that he would wake up for the first time in the morning to find her by his side. He leant over to kiss her goodnight but found that she had fallen asleep instantly.

* * * * *

The buzz of excitement and the tingle of nerves when they woke up the next morning infected them both. The hugs and early morning kisses might have turned into something else but their shared sense of urgency of purpose dominated all else. Adam got up, had his usual two minute shower and made the coffee. Rosaria sacrificed her usually lengthy ritual meeting with hot water and was out, dried and dressed within fifteen minutes. 'Little short of martyrdom,' comment Adam teasingly. Outside, the April sunshine had barely raised the air temperature above a modest 8 or 9 degrees – winter by Puglian standards.

They organised what they imagined they would need for this crucial day; mobile phones had been charged up overnight. Adam found a small rucksack into which he packed his digital camera, a notebook and pen – on the basis that he would inevitably need these items if he *didn't* take them. Rosaria entrusted him with the envelope containing the photos of Diletta's wedding, which he would study on the journey up to London. 'Don't forget to take the sixth letter,' said Rosaria. Adam handed it to Rosaria.

'You're the one most likely to need it today, Rosy.'

'How do you know that, Adam?' asked Rosaria.

He could not give precise reasons but, true to character, Adam had already formed mental pictures of the likely scenarios of the day ahead, whereas Rosaria had no preconceived notions as to how the day would pan out.

'Grazie a Dio you are with me, Adam. Today, I know I am going to need you.'

'I think that, if today is going to be successful, it will be equally thanks to both of us,' Adam assured her. A final hug and they were off.

Rosaria nearly went into revolt mode when Adam retrieved his custard-coloured Panda from the garage. She had the same expression of outraged aesthetic scruples as when she had first seen him in the green cardigan. She did not say a word, but the look on her face clearly stated that the car would have to go if there was to be a future for them together.

Adam merely laughed at the distaste on her face. A car as status symbol was an alien notion to him. 'Don't worry, Rosy,' he reassured her. 'It's only a short ride to the station.'

They were on the train to London by half past nine. As they passed through the Buckinghamshire countryside, Rosaria seemed more impressed than anything else by the height of the trees.

'I'm so used to olive trees which hardly ever stand higher than a single storey house,' she commented. 'These trees are like giants. They are beautiful but they feel *threatening.*'

Adam could understand her point of view. When he had first arrived in Puglia, he had looked at the olive trees and had the impression that he had arrived in a land of dwarves. She looked more and more intrigued as the countryside gave way to the suburbs of London and, five minutes later, the conglomeration of buildings that was London proper. She commented on the quaint station names as the train passed through Swiss Cottage and St John's Wood. Adam experienced a brief flash of something disconcerting as he read the last station name before the train branched off to Marylebone. The sensation dissolved into thin air before he could identify it as a thought.

'The photos!' he said, remembering that he still had no idea what Diletta or Enrico looked like. 'I must look at them when we are on the underground train.' It had seemed the obvious first step that they should head immediately for Southwark Cathedral and its adjoining market. Adam remembered from a previous visit many years ago that the station for Southwark Cathedral was London Bridge, not Southwark – confirmed by a member of staff at Baker Street. For Rosaria, travelling on the London Underground felt no different to the *Metropolitana* in Rome – until Adam told her that they were travelling deep under the River Thames between Westminster and Waterloo.

Adam drew out the photo of Diletta taken at her wedding. She looked stunning in her bridal dress, taller than Rosaria but equally as beautiful. But she had a petrified smile on her face which betrayed her inner feelings. Adam could well understand why Rosaria had wanted to avenge her cousin's death. He shared Rosaria's deep anger at the utter waste of a precious life. The sensation was reinforced when he turned his attention to the photo of the man standing by her side, appropriately holding a knife in his left hand, with which he was about to cut the wedding cake. It reminded Adam of someone he had seen in a film – maybe The Godfather. There was a cruel arrogance about his face, a kind of noble corruption which sent a shiver up and down his spine. He stuffed the photo back into the envelope with a sharp intake of breath – a gesture which did not escape Rosaria's attention.

'Now you know, Adam,' was all she said.

They alighted at London Bridge. As the train pulled out of the station with that eerie whine, increasing in pitch, which appears to be peculiar to the Jubilee Line, they stood on the platform looking at each other. They were both feeling the same sensation of apprehension, both facing the unfolding of events shrouded in the indecipherable shadows of this long awaited moment. Another quick hug as other passengers pushed past them on their way up or down the platform, some looking distractedly at this disparate couple. In London, everything and nothing is remarkable.

They emerged, hand-in-hand, from the bowels of the earth one hundred feet below the surface of the city to be greeted by an edifice which rose skywards like a declaration of war on the heavens above; a jagged glass finger that tore into the fabric of the blue sky. An airplane heading for Heathrow passed over it, seemingly about to be lacerated on the giant splinter of glass. Adam was thinking of their flight over the Alps the previous day, with the perspective alarmingly reversed.

'What is it?' asked Rosaria in awe.

Adam explained why it was called The Shard.

'Do you like it, Adam?'

Adam replied that he would rather not expend emotional energy at that moment when he needed to reserve it for their shared undertaking. But in his mind, he had images of starving children who could not even hope for a sip of clean water in their stunted young lives. Why should they starve while money was squandered on such an obscenity?

'The folly of the modern world masquerading as progress!' he muttered hoping that Rosaria would not ask for a translation. By the expression on her face, he saw that she had captured the essential message.

'*È orrendo!*' she agreed. She squeezed his hand and he kissed her softly on the forehead – as it turned out, it was to be the final kiss of the day.

They turned their attention to the ordinary bustle of London traffic. It took Adam a minute to get his bearings before they headed off in the direction of Southwark Cathedral. The contrast between the glass monstrosity and this gracefully noble building, reaching modestly towards God's heaven, was startling.

'What a beautiful church this is!' exclaimed Rosaria. 'It's reassuring to find a lovely place like this so near that other monstrosity.' Adam nodded in silent agreement.

'But where's the market?' she asked coming back to the business of the day. By way of response, Adam took her by the waist and turned her through a ninety degree angle. 'You're looking at it.'

'Come on, Adam.' He was disconcerted to find that she withdrew her hand from his without ceremony and strode off in the direction of Borough Market without a backward glance. As he caught up with her, she said:

'From now on, *amore*, we cannot afford to be seen too obviously together. If things work out right, I may need you to follow her to see where she goes.'

The love of his life had become instantly focussed on the business in hand. It was no longer a cosy walk round London but a deadly earnest mission. 'Stay close to me, Adam. But we must be ready to act as if we do not know each other at a second's notice.'

And so they walked around all those vibrant market stalls, selling cheeses, salami and hams of every description, wines and olive oil from Puglia and a luscious selection of fruit and vegetables. The predominance of Italians was noticeable amongst the presence of French, German and sometimes English stall-holders. There was even a Chinese couple – manning an espresso coffee stall. They walked around a second and third time but there was no sign of anyone remotely like Diletta – or even a young Italian woman who might have been a likely candidate.

'Maybe she isn't working here today,' suggested Adam despondently. He felt deeply sorry when he read the dejection on Rosaria's face. He went to kiss her but she shrugged him off almost angrily.

'Perhaps she is working later today. Come on Rosy. Let's go back to the cathedral and seek inspiration there. It has worked before,' he said thinking of the sixth letter which had arrived so soon after their pilgrimage to the now so distant hilltop church in Campanula.

'Is it a Catholic cathedral, Adam?'

'No, it's Anglican, I'm afraid. But I don't suppose God has turned his back on it because of some small historical blunder,' said Adam light-heartedly.

'Alright Adam, I suppose this was never going to be a straightforward venture,' she added resigned to the inevitable.

They spent a tranquil fifteen minutes inside the cathedral, listening to the magic notes of someone practising for an organ recital. They implored the invisible spirits that surround us to heed them. Just as before, the other world appeared to be indifferent. They did another tour of the market stalls but to no avail. Rosaria began to grow despondent again. It was midday and Adam was feeling hungry. He had spotted a sandwich bar down an arched side alley that led back towards the main road. Rosaria was not hungry and said she would wait for Adam where she could keep an eye on the big vegetable stall, called *Zucchini*, where there were four or five Italian men and women serving customers. Adam went for his sandwich. The snack bar was called *Altamarea*. More Italians, though Adam. He ordered his sandwich in Italian. There followed the usual surprised comments from the lads manning the stall that an Englishman could manage to speak Italian fluently.

'How come you speak Italian so well?' asked one of them.

'I teach English near Lecce,' he answered. They expressed interest but there had been a fleeting glance that passed between them that did not escape Adam's notice. Acting purely on impulse, Adam said in Italian:

'In fact, I have a message from someone called Rosy to her cousin Diletta who works in this market. But I can't find her. Do you know anyone by that name?'

Adam held his breath. Again, there were hesitant glances between the three young men. They seemed to convey the sense that Adam did not pose a threat. Adam continued to look expectantly at each one of them in turn.

'Diletta works in the Italian restaurant. You'll find her there for certain. We've seen her today.'

'Quale ristorante?' asked Adam with a feeling of suppressed elation.

'It's called *Don Giovanni,'* came the reply. 'It's on the main road opposite the station. The entrance to the restaurant is down a side street.'

'Grazie! Grazie mille, ragazzi!' said Adam smiling broadly. 'You might have saved somebody's life.' He shook each one of them by the hand and hurried back to find Rosaria, still standing where he had left her, looking more despondent than ever. He had forgotten to pick up his sandwich.

'She's here,' said Adam simply and he told her what he had discovered.

'Oh, Adam! *Bravissimo!'* she said admiringly. She went to kiss him but stopped herself in time. She had to calculate whether her germ of a plan had been compromised. On balance, she thought, the advantages of finding the girl far outweighed any risk of her being associated with Adam. 'We must go immediately. One of those lads at the sandwich bar is bound to phone her and warn her of the arrival of an Englishman.'

They found the restaurant within minutes. Rosaria held out a restraining arm as they were about to cross the road. 'Look Adam!' she exclaimed without pointing at what she had seen. She made him turn towards her so that they both had to look obliquely across the road. Fortunately, the usual lunchtime crowds were starting to mill around so there was little risk of being spotted by the girl wearing a black and white waitress's outfit talking on her mobile phone whilst gesticulating animatedly. Her general appearance, hair colour, height and good looks were strikingly similar to the photo of Diletta.

'Not quite a *sosia*,' said Rosaria excitedly, 'but near enough. We've found her, Adam.' The girl who was almost Diletta went back through the door and downstairs to the basement restaurant. Rosaria's mind had covered all the possible outcomes in a split second. She had worked out that, whatever the scenario, whatever part Diletta's double had to play in this drama, the girl would need to talk to her. She would not attempt to avoid any encounter.

'Adam, I'm sorry to leave you. But I shall have to go down there on my own. I'll be as quick as I can.' Rosaria was speaking so rapidly in Italian that Adam had difficulty following what she was saying. 'I shall try to send you a text message from *her* phone so that we have a record of her number. Then you must follow her wherever she goes.'

'But what about you...?' began Adam anxiously.

'Don't worry about me. We'll meet up later. This is *it*, Adam.' And she was off across the road before he could think of any further objections.

In point of fact, Adam was left to loiter in the street, drink a succession of coffees in a nearby bar, prop up street lamps reading a newspaper for almost three hours. 'Diletta', Rosy would tell him later, had had to serve customers for an hour before she could sit down and talk in earnest. Adam hardly dared go to the toilet in case he missed the vital moment or for fear that the mobile signal might fail to penetrate the basement toilet in the coffee bar. By chance, there was an intriguing article in his Guardian about mafia infiltration in London. The major mafia clans, including *La Sacra Corona Unita,* it was reported, were establishing themselves in various districts of the city in order to invest in legitimate businesses with the sole purpose of laundering their vast fortunes. He became so involved in his reading, as he sipped his umpteenth coffee, that he almost missed the tell-tale bleep of his mobile phone just before four o'clock.

It was the long-awaited text message from Rosaria. 'Adam, follow her home', was all it said. The number on the screen was not one he recognised. Adam shot out of the coffee bar in time to see Rosaria and 'Diletta' walking out of the restaurant, arm-in-arm like long-lost friends, chatting and smiling, completely at ease in each other's company. Now they were crossing the road and coming towards him. He was on the point of speaking to them but remembered his mission instructions just in time. Rosaria walked right past him without a flicker of recognition.

'It looks as if I shall be trailing both of them,' he thought, as they descended underground once again. 'That should make things easier. Two birds with one stone, so to speak.'

16: Springing the Trap

Fortunately, rush hour had not got underway on that Thursday afternoon, so Adam found it easy to follow the two women down the escalator on to the westbound platform of the Jubilee Line, retracing their steps from that morning. He easily managed to get in to the same carriage as they did, but he remained standing while they sat down side by side still deeply engrossed in their conversation, despite the clattering of the wheels as the train sped back under the Thames towards Westminster. Rosaria's ability to ignore Adam was disconcerting. Not for one instant did she divert her attention from her new-found friend. Her ability to engage with other people was impressive, Adam concluded. He realised with embarrassment that the other passengers might have assumed that he was ogling these two attractive girls. He tried his best to remain detached from his task of keeping an eye on 'Diletta'. He supposed Rosy must know her real name, by now.

As the train drew into Bond Street, the 'cosy' situation ceased abruptly. Diletta stood up to get off the train. Rosaria stood up but only to embrace her companion fondly. Adam heard Rosaria saying: 'Don't worry, Sofia! You must be brave for another few days. Remember everything that we have decided. I'll be in touch soon.' And as the train doors slid open, the girl got off followed closely by Adam, who had given a brief sideways glance in Rosaria's direction. She, however, with single-minded purpose, kept up her act of ignoring him to the bitter end.

Adam's worst fear, apart from leaving Rosaria on her own in a city that she was unfamiliar with, was the thought that 'Sofia', as he would now have to think of her, was intending to go shopping down Oxford Street. Not only would it be difficult to follow her unobtrusively, but the very thought of following a woman on a shopping spree was a nightmare. He had had ample experience of this in his past life; women out shopping *never* walked in straight lines but in ever widening circles before returning to their point of departure and starting all over again. On the way, in his experience, they touched every item of clothing, sifted through endless hair-colouring products and body lotions but never made a decision about purchasing anything. Adam's greatest fear did not materialise, however. Sofia – he had to repeat her name several times to himself – headed purposefully down Davies Street without sparing a glance in the direction of any shop window. Adam's next fear was that she was going to visit a friend. This might mean that he would have to stand in the street until midnight. He would draw the line at that, he decided.

But Sofia's destination was far more obvious, as he discovered a few minutes later. She turned right into Three Kings Yard, a gated mews with a side entrance for pedestrians. She got out her mobile phone and stopped in her tracks half way along the cobbled street to speak to someone. Adam had to walk straight past her so as not to seem to be following her. He looked towards the end of the mews and understood immediately where he was. The vertically striped red, white and green flag was hanging, inert and damp, from a flagpole. The Italian Embassy, of course.

He walked on towards the Embassy simply because there was no other choice. He couldn't just do a sudden about-turn and risk running headlong into Diletta – no Sofia. He reached the building just as someone the other side of the big black door was manipulating the locks. He turned and walked smartly along the front of the building and to the left just as the door was opened. It was a dingy alleyway enclosed by houses. One old street lamp, which somebody had forgotten to turn off, seemed to intensify the gloom. He had the presence of mind to fish out his mobile phone and pretend to be engaged in a conversation during which he did a lot of head nodding. It was just as well that he had made himself inconspicuous since he instantly recognised the man who was standing on the top step of the Embassy. Enrico was taller than he had imagined. Sofia was standing at pavement level, which emphasised the man's height and made her look overpowered by his presence. Adam, with heart in mouth, began to walk back towards them still holding the phone to his ear. The few words that Enrico uttered were delivered in a gruff voice that was never raised. There was no gesture of friendliness, let alone affection. Sofia looked ill-at-ease and nodded or shook her head as appropriate. As Adam walked past them, shielding his face with his left hand holding the cell-phone, he heard Enrico saying brusquely: *Adesso va' a casa!* 'Now go home!'

She turned and walked back the way she had come while Enrico went back inside the Embassy and closed the door. Adam allowed Sofia to overtake him as he finished his mimed conversation with a cheery: 'See you later.' Her head was bowed as she walked past Adam. It was difficult to make out the expression on her face. She could have been suppressing tears or was it a secret smirk? Adam wondered what had been the purpose of her seemingly pointless visit to see Enrico. As he began to follow Sofia again, he intuited that her detour was most likely imposed on her by this bully of a man with the sole purpose of reasserting his hold over her. In all probability, she was forced to repeat this ritual humiliation every time she came back from work. Adam had already conceived an instinctive hatred of this arrogant individual. Adam's intuition appeared to be confirmed by the fact that Sofia headed back towards Bond Street station, her head bowed in deep thought. She must have a lot to think about since she had met Rosaria, considered Adam. She headed directly for the westbound platform of the Jubilee line whence they had so recently alighted, leaving Rosaria to plunge onwards into the murky tunnel. He dreaded to think where the love of his life might have ended up before realising that she should have got off at the next stop.

Adam looked at his mobile to check that Sofia's number had registered on his phone. He wrote the number down in his little notebook while they were waiting for the next train. He did not trust himself to use the gadget's ability to store the new number in case he accidentally obliterated it. For a brief instant as they got on to the train, he entertained the insane notion that he should call Sofia and ask her where she was heading. 'I must be getting weary!' he thought. He did not have long to wait before he discovered the answer. At Baker Street, a crowd of people got on and he had to reposition himself quickly so as not to lose sight of his beautiful quarry; yes, she was a very attractive young woman, thought Adam, before dutifully suppressing the thought.

At the very next stop, Sofia stood up well before the train drew in to the station and made her way through the throng of people towards the double doors. Adam followed her. He was so close behind her that he was afraid that she would recognise this man who had been trailing her for the past hour. But Sofia must still have been too deep in thought to notice specific strangers in her vicinity. With a shock of surprise, Adam noticed that they had got out at St John's Wood station. He tried to identify the fleeting sensation of recognition that he had experienced that morning. Just one of his occasional flashes of prescience, he assumed.

Sofia crossed the main road and walked rapidly down Grove End Road. Adam briefly entertained the reprehensible thought that he would be happy to follow Sofia's long shapely legs all the way round London but quickly dismissed the unbidden thought as ignoble. The legs in question turned right into Loudoun Road and then left into Langford Place. Just before the end of the road, she turned into the driveway of the last house. Adam had to speed up to make sure that she really did go into the house. Yes, she did! It was number 42. Sofia paused to look for the key in her handbag as she walked up the short flight of white steps leading to the front door. It was a spacious, three storey semi-detached house. Adam saw the hall light being switched on and then the room to the right was illuminated for an instant before she drew the curtains to shut out the world even though it was not yet nightfall. He had accomplished his mission. He took a photo of the house before returning to the station, making a scribbled note of the street names as he went. The accumulated effect of the tension and the many coffees that he had consumed suddenly made an urgent call of nature imminent. He was saved from any embarrassment when he found – to his relief – that St John's Wood station had a toilet. Only then, did he remember that his beloved Rosaria was waiting somewhere for him in this vast city. He sent her an urgent text message.

She had found her way back to Marylebone station, having had great difficulty pronouncing the name of the station when asking directions of an Italian waiter in a coffee bar in Baker Street. She had not had to wait too long for Adam, who found her sitting on a bench gazing vaguely at the departures board.

'Let's go home, Adam,' she said wearily. They stumbled on to the train and hardly spoke to each other for the first ten minutes. They agreed to save the 'debriefing' until they were back home. But when Rosaria stood up to get off the train, she nearly collapsed. The blood had drained from her face.

'You haven't eaten all day, Have you Rosy?' She shook her head. Adam supported her as they walked across the road to an Italian restaurant on the opposite side of the road. They both tucked into a large bowl of pasta and Adam, casting caution to the winds, ordered a half litre of red wine. The colour returned to Rosaria's cheeks and, first of all, she wanted to know what had happened to him since he and Sofia had got off the train at Bond Street. She already knew where Sofia had been heading – and why. Adam's intuitive guess about the reason behind her visit to the Italian embassy had been entirely correct. He related how he had followed Sofia home and showed Rosaria the piece of paper on which he had written the address in St John's Wood. In return, Rosaria handed him a letter which she had in her handbag. At the top of the letter, he read: 42 Langford Place, St John's Wood, London NE8 2PQ. Adam looked puzzled.

'But it's the same address!'

'Yes. I'm sorry to have made you work so hard and hang around so long today, *amore*. But we just *had* to be sure that she was telling us the truth. Now I know for certain that we can trust her.'

'But what's this letter about, Rosy?'

'Read it, Adam. Then you will understand.' He skimmed through the formal letter which began: *'Cara Rosaria...'*

'Oh, good heavens! Now I understand! This is the original sixth letter which was supposed to be sent to you, isn't it?'

'Yes, Adam. Sofia took a huge risk when she substituted the letter which Enrico had already composed for the letter she invented and sent to me. No wonder she was scared when she heard him coming back into the room. She had to seal up the letter quickly before he had a chance to see what she had done. She kept the original letter hidden in the restaurant for weeks.'

The original letter was a very unsubtle invitation to Rosaria to come and meet her 'cousin' Diletta, presumably with the sole purpose of tidying up the loose ends, or at the very least, to ascertain that Rosaria suspected nothing of the crime that Enrico had committed.

'So are we any clearer as to why Enrico went to the trouble of killing Diletta?'

'No, not really, Adam. But it must have been as I thought. Diletta discovered who Enrico really was and threatened to expose him. He found my address amongst Diletta's things and remembered that I had seemed suspicious of him. So he decided to send those letters to put me off the scent.'

'So you probably owe your life to Sofia, Rosy. I gather that Sofia is her real name?'

Rosaria nodded. 'She's a lovely person, Adam. We got on really well, like two...cousins, no, two friends. She is just as trapped as Diletta was but Sofia has been much more skilful at hiding her feelings and acting out her part. To cut a long story short, Enrico picked her up in a village in Calabria before returning to London. He chose her because of her similarity to Diletta. As far as the ID card is concerned, the likeness is near enough to get her through any passport check. She had little choice, Adam. When she objected that her parents and younger brother and sister needed her, Enrico told her in *'ndrangheta* language that her family would be taken care of. 'If you don't come to London with me,' he added, 'your family will be taken care of in other ways.'

'What an evil bastard the man is!' exclaimed Adam angrily. Having seen Enrico in the flesh and had a glimpse into his twisted soul, he found it far easier to accept the idea that retribution should figure in the outcome of events.

'He deserves to...' He left the sentence unfinished. Yet Adam felt, for the first time in his life, a profound desire to seek vengeance. Well, not quite for the first time, he recalled. He had often wished a dire fate on Marjory Rubberstamp and Mr Norman. He had even stuck a pin into a school photograph of Mr Norman where his private parts should have been, whilst evoking some Voodoo curse. When nothing untoward happened, he assumed his choice of the positioning of the pin had been misguided. But Enrico was different. The desire to see this man get his just deserts was potent. Rosaria was smiling darkly at him over the table.

'We *are* certain that Enrico lives at number 42, I suppose?' he asked.

'Oh yes, Adam. He...*uses* her without mercy. On more than one occasion, he has expected Sofia to 'satisfy' visiting members of his clan. That's one of the main reasons she needs to escape. But she's too scared of him to do it on her own – especially as she knows there could be repercussions for her family back in Calabria.'

'So, Rosy, any plan of action has to make her safe too. In one way, she complicates the task. But we *must* help her too, mustn't we.'

She stood up and came round to Adam's side of the table and hugged him. As the waiters had nothing else to do in the deserted restaurant except stare at Rosaria, she stopped short of kissing him.

'*Grazie,* Adam. In fact, Sofia and I discussed how we should rescue her. That's what took up so much of the time in the restaurant.'

'She must have been surprised to see *you,* rather than the Englishman who had enquired about her at the sandwich bar.'

'Oh, I told her all about us, Adam. But I said you had another engagement. I didn't want her to be on the lookout for you.'

Adam pressed her for further details of their three hour conversation, but she just smiled enigmatically and avoided going into details. 'Let's go home, Adam. I feel much better now, but I want to lie down.' Adam paid the bill and the waiter told him that his daughter looked very beautiful. The luckless waiter received no tip. Rosaria herded him out of the restaurant before he could think up a suitable retort. 'Come on, *papà!* It's getting late,' she said pointedly in earshot of the offending waiter. It was the first time that he had appreciated what their relationship must look like from a public perspective – and he didn't particularly like it.

'Don't take it to heart, Adam! I love you the way you are and I take it as a compliment that I look like you.'

Adam smiled grudgingly and put the waiter's intended compliment out of his mind as they drove home. 'By the way, Rosy, your real *papà* is a good-looking man - even if he is a little daunting.'

'Everybody finds my father daunting. Beneath the surface, he is really soft-hearted and insecure. Believe me! You may have to face *him* in the near future. You do realise that, don't you?' Adam was horrified at the idea. He was still attempting to cope with the idea of confronting Enrico. Now, he was faced with the prospect of a second ordeal – maybe far more challenging than the first. He told Rosaria what he was thinking. Despite or because of her fatigue, she found the notion of her *papà* posing more of a threat than the *'ndrangheta* enormously funny. To Adam's consternation, she broke into uncontrollable giggles that lasted until they reached home. He put it all down to nervous reaction after the stresses of the day. In the end, her laughter was infectious and they let themselves into Adam's flat in buoyant mood.

* * * * *

What a glorious sensation it was to be able to relax after the stresses of the day gone by. It was not late but they went to bed and lay there talking, analysing the events of the day and cuddling until sleep overtook Rosaria at least. She had filled Adam in on much of what had come to light during her long talk with Sofia in the restaurant. Adam had remembered the article that he had read during his long vigil and outlined the main points to Rosaria. He had torn out the article and brought it home with him, leaving the rest of the paper on the seat in the coffee bar.

'Then you won't be surprised to learn that Enrico, using laundered *'ndragngheta* money, has bought up that restaurant, which had been a happy, family run business for decades. The owner was, of course, generously allowed to stay on as manager in his own restaurant. But he says his heart has gone out of it since *they* took over. He says that no amount of money can ever substitute the feeling of pride that he felt when he was his own boss.'

'But why did he agree to it? This is London, not Naples or Reggio Calabria!'

'I asked Sofia the same question. She told me that he was promised a future free of financial worries. He has a daughter of university age who wanted to study medicine. The cost of sending her to university for five years would have been exorbitant. He hesitated for weeks, so Enrico sent his 'boys' down there to have lunch on a number of occasions. They arrived with their D and G suits and their designer sunglasses, flashing their Rolex watches and then they swaggered out without paying. Soon the regular customers began to drop off – not wanting to share their meals with mobsters. In the end, Giovanni had no option but to accept the deal. It was all done neatly and legally.'

Adam felt the rising tide of impotent rage at the cruel injustice of it all. 'And this sort of thing is beginning to happen all over London, I suppose – a slow, insidious invasion.'

'Yes, a bloodless revolution at the moment, although even that is inevitably changing; there are parts of North London where the mobs are taking over the drug rings. Sofia said she has heard Enrico giving out orders over the phone – and then bodies of rival gang members would be found washed up on the banks of the Thames. The local gangs just aren't geared up to deal with that level of organisation and ruthlessness.

'But Enrico works at the Italian embassy,' exclaimed Adam in disbelief.

'What better cover for his real purpose for being in London, Adam? He only works there a few hours a day. The rest of the time, he can devote to expanding the *'ndrangheta's* activities, legal and illegal. They are accumulating properties and businesses step by step – always in competition with the other mafia organisations like *Cosa Nostra, La Camorra...*'

'And *La Sacra Corona Unita,*' added Adam waving his newspaper article.

To his surprise, Rosaria did not comment on Adam's interruption but continued her narrative as if nothing had been said.

'Yes, Adam. The *'ndrangheta* is trying to gain a monopoly of all supplies sold at market stalls and small shops dotted round London. They specialise in selling fake designer goods – that is becoming very profitable, it appears. But the rivalry between the different mafia clans is always fierce...'

'And Sofia – poor girl – is caught up in all this, too scared to do anything, or too powerless I suppose,' said Adam.

'Exactly! But she has reached breaking point now, Adam. There is nobody that she could trust enough to confide in; the restaurant owner, the other girls who work in the market, the boys in the sandwich bar... Any one of them could have dropped a word in Enrico's ear hoping to curry favour with him. So she thought of me, in desperation. She had become really alarmed when she had to include that ultrasound scan in with the letter. She had already worked out that something really bad must have happened to the girl whose ID card she is using...'

'But didn't Sofia ask Enrico questions about Diletta?' Adam pursued.

'Yes, and she did not like the answers that she got. Enrico threatened to hurt her family if she kept asking him questions. 'The past is the past,' he told her and refused to give any details. Significantly, Adam, Sofia is convinced that Enrico is a ruthless, *prepotente* – a domineering bully who will stop at nothing to please the 'clan' back home. He belongs to the *Anacro* clan, which is one of the most violent. But she does not believe that he is all that perceptive. She has the distinct impression that Enrico has completely failed to understand how close a relationship I had with my cousin. He imagines that we met up again just because of their wedding. We decided we should take advantage of his ignorance when we...' Rosaria paused to choose her words carefully so as not to alarm him, Adam suspected. '...go and rescue Sofia,' she concluded. Adam thought that this might be a very euphemistic statement of her intentions. But she would not be drawn and soon after took refuge in sleep.

The following day, Friday, Rosaria became so involved in sending text messages and making phone calls that Adam decided he was redundant. He decided to go out for a long walk across the Chilterns. Rosaria told him she would feel a lot less uncomfortable if he was not there. She kissed him warmly and sent him on his way. By late afternoon, she seemed satisfied that all her plans were in place.

'Only one more phone call left now, *amore mio. And I definitely* want you by my side when I make *that* call.' She made the call to St John's Wood on her mobile, making sure that the caller's number had been concealed. It was a very brief call. Adam was full of admiration at the way she handled the conversation with Enrico. 'You should have been an actress – or, of course, a detective!' he said mindful of Rosaria's past achievements. 'That call was flawless. Your duplicity is *impressionante,* my dear!'

'Thank you, Adam,' she said warmly and led him off to the bedroom. The tension of the last few days melted away for the time being as both of them discovered the need for physical release.

So, the *coup de grâce* was fixed for Sunday evening, when they would have to make the journey to the house in St John's Wood. There was nothing else to be done except wait in knife-edged anticipation for events to unfold as they were destined to do. Adam felt that he would only be playing a minor part. Rosaria reassured him that, now certain elements had been set in motion, they would both become mere supporting actors in the drama that was about to unfold.

'I could never have gone through with all this without you by my side, Adam,' Rosaria reasserted. Adam considered that this might well be true and took some consolation from the thought.

Saturday morning. That meant there were about thirty-six hours, or two thousand one hundred and sixty minutes, to go before they would have to confront Enrico. Adam dismissed this pointless calculation from his mind as being purely negative and quite neurotic into the bargain.

Rosaria was less nervous than he was. He felt envious of her ability to block out the future until the future caught up with her. She was looking at Adam, appealing for him to be strong. She had that 'you-are-my-rock' expression on her face, which was irresistible.

'Why don't we go shopping?' he suggested in desperation.

Rosaria was never one to refuse a shopping trip so, after breakfast, they set off to the nearest branch of John Lewis, where Rosaria persuaded him to part with a lot of money on a lap-top computer – an item which he did not possess. Then they spent a couple of hours looking round this latter-day Aladdin's Cave, choosing imaginary furniture, curtains and carpets for their future home. They had lengthy discussions about what constituted the ideal fitted kitchen. Needless to say, there was barely a single point in common between them, Rosaria preferring modern surfaces with bright yellow wall tiles and black floor tiles, whereas Adam went for the traditional rustic stone finish and terracotta floor tiles. Of course, Adam conceded, Rosaria being the woman, should be the one who had the final choice – even against his better judgement.

The therapeutic effect of spending hours and a lifetime's savings all in one fell swoop was more relaxing than a dozen tranquilizers apiece. They had lunch in a country pub, went home, made love, set up Adam's new computer – all without a thought for the morrow. By the time they clambered into bed, tired and carefree, they had reduced the waiting time by half – and eight of those hours would be taken up by sleep.

The peace was broken just as they were about to fall asleep by a phone call from Benedetto, asking his usual barrage of questions. Rosaria did her best to fend off his persistent enquiries.

'The trouble is,' said Rosaria when he had rung off, 'he will notice that the call has cost him treble what it should have done. He is bound to contact my mother who will start badgering Martina. In point of fact, Martina phoned some minutes later, saying that she was running out of excuses as to why Rosaria could not come to the phone.

'We'll be home in a couple of days, Marti,' Rosaria promised optimistically. They fell asleep in each other's arms that night.

Sunday morning inevitably arrived. They felt calmer now that the waiting period was almost over. Adam suggested going to church. It would be tempting providence *not* to go on that fateful day, he suggested. As it was approaching Good Friday, the priest had chosen as his text the words of Christ: *'Let this cup pass from me: nevertheless, not as I will, but as Thou wilt.'* The sermon was all about facing up to our mortality and not being frightened about the prospect of death. Adam looked at Rosaria sitting on his left. She smiled her brilliant smile and held his hand tightly throughout the rest of the mass. 'Other brain,' silent for so long, pointed out that he was up to his neck – and probably beyond – in this affair.

'So be it,' repeated Adam with all the conviction that he could muster.

17: Face to Face with Enrico

It was time to go up to London. He put on his dark suit for the occasion. Rosaria was wearing a black trouser-suit. 'We look as if we are dressed for a business meeting,' commented Adam.

'*Già!*' she replied. 'Precisely!' After a muttered prayer about 'cups passing from him' – possibly in the form of a train strike – he drove them both in his yellow Panda to the railway station. He was surprised that he felt relatively calm and was congratulating himself on holding his nerve. 'Other brain' was not impressed, pointing out that he was shielded from fear simply because he was underestimating the danger to himself and Rosaria through his sheer lack of awareness of the ruthless nature of the enemy. He put his foot down hard on the accelerator and drove to the station as if he had been on the Monte Carlo circuit. Rosaria was in admiration of his driving for the first, and perhaps the last time.

They arrived early at Marylebone station and decided to walk up and down Baker Street for a while before taking the tube train one stop up the line to St John's Wood. A chance linguistic error transformed their tension into laughter. Rosaria had been intrigued by the little cards left in all the telephone booths by the calls girls – *le ragazze squillo,* she translated at Adam's request. This discovery led to an animated discussion as to whether the girls acted independently or not. Lots of them did, claimed Adam. 'Nonsense, Adam,' stated Rosaria categorically, speaking in English for a change. 'Every prostitute has a pimple!'

When Adam had stopped spluttering with ill-suppressed laughter, he explained the difference in meaning between 'pimp' and 'pimple'.

'All your English words sound the same!' declared Rosaria disparagingly, returning to the use of her own language.

By way of rebuttal, Adam felt obliged to point out that, in the Italian language, there was only one letter different to distinguish between the word *penne* for that pasta shape and *pene,* the word for penis. He considered that he had made his point. They were still chatting amiably about the fascinating subject of paid-for sex when they turned into Langford Place. It was three minutes to seven. They had not had time to start panicking – right up to the last minute when the reality of what they were doing struck home with full force.

Adam was the first to notice that there was a black Audi Q7 with tinted windows parked in the road just before the house towards which they were heading. He could see four or five shadowy figures inside, filling Adam with dread. 'Enrico's mob!' he thought, terrified. He was walking slightly ahead of Rosaria in order to pass a tree which was growing in the middle of the pavement. He did not see the window of the Audi being wound down nor the hand which emerged briefly holding out a small object to Rosaria, which she took quickly before catching up with Adam. Thus, Adam could not understand why she was looking relieved and smiling darkly to herself.

'Rosaria?' he whispered. But she linked her arm in his and urged him forward into the drive of number forty-two.

'It will be alright now,' she said quietly. Adam felt far from being reassured. 'Lambs to the slaughter,' other brain interjected.

The front door was opened and they found themselves facing a smiling Enrico. He did not seem quite as tall as Adam had remembered him on the steps of the Embassy, but he was thickset and that smile could hardly be described as reassuring. It had something predatory about it as the *mafioso* ushered them into the large living room in which the predominant piece of furniture was a solid mahogany desk. There were one or two comfortable armchairs but Enrico did not bother to offer them a seat. The atmosphere was charged with uncertainty and conspiracy. Adam and Rosaria stood side by side facing Enrico who was standing staring at them both with that cynical smile on his face. He felt no need to make them feel at ease. Indeed, it appeared to serve his purpose to maintain the sense of unease. Adam understood at once that it was done deliberately to unnerve them. In the end, it was, to Adam's shocked surprise, Rosaria who spoke first.

'Well, Enrico? I have come a very long way to see my cousin Diletta. Where is she?' Adam was amazed at the coolness in her voice. Enrico glanced at his Rolex but did not reply immediately. 'Well?' repeated Rosaria. 'I'm waiting!' Her boldness took Adam's breath away. But it worked. Adam vaguely understood that, had Rosy been timid in the face of this man, he would have continued to play cat and mouse with their fears for as long as he could, just for the sadistic pleasure of watching their growing unease.

'She will be down in a minute, *signorina.* Unfortunately, she has to work in the restaurant this evening. She's getting ready.' He continued to stare hard at Rosaria as if calculating what would happen when 'Diletta' appeared in the room. From that point on, Enrico pointedly ignored Adam, who felt invisible, powerless, redundant.

Footsteps coming downstairs! Adam felt the tension mounting. And then, she was there in the room, running towards Rosaria with her arms wide open.

'Rosy, Rosy, Rosy!' she cried. They hugged each other warmly for what seemed like ages to Adam. 'But, Diletta,' said Rosaria in surprise. 'I expected you to be...' At this point, Rosaria made a gesture in front of her belly to indicate an advanced pregnancy. 'Diletta' burst into uncontrollable tears and they renewed their close embrace. Rosaria was comforting her 'cousin' and pouring out words of consolation and sympathy. Adam could not believe what he was witnessing. This was more than just a theatrical performance, it was totally convincing. The clever part of it was, Adam realised, that their faces were always hidden from Enrico's view. Adam chanced a glance in Enrico's direction and was amazed to see a sly, self-satisfied leer on his face. The deception was working.

'Rosy, I'm so sorry. I have to go to work now. The restaurant where I work is always at its busiest on Sunday evenings. But I have a day off on Wednesday. Can we meet up somewhere nearby?' They went through the charade of exchanging mobile phone numbers like a couple of excited school-girls who had not seen each other for ages. 'Yes please, Diletta,' said Rosaria full of girlish glee. 'We have so much to talk about, don't we?'

'Diletta' hugged Rosaria again and then, staggeringly, went up to Enrico and put her arms round him. *'Grazie amore per avermi resa tanto felice.'* She was actually thanking him for making her so happy, translated Adam to himself in astonishment at the thoroughness of their play-acting. Another quick hug and a kiss with Rosaria, a quick *'Arrivederci, signore'* in Adam's direction and she was out in the hallway. They heard the front door opening and her footsteps going down to ground level. The sound of her shoes on the gravel path was quite distinct. There was a marked pause before the front door closed again with a click.

Enrico was looking smugly at Rosaria. 'There, *signorina*. Now you have seen your cousin and you know she is well. I hope that your doubts have been put to rest and that you can reassure her family back home.'

The arrogantly expressed and entirely false sentiment was delivered with the same cynical, self-assured smirk as before. Enrico was feeling safe. 'And now if you and your...English friend will excuse me, I have important business matters to attend to,' he added dismissively. Rosaria did not move an inch. 'Now what is she up to?' wondered Adam. He had been beginning to relax as it had become apparent that, contrary to his worst fears, the deception had worked like a dream. Rosaria continued to hold her ground. Then Adam, in consternation, understood what she was doing – giving Sofia time to get clear of the house. Now she was looking boldly at the *mafioso* with no obvious intention of leaving.

'*Signorina*,' continued Enrico coldly. 'It has been a pleasure meeting you again, but now there is no need for us to continue this conversation. You have seen for yourself that your cousin is as well as can be expected after her...grievous disappointment. Now, if you don't mind...'

If Adam had entertained the hope that their ordeal was over, Rosaria's next words put paid to any illusion that this was the case.

'But there is one more important matter to be settled, isn't there, Enrico Anacro?' The change of facial expression, the alteration of body language was so marked that, to Adam, it appeared that the man had been transformed into another being. The manifestation was diabolic in its suddenness.

'What did you just say, *signorina?*' The words were spat out in a rasping snarl. His eyes had become hooded while suspicion, fear and anger passed from one to the other in rapid succession. To Adam's horror, Rosaria seemed completely unperturbed by the transformation to the man standing a few metres in front of them.

'The girl who has just walked out of your life for ever is not my cousin Diletta, as you well know,' said Rosaria, her voice as cold as ice. 'The body of my dear cousin was discovered months ago at the bottom of the well where you dumped her. She probably did not die from the fall but suffered hours of terror, agony and suffering, all alone...because of *YOU.*' The last word had been infused with such disdain and pent up hatred that it struck like a serpent's bite in the vital organ of Enrico's pride and self-assurance.

There was a look of such cold hatred on his face that Adam turned to jelly. He could feel his legs shaking uncontrollably. Enrico walked round behind the mahogany desk and a revolver appeared in his left hand as if by some conjuror's sleight of hand. He was calmly screwing a silencer on to the end of the barrel.

'You made a fatal mistake coming here, *signorina.*' The words were uttered with a matter-of-factness that petrified Adam. 'It has cost you your life – and that of your...friend.' He had merely gestured with a curt, oblique nod of his head in Adam's direction as he began to raise the pistol. Adam never knew where he found the vestige of real anger that momentarily gave him the courage to step in front of Rosaria, shielding her and sparing her life for another five seconds. At least, he had the satisfaction of seeing a split second's look of surprise cross Enrico's face before it was replaced once more by the cold sneer that had been there before. Enrico shrugged his shoulders with indifference and Adam found

211

the pistol pointing at *his* forehead. In a few seconds' time, he would experience a brief, searing pain as his skull was splintered and his brain exploded into infinity.

'You don't imagine that we came here without telling the police where we were going, do you, Enrico Anacro?' How had he managed to croak out those words seconds before the end of his life? What mechanism of self-preservation had prompted his nearly obliterated brain to formulate those pointless, hackneyed words? He could see the look of doubt which fleetingly crossed the face of his executioner, before the cynical leer once again distorted his mouth. Enrico's enjoyment at the prospect of killing overpowered any fear of being apprehended.

In the instant that followed, there was a flash of light from somewhere behind Adam. This struck him as being in the wrong place for the fatal shot. He was surprised too because he had imagined that his violent departure from this life would have been infinitely more painful. The flash had temporarily blinded Enrico.

Instead of the expected shot, he heard somebody behind them shouting out the words: *'GIÙ! A TERRA!'* Rosaria leapt forward doing a kind of rugby tackle which brought Adam to the floor – easy, since his legs were shaking so violently that a feather would have had the same effect. He heard the *phut* of a silenced bullet flying over his head. How absurd that he should think of his silly mime, a lifetime ago, when Glenda had called him 'duck'.

Adam looked up, with Rosaria's arms still enveloping his legs. Enrico was clutching his left shoulder, a look of shocked surprise on his face. He seemed more puzzled that he had so unexpectedly lost control of the situation than upset by the pain he must have been feeling. In the next second, four figures raced across the intervening space. They were wearing black track-suits. On the back of the jackets, Adam could see white letters spelling out a word which seemed inappropriate in the circumstances. In a second, Enrico was pinned to the floor. One of the four men had his knee firmly planted in the small of Enrico's back. As soon as he realised that he had been effectively immobilised, the language and the curses began pouring out in a dialect that was quite incomprehensible to Adam. He managed to make out the words: 'You are DEAD, Rosaria Miccoli. And so are all your family.' There was a hatred and rage in the words that Adam would never forget as long as he lived. Enrico continued his imprecations, although muted, even after one of the four men had plastered a strip of silver adhesive tape over his mouth.

One of the men turned to Rosaria, who was slowly trying to stand up whilst still clutching on to Adam in an attempt to help him to his feet, and said to her: *'Può andare, signorina. Brava! Bravissima! Anche Lei, signor A-damn – bravo!'*

'How does he know my name?' muttered Adam, his voice slurred with shock. In a daze, they both staggered out into the hallway and down the steps into the cool evening air. They could hear the mercifully welcome sound of London buses travelling down the main road at the end of Langford Place. They glanced back at the black Audi Q7. There was one man sitting nonchalantly in the driver's seat, smoking a cigar. Adam was suffering from emotional shock and could not manage to speak. He looked at Rosaria. She was pale but otherwise quite composed. He tried to take hold of her hand but found her fist clenched round some metallic object. 'What's that you're holding?' he managed to croak. 'A token of our safe passage through those last few minutes, Adam,' she said. She linked her arm through Adam's and led him towards the main road instead of walking back the way they had come.

She ushered Adam into a waiting taxi. The driver knew where to take them without being told. Sitting in the back seat of the taxi, Adam could feel Rosaria's body shivering. She must be in delayed shock too! But when he looked at her, he was disconcerted to find she was shaking with suppressed laughter. She hugged him tightly and said: 'Adam, you are my hero! You nearly got yourself killed trying to protect me. I shall love you for ever for that moment.'

Adam found his voice again. 'You had everything planned to almost the last detail, didn't you?'

'All except that final gesture of yours,' she replied no longer laughing.

'But why didn't you tell me what you had planned?' he asked, knowing that he ought to be feeling angry. 'That performance with Sofia was more than just play acting. It was professional.'

'I didn't want you worrying, Adam. If you had known what was going to happen, you might not have reacted in the way you did. Enrico would have suspected something.'

Adam thought for a moment and decided that she was right. He would have spent the intervening time imagining every possible negative outcome and would have sabotaged the whole operation.

'But why did those men all have the word Paris written across the back of their track-suits? They didn't have much to do with being French.' Adam was aware that this was quite a minor detail in the great scheme of things, but the matter had aroused his curiosity. Rosaria hesitated for a moment, choosing her words diplomatically.

'I think, in your state of surprise, Adam, you didn't notice there was another letter on the end of the word PARIS.' Adam opened his mouth to ask for further clarification but the taxi had stopped outside Marylebone station. To Adam's mild surprise, the taxi drove off without the driver expecting to be paid. He had a hundred questions still to ask but was still too shaken by the whole episode to go into precise details.

'Adam,' began Rosaria in that cajoling voice children use when they are unsure what the adult's reaction will be. 'I have one more little favour to ask you and then we are done.'

'As long as it doesn't involve being shot at, I don't mind,' he replied with a note of asperity in his voice signalling his partial recovery from shock.

'Can we take Sofia home with us, please? She is coming back to Italy with us.'

Adam was feeling so euphoric at the discovery that he was still alive that he would happily have agreed to host all of Sofia's family as well.

'Of course!' he said beaming. 'But where is she?'

Rosaria pointed to a solitary figure standing in the shadows under the archway which led into the station, a trolley suitcase keeping her company. They walked up to her and she and Rosaria hugged again briefly before Adam was introduced to her. He found himself being hugged warmly in his turn. He felt he knew Sofia well already, forgetting that she would not have recognised him from their previous one-sided encounter.

'I am so happy you are safe and sound, Sofia,' he said in Italian.

There was a thirty minute wait for their train. Adam excused himself briefly from their company, ostensibly to purchase a ticket for Sofia. He headed for the toilet and the bar, where he downed a double scotch. As he was walking back from the ticket office to rejoin the girls, he remembered the Guardian article that he had read three days previously. The shock of realisation was almost enough to send him back to the bar for a further dose of whiskey. PARISI was the surname of one of the major Puglian mafia clans who had set up in business in West London. It hadn't said PARIS on their jackets at all.

There would be a lot of questions to be asked over the next few days, he decided. But now was not the moment. How ironic, he thought, that his life had been saved so efficiently by such people - by men who knew his name and even complimented them both on their courage.

He smiled at Rosaria and Sofia as he went up to them and led them to the waiting train that would whisk them away from London to the relative safety of the English countryside.

As the train sped away from the city, a silence fell as they began to absorb what had happened – as well as what might have happened if some vital part of the plan had misfired. But Adam's curiosity was aroused by too many unexplained aspects of the drama that had been enacted. He happened to look up at the baggage rack where Sofia's trolley-case was stowed.

'Wasn't it risky going out of the door wheeling a suitcase, Sofia?' he asked. This minor detail had begun to worry him. 'Surely *he* could have spotted you leaving the house with it?'

Sofia and Rosaria both smiled that Adam should be bothered by such a trivial detail in the midst of a series of events that might have ended in his death.

'We thought of that, Adam,' replied Rosaria smugly.

'If I was working late at the restaurant, I always took a suitcase with me and slept in a room above the restaurant. So when I left the house as usual, I just...let the other men in.' Adam nodded. It all seemed very simple.

'Congratulations, you two! Your planning was meticulous.'

On reflection, Adam considered that Enrico's attempt at covering his tracks had been amateurish, tending to confirm Sofia's impression that he had not been at all perceptive as to Rosaria's close relationship with Diletta. It had been easy enough, with a bit of skilful acting, to dupe Enrico into believing what he had wanted to believe.

Adam turned his attention to Rosaria sitting by his side still clasping the mysterious object tightly in the clenched ball of her fist. He gently tried to prise her fingers open but she resisted. Adam decided to take a stab-in-the-dark guess.

'I think it is a crown with maybe a crucifix on it.' The expression on Rosaria's face was a mixture of fear and admiration. Fear, that he had guessed who their rescuers had been and the consequences that might ensue; admiration, that he had been so perceptive.'

'You must be a *mago*, Adam – a wizard!' she exclaimed.

'*La Sacra Corona Unita,*' he whispered.

Rosaria unclasped her hand to reveal the symbol that had guaranteed their safe passage out of the house. Adam noticed that the sharp metallic cross, gripped so tightly in the palm of her hand, had drawn a tiny amount of blood. The religious significance did not escape either of them. A sacrifice had been made, a service rendered that might well have to be paid for later. Had it been worth it? They both simultaneously looked at each other and then at the girl sitting opposite them, looking tired but at peace for the first time in months. Rosaria's grip on Adam's hand tightened imperceptibly. Whatever the consequences might be, they had saved one innocent woman's life.

'What if Enrico tells someone about Sofia's disappearance?' he was about to ask. But he was not naïve enough to believe that Enrico would survive his encounter with the rival clan for longer than a few hours,

* * * * *

Two days later, Adam was standing in the departure Lounge of Heathrow's Terminal 4. They had decided that Rosaria and Sofia should fly back to Puglia together as soon as possible, while Adam would stay on for a couple more days to wait and see if anything was reported in the news. Rosaria was becoming anxious that Martina was bearing the brunt of her unexplained absence. Martina had grown weary of fending off phone calls from her parents and from Benedetto and had resorted to switching off her mobile altogether.

Rosaria was holding Adam tightly in her arms just before they disappeared into the security area. 'You *are* going to come back, aren't you Adam?' she asked anxiously. 'I couldn't live without you now.' Adam had already booked his flight to take him 'home', as he put it, in three days' time. They kissed and hugged. Sofia hugged Adam too. He noted the different sensations that he felt – Sofia being taller than Rosaria. How could the identical gesture feel so *distinctly* different with someone else, he wondered? Sofia had a different smell to Rosaria – the smell of someone else's skin, hair – but also a different pressure of her arms, a different tension in her body. His experience of a few days previously had made him far

218

more aware that small, seemingly trivial things were infinitely important. It was all very wonderful and mysterious, he thought.

The realisation had dawned on him that he had become more like the human being that he had always aspired to be. And it was all thanks to one other, unique human being – who had nearly brought about his removal from Planet Earth.

A last wave to Rosaria as the two figures were swallowed up in the crowd of travellers...

'A *prestissimo, amore,*' he said under his breath. 'See you very soon.'

18: *Adam versus Puglia*

Ten days later, in total contrast, Adam found himself standing in the shade of an olive grove a few steps away from Rosaria's family's country house. For the first time, he was looking at the well in the centre of the meadow. The scene looked so serene in the bright spring sunlight that it was difficult to imagine the sombre events which had overshadowed it.

Adam had spent his remaining few days in England attempting to glean what he could about the fate of Enrico from the snippets of news concerning events at 42 Langford Place. He gathered that an elderly lady, who lived on the second floor of a block of flats opposite number 42, had seen suspicious figures going in and out of the darkened house. She had called 999, but the police had obviously decided that it was the fanciful ramblings of an old lady and had shelved the investigation until the following morning. But the local police station in St John's Wood had received an anonymous tip-off from a man with a 'foreign sounding' European accent, which had prompted them to investigate sooner than they might otherwise have done. The anonymous caller had evidently wanted the crime to be discovered as he had alerted the 'serious' newspapers too.

What the police had discovered prompted a major murder enquiry involving Interpol supported by the Italian anti-mafia squad. The victim had been found, dead. But, what was unusual about this crime, was that the man had been *incaprettato* – goat-tied. The newspapers went into gruesome details about this method of execution, which involves the victim's ankles being tied together with his legs bent up painfully behind his back whilst the other end is attached round his neck. The result is a slow and painful death by self-strangulation as the victim's legs inevitably start to unbend. The article pointed out that this is the method of assassination favoured by the Sicilian mafia, *Cosa Nostra*. Adam also found out that the victim, a stocky man in his thirties – an employee at the Italian embassy – would probably have died from a bullet wound before he died from strangulation. A police search of the house revealed one bedroom containing a wardrobe full of woman's clothes and a dressing table with all her make-up on it. But of the occupant, there was no sign. The victim's computer, mobile phone and memory stick had all been removed. To Adam, this all added up to the obvious conclusion that the killing of Enrico had been dressed up to look like an act of provocation or retaliation by the Sicilian mafia to cover up the real perpetrators who thereby hoped to gain an advantage over rival clans. It also ensured that Sofia would be free of blame in the eyes of the 'ndrangheta. Adam could not help thinking that the Puglian clan had been remarkably astute in the way its 'charitable act' had been fully exploited to its own ends, whilst leaving the innocent protected.

The Guardian ran another article about the increasingly violent infiltration of southern Italian mafia gangs in London. Adam meditated on the irony that their mission had succeeded on a personal level but that, on a grander scale, they had merely helped to redistribute the power of the mafia gangs operating in London in favour of the Puglian clan. It did not bear thinking about too deeply.

Like any normal, sentient being, Adam could not help feeling a sense of revulsion at the way in which Enrico had been dispatched from this life. He was pleased that a murderer had had rough justice meted out to him, happy that Sofia had escaped a fate she had not deserved. But, like the killing of Saddam Hussein, Adam did not believe that any man should have his life taken away from him in that manner. There was something brutal and atavistic about Enrico's death which left him with the sensation that a darker creed still held sway beneath a veneer of civilisation; codes of conduct that two millennia of Christianity had failed to extirpate. In his head, he could hear a thunderous voice from an Old Testament heaven intoning: *An eye for an eye. A tooth for a tooth.*

Adam shook himself out of these sombre thoughts and turned back towards the house where members of Rosaria's family were gathering for an outdoor lunch. Sofia's parents had travelled across the mountains of Calabria and Basilicata to meet up with her again. Rosaria's family were all present to celebrate the fact that the violent death of a close family member could finally be put behind them. Equally, Adam understood, the *festa* was to rejoice in the safe return of Rosaria whose act of foolhardy courage had to be secretly admired even if overtly censured. Even the *carabinieri* captain, who had stalled the investigation, was going to be present. Benedetto was working and might not be there until later, Rosaria had informed Adam – who was not particularly bothered either way. Today was the day when Adam would meet Rosaria's parents for the first time – the brief glimpse of her father through the train window hardly counting. Adam was experiencing only slight apprehension since, after his near death experience, no encounter with relatively normal mortals was going to concern him unduly. Besides which, Rosy had gaily informed him, she had stressed to her parents that Adam had heroically saved her life; a slight, but welcome, embroidering of the truth which he hoped would stand him in good stead in their eyes. Adam doubted whether his objective *should* be to impress them. After all, as far as they were concerned, he was only Rosaria's English teacher who had also, incidentally, accompanied her to London. The only two people at this family gathering who knew for certain that they enjoyed an intimate relationship were Sofia and Rosy's sister, Martina. Otherwise, their intimacy was a secret that Rosaria had been at great pains to conceal from the world. No, Adam decided, he would just try to be his normal, sociable self and see what happened.

What happened was that Rosaria's father spent the whole of lunchtime staring fixedly at Adam while he, Adam, was eating and sipping his glass of more than drinkable home produced red wine. Adam found the experience so disconcerting that he forgot to enjoy the taste of either the food or the wine. Adam had been placed, as a guest of honour, at the 'head' of table; that was to say, at the narrow end of one very long table that seemed to Adam to stretch to the horizon before it reached the various aunts, uncles and Rosaria's father, diametrically opposite Adam at the far end. No, Adam realised – it was *papà* who was sitting at the head of table. Adam was only the tail-ender. It was from this distance that Adam felt himself being observed. *Papà* had introduced himself as Umberto before they had sat down to eat and had formally shaken Adam by the hand. Rosaria's mother had pointedly avoided introductions as she busied herself with the preparations for lunch. At Adam's end of the table, there were seated Rosaria, Sofia with her parents, Martina and the twins from Milan – all of whom were in talking distance. In between trying to eat and fending off the usual questions about Prince Charles, Camilla Parker-Bowles and the rather late Princess Diana, Adam was aware of Umberto studying him thoughtfully. It fell short of being a hostile stare, Adam reasoned. It was more of an intense scrutiny.

Adam looked at Rosaria sitting a few places down from him on the right hand side of the table. She was talking animatedly to the twins and Martina, as she recounted what had happened in London. She looked at Adam, smiling every so often, as if to confirm some point she was making. She held her audience spellbound as she related the final moments of their confrontation with Enrico and Adam's heroic display of petrified courage before the intervention of Enrico's assailants. Adam was gazing longingly at her, momentarily oblivious of all those around him.

He was jolted out of his reverie by words spoken quietly in perfect English. 'You two really are in love, aren't you?' He was so startled that he knocked over his glass of wine – fortunately nearly empty. The words had been spoken by Sofia.

'Sofia!' he exclaimed. 'You've been holding out on me. You speak English.'

'Only when I have to,' she replied. 'I did an English degree at university – and I did work in London, don't forget. I wish you both luck,' she added sincerely. 'You are certainly going to need it.'

Adam looked quizzically at her, seeing the girl he had helped rescue in a new light.

'They are talking about you down the other end of the table,' she stated simply. 'They strongly suspect there is something going on between you. Rosaria's father is looking at you full of suppressed jealousy. He sees you as a rival.'

'But how do you know all this, Sofia?' asked Adam who, nevertheless, sensed that she was speaking with authority.

'Because I am Italian - even worse, I am Calabrian. I know how these people think - especially the older generation. You are different, Adam. You have an Anglo-Saxon perspective of the world.' Adam seriously doubted whether his Anglo-Saxon perspective had any relevance down here. He would have loved to continue the conversation with Sofia but her parents were talking to him and he had to concentrate hard on what they were saying. They spoke with a very marked Calabrian accent, which Adam recognised from his vivid memories of the few words Enrico had spoken.

They were thanking him, expressing their deep gratitude for the part he had played in saving their daughter's life. All at once, Adam was looking at a mother and father who were pouring out their soul to him. He saw them clearly for the first time. He felt a surge of affection for these two decent, honest people from another world to his; a couple untainted by the corruption which surrounded them in their everyday lives. The full significance of what Rosaria and he had achieved came home to him. The depth of sincerity in their eyes was unmistakable. He stood up and embraced them both spontaneously. His gesture did not go by unnoticed. Adam's end of the table cheered. Rosaria was looking at him lovingly.

'*Un brindisi!*' someone said as they raised their glasses. '*A Rosaria ed A-damn! Bravi! Bravissimi!*' Adam went round and hugged Rosaria as they were toasted. The other end of the table looked on darkly. Their moment would come.

The moment came very soon afterwards. Benedetto arrived minutes later. Significantly, he headed to the end of the table where Rosaria's parents were seated. After a brief exchange of words, Benedetto made as if to approach Rosaria – or Adam – but

Rosaria's mother laid a restraining hand on his arm. It was Umberto who walked solemnly down the length of the table, wearing the full weight of his paternal authority like a cardinal's robe. The festive atmosphere at their end of the table faded like the sun being concealed behind a dark cloud. Umberto came directly up to Adam and said with ecclesiastical solemnity: 'May we take a walk together, *professore?*'

Adam nodded. Rosaria was looking anxiously at him, a pinched look on her face in contrast to the exuberance of a few minutes ago. Her look appealed to him to be discreet. They were walking downwards towards the well. If Adam had been expecting to discuss weighty personal matters, he was disappointed. Umberto-the-Disconcerting began a lengthy monologue about how the water supply in Puglia arrived via a huge underground aqueduct from the hills of neighbouring Basilicata. He told Adam about how he remembered, as a child, his grandfather telling him how they drew water up from the depths of the well and were able to drink it without fear of contamination. Adam agreed that it was a tragedy that such a simple era had disappeared for ever. It was all very interesting, thought Adam, but certainly not the direction he had feared the conversation would take. The subject of his relationship with this man's daughter was not touched upon. As they leant on the parapet of the well, talking about the oil and the wine that the family produced, Adam understood that he was dealing with a very reserved man with dark and complex thoughts and emotions that it was not natural for him to express to a stranger. Umberto changed the subject and asked Adam what his plans were for the immediate future. Adam informed him that he intended to stay on in Puglia where he felt he belonged. He answered questions about his sons and the fact they were beginning to have children of their own. Umberto-the-Disconcerting had a deep and gentle voice which, Adam had the strong impression, he was controlling carefully.

'Yes,' he was saying to Adam, looking at him with that particular intensity with which he had studied him over lunch. 'It is good, at our age, is it not, *professore,* to see our children getting married and having children of their own. It gives us a feeling of deep satisfaction in our brief time upon this earth.'

It had been beautifully and skilfully performed, with Machiavellian precision. Adam had to admit to a grudging respect for Umberto's diplomacy. He looked straight into the eyes of the man who was Rosaria's father to tell him that he had received the unspoken message. To say nothing further to Umberto would have been to capitulate. This would be a betrayal of his love. To openly declare what he felt and intended would have been an act of grave indiscretion. He was walking on verbal eggshells, in a minefield of moral values and traditions whose significance he perceived but did not share.

'Of course, *signore,*' began Adam, choosing his words with great care, 'over the past week, Rosaria and I have come to understand each other very well. It strikes me that she is not convinced that her happiness is to be found by sharing her life with her present fiancé.' By choosing these words, Adam had calculated that Rosaria's father was not likely to react adversely, bearing in mind what he had learnt about Umberto's jealousy of Benedetto. The sigh that he let out was indication enough that his calculation had been correct. By the look that Umberto gave him, he could sense the dawning of a mutual respect.

'But, *professore,* I think that a marriage to Benedetto would be an easier alternative for me to bear, don't you?'

'I cannot agree with you entirely, *signore.* With all due respect to your traditions, it cannot be right to believe in a marriage that is contrary to a woman's wishes.'

Umberto gave the first hint of a sad smile. 'I have known Rosaria longer than you, *professore.* Much longer! Rosaria needs a little *spinta* – a push in the right direction. She can be very headstrong, as you have discovered. But, conversely, she can delay making important decisions for ever.'

'Nevertheless, *signore,*' pursued Adam, not wishing to relinquish an argument that ought to decide his and Rosaria's future. 'Rosaria should surely be given the right to decide, or even *not* to decide, for herself. I could not wish any other fate on a daughter of mine.' Adam was convinced that he had overstepped the mark this time. He felt a little hypocritical in view of the fact that he did not have a daughter. Umberto's reply came quietly but cuttingly.

'If you love our country so much, *professore,* maybe you would find life in the north more in keeping with your beliefs.' He had spoken in a tone of regret that he had betrayed a host's obligation to be courteous. But the words had been said and could not be retracted. Adam realised that they had both stated their points of view unambiguously. At this point, any further words would have been inflammatory. They were once again in full sight of the assembled company. Umberto held out his hand to his adversary from another world. It would have been a breach of hospitality for Adam not to have taken the proffered hand. He gave Umberto a brief but firm handshake, knowing full well how the gesture would be interpreted by all who were observing them. There was a look of slight relief in Rosaria's father's eyes, Adam thought, as they walked slowly back towards the expectant family gathering. To anyone else, it would be assumed that Umberto and Adam were in complete accord.

In Puglia, nothing is as it seems.

* * * * *

Rosaria had not noticed Adam's return because she was engaged in close conversation with a young man who, Adam assumed, must be the police captain without his uniform. He was holding Rosaria's arm at the elbow and she was showing no signs of wishing to withdraw her arm. To his own stupefaction, Adam felt a stab of jealousy. What was happening to him? Was he undergoing some unconscious metamorphosis as a result of living too long in this place? Could jealousy actually be catching, he wondered? Ridiculous, he thought! He should be far more concerned about his recent encounter with Rosy's father. It was evident that the course of their continuing relationship was never going to run smooth. As if to confirm this, Martina came up to him with a rueful smile on her face. She came straight to the point, in concerned sisterly mode.

'Adam, you are a good person and my sister truly loves you. You *do* know that, don't you? But my parents will never agree to...' She left the sentence unfinished. There was no need for her to complete it. 'Has Rosy told you about the house in Campanula yet?' Adam shook his head, puzzled.

'Our father has promised her this house. It needs modernising and decorating, that's all. But the deeds of the house remain in my father's name. He will settle both matters – but only when Rosy is married. Do you understand what I am saying, Adam?'

'*She* pronounces my name correctly,' thought Adam irrelevantly.

'You are dealing with a completely different mind-set down here, Adam. If it was only you and my sister to think about, you would both be happy together – of that I am certain. But you are up against two extended families, not just two individuals.' Martina broke off as her mother approached in determined manner. 'We need help, Martina,' she said with a curt nod in Adam's direction.

Suddenly, Adam did not want to be in this place any longer. He went in search of Sofia and her parents to say his good-byes to them.

'Are you going back with your parents, Sofia?' he asked in English.

'No,' she replied reverting to Italian. 'We have decided I should stay here a while longer, Adam, until we are sure there is no danger. Besides, Flavia seems to have adopted me as her daughter. She would love me to stay a little longer.'

'Then, I am sure we shall see each other often, Sofia.' Adam realised that he had hold of her arm in exactly the same way as the police captain whilst he had been in intimate conversation with *his* Rosaria. He had to smile at the thought. Sofia was returning his smile, having misinterpreted its intention. Adam was not about to spoil the moment by telling her what he had been thinking. Sofia's parents invited him to visit them in Calabria.

'You will come, won't you, A-damn?' they pleaded. Adam promised he would. He seemed to making a lot of important promises these days – none of them to be taken lightly.

He added another secret promise to himself; he was not about to relinquish his love for Rosaria – even in the face of opposition from the whole of Puglia.

Rosaria had noticed the gesture between Adam and Sofia and thought it was about time to reclaim him. There followed brief but unambiguous 'good-byes' to the twins, who decidedly seemed to be on the side of righteousness.

'It must be because they live in Milan,' thought Adam, thinking again how Umberto had relegated him to those dark northern lands where traditions had been so fatally abandoned.

In the car going back to Campanula, Rosy and Adam's private lives were free to be resumed.

'Do you fancy Sofia, Adam? I think so,' stated Rosaria in playful accusation. At least, she was attempting to *sound* playful.

'Absolutely!' replied Adam recklessly. 'What gave the game away, Rosy?' She was momentarily nonplussed by his reaction.

'The way you were holding her arm while you were looking so intently into her eyes,' she replied on the verge of a jealous outburst.

'Ah, that! You mean the same way that *you* were holding on to that good-looking, young *capitano* while I was coping with your father.'

'That's completely different, Adam.'

'Oh yes? And how do you explain the difference *mia cara* Rosy?'

'Simple!' said Rosaria, always ready to defend her position. 'Because it was *him* who was holding *my* arm,' she rounded off triumphantly.

'Your ancestors were surely brought up by Jesuits, Rosy. By the way, I did feel jealous when I saw you with that police officer – for the first time.'

Rosaria was jubilant. There was no other word for it. She felt *reassured,* Adam realised.

'Don't you want to know what your *papà* and I talked about?'

Rosaria thought about this and shook her head.

'No, Adam, I don't want to know. We must try hard to create our own small world of happiness for now. We have to ward off the future.' He placed his left hand on her unresisting thigh until they arrived at Adam's house in Campanula. Now that Rosaria had seen Adam's cosy place in England, she could better appreciate the discomfort that he must be suffering. 'We must find better accommodation for you here,' she said.

'What about your house in Campanula, Rosy?' he challenged her. 'It's alright,' he added seeing the expression of mild shock on her face. 'It was Martina who mentioned it.'

'Let's go and see it tomorrow, Adam. I'll get the keys off my father. I wanted it to be a surprise. We can go and dream about our future together and decorate it any way we want.'

So, Adam kissed her and told her for the first time since his return from England that he loved her. 'Just the way you are – with your missing future gene and all.'

'I know, I know, Adam!' she interrupted, not liking to have her idiosyncratic philosophy of life pointed out too plainly.

By mutual consent, they did not make love. The strain of meeting Rosaria's family had left him drained of energy. Besides, if she had stayed with him, the reason for her absence would have confirmed her parents' suspicions. No, they knew what was going on but, as long as the matter remained firmly swept under the carpet, appearances could be maintained.

In Puglia, nothing is as it seems.

Adam-Rosaria kissed fondly and they promised to phone each other later.

'*A domani, amore.*' they said.

That night, Adam had a strange dream that he still remembered when he woke up in the morning. It had reminded him of a scene from Alice in Wonderland.

He was playing in a weird kind of contest on a sloping terrain. He was the only player in his own team. There was a well instead of a goalpost behind him. The opposing team consisted of various members of Rosaria's family, who all had the advantage of being on the higher ground. The idea seemed to be to force Adam back to the parapet of the well whenever he tried to climb up the slope. He heard a loudspeaker announcing the scores as the game progressed. 'Adam, one,' proclaimed a voice. A few people, such as Sofia and her parents raised a feeble cheer. 'Strange,' thought Adam. 'When did I score even *one* goal?' 'Puglia, three,' continued the commentator. A huge football crowd cheered enthusiastically as the players, who appeared to outnumber Adam ten to one, bore down on him before he woke up, relieved to find himself in one piece. The nocturnal dog was yapping again. Some things never changed.

When Adam woke up at 8 o'clock the next morning to the sound of the beep-beep of a text message from Rosaria, welcoming him to a new day, he felt positive about life despite the unusually graphic dream. He was never going to change Puglia nor resolve the situation with Rosaria's family overnight. For the time being, he and Rosaria would have to live out their love hidden from the eyes of the world, until fate decided otherwise. This was going to take patience and long term faith.

If he had been anxious about explaining his newfound philosophy to Rosaria, he need not have been concerned; her own way of viewing life was already much closer to this perception of things – and she had time on her side for now.

And so, they squeezed every available instant of time together into a meaningful and love-filled existence. They went to see Rosaria's apartment in Campanula – not the following day because she forgot to bring the keys.

The house was spacious. It had three bedrooms and two bathrooms. This one is mine, of course, she said indicating the larger bathroom of the two. 'I need room for all my make-up, perfumes, soaps, skin creams...' Adam held up his hands in surrender. 'All the usual female paraphernalia,' he said in order to curtail the endless catalogue.

The kitchen was in sore need of modernisation. The tiles were a chocolate brown colour, which had been, inexplicably, the 'in vogue' colour of the nineteen-seventies in both England and Italy. 'Maybe people thought that the gravy and curry stains wouldn't show up so much,' suggested Adam.

As in their visit to John Lewis before the confrontation with Enrico, they spent all their imaginary money creating a beautiful living area where they would live happily ever afterwards. Adam cringed at the thought of yellow leather sofas and Rosaria rejected, yet again, Adam's traditional rustic stone tiles in the kitchen. The allocation of household tasks was clearly laid down. 'I'll do all the cleaning and housework if you do the cooking and empty the rubbish bins,' stated Rosaria. Thus, their future domestic life was easily agreed. They kissed, hugged and left the house to regain its sombre, unlived-in, undecorated state of gloom.

Rosaria wanted to show Adam the rest of Salento and beyond, so every available bit of free time was spent exploring the wonders of this part of Italy that they had not already visited. On some occasions, they took Sofia with them, assuring her that her presence only added to their joy at being together. They went to places that Adam could never have imagined existed: Ostuni, the 'white city' just to the north of Brindisi, with its maze of narrow cobbled side streets where real people lived out their daily 21st century lives in little white houses which had not changed since medieval times; Alberobello, whose centre was crowded with 'Trulli', those mysterious, circular, white stone houses with strange, hieroglyphic symbols painted in white on their inverted, cone-shaped roofs. Adam and Rosaria would walk hand-in-hand, far away from the war zone of Campanula or, sometimes, the three of them linked arms and marched through ancient Puglia like fearless warriors defying the Turks – or the army of Japanese tourists brandishing their video cameras.

As April turned to May, Adam, Rosaria and sometimes Sofia visited the sun-soaked Salento coastline with its myriad rocky coves alternating with long sandy beaches. They visited Porto Selvaggio, near Nardò – a beauty spot on the steeply sloping cliffs tops above the scintillating Ionian Sea. They walked down through a pine wood to the rocky shoreline. Adam dipped his foot into the clear water. It was cold. Rosaria explained that there was a freshwater spring which fed the water in the bay. They walked round the headland and looked up at one of the many stone watchtowers dotted round the Salento coastline to warn of invading foreigners or protect lovers from the intrusion of the outside world.

'La Torre Uluzzo,' said Rosaria. Even the name had a magic ring about it, like the call of owls in the middle of the night. Adam held

Rosaria tightly in his arms in a protracted embrace – to ward off the relentless passage of passing time.

By the time June arrived, Rosaria dared to put on a swimming costume although she was convinced the water would still be too cold. Adam told her about a documentary he had seen on British television which proved that populations adapted to a Mediterranean climate are physically unable to bear cool water on their bodies. Northern Europeans can tolerate much colder water temperatures. Rosaria and Adam had provided comical proof of this premise when, back in Adam's flat, Rosaria had seductively invited Adam to share a shower with her. He had leapt out of the shower with a yelp as the hot water scalded his skin.

Rosaria had wanted to show Adam the *Grotta Zinzulusa* on the Adriatic coast below Otranto. There was no beach. One had to jump straight into deep water from a narrow ledge just above surface of the sea. Rosaria was already in the water while Adam was still plucking up courage to jump in. He did not like to tell Rosaria that his ability to swim distances out of his depth had never been put to the test. It was apparent to Adam that the love of his life was able to swim with the same consummate skill with which she danced the *pizzica.* She was totally at home in water, ducking, diving and turning like a mermaid. He reminded her of the legend of the *sirena* who lured hapless mariners to their deaths with her seductive and fatal charm. She flashed a beaming smile in his direction as she rolled provocatively over and over in the water. No risk of snagging ones feet on the rocks below the surface, thought Adam. He could not even see where the bottom was. Nothing for it, then! He jumped in and began swimming the only stroke he could reliably do – a steady, more or less dependable breast stroke. He knew that, if he began to think about the depth of the water beneath him, he would be lost. So he swam calmly after Rosaria covering the hundred metres or so to the lofty, blue grotto. Their voices echoed eerily round the rocks, so they shouted silly things to each other about eternal love, clinging to each other while treading water. Rosaria began to feel the cold before Adam. The water in the grotto never saw the sunlight and they began to shiver. So they swam out again towards the rocky ledge. Rosaria hauled herself gracefully out of the water leaving a breathless Adam clinging on to the ledge below. Another couple good-humouredly helped her pull Adam out on to the safety of the ledge. But Adam was radiant from his successful swim. He confessed to her that he had never swum out of his depth before. She was horrified. 'Why didn't you tell me? You could have drowned!'

'But I didn't. That is the important thing. Thank you, my love, for leading me to the brink yet again!' he added with only a hint of intentional irony.

They had a sandwich on the way back to Adam's flat. There, they shared the most intimate part of their love once again and fell asleep until late in the afternoon.

'Do you know what I want to do next time, Adam? Spend a whole day in bed just talking, hugging and...'

'Agreed!' said Adam. The remarkable thing was that, the more time they spent together, the more natural being together seemed to become.

'We are made for one another,' said one of them. 'I know we are,' said the other.

And so, they continued to build romantic castles in the air behind whose ethereal walls they could live and dream in cosy intimacy.

19: The Parting of the Ways

It was time to say farewell to Sofia, who had decided that it was safe to return to her village in Calabria. She was even talking about going back to London to work one day, now that the threat to her life had been removed. It was Sofia's idea to treat Adam and Rosaria to a meal – an offer which Adam leapt at with alacrity. Rosaria was unusual in that she did not like eating out and lived in the perpetual fear of being seen in Adam's company by one of her family members.

Added to this, Benedetto had begun to become more persistent in his attentions again, reluctant to let go of his prey. Adam was convinced that Rosaria's mother was behind this campaign to wear down her daughter's resistance.

They chose a restaurant named *A Casa Tu Martinu* - Martin's House - in an obscure little town called Taviano. Adam disgraced himself by letting the girls do all the talking while he concentrated on the seemingly endless stream of fresh *antipasti* dishes that arrived at the table: sweet yellow peppers laced with capers, baked cherry tomatoes in oil and herbs, tiny meat balls, potato croquettes that tasted of mint and parmesan cheese, anchovies marinated delicately in vinegar and dough balls the size of golf balls filled with tomato and mozzarella cheese. It was difficult to find room for the best rabbit stew he had ever eaten in his life. He also became a devotee of Salento wine during the course of the meal. Adam found the time to propose a toast to Sofia on this, the eve of her departure. Sofia, in her turn, proposed a toast to Rosaria and Adam to wish them a safe passage through the minefield of southern Italian prejudices. Rosaria looked particularly solemn as the meal drew to an end, the shadows of the future gradually resolving themselves into the images of the present.

There were final fond farewells outside *zia* Flora's house and Adam and Rosy were on their own again. They went back to Adam's flat and Rosaria phoned home to say that she was staying with a friend that night. She switched off her mobile phone so that their intimacy was not disturbed by intrusions from the outside world.

Adam had to find the mental energy to complete the English courses that were still outstanding. It had been difficult to pick up from where he had left off after his return from London. Adam and Glenda continued teaching into the first week of June to recuperate the time lost during the school year.

One day, soon after his return to Campanula, Glenda and Adam sat down to have lunch at their usual restaurant.

'Don't you think it's time you told me about your trip to London, Adam? You've been very secretive about it ever since you came back.' Glenda had that hunger-for-gossip expression on her face as she attempted to suppress her curiosity as best she could.

'You took Rosaria with you, didn't you, Adam? Don't try to deny it, I can see by the expression on your face that I am right,' she added triumphantly. Adam secretly cursed the fact that his face always gave away what he was thinking. But Adam decided that it was time to take his revenge – even if the satisfaction he derived from it was likely to be short-lived.

'Very well, Glenda,' he said with a contrived expression of seriousness on his face. 'But I must be able to rely entirely on your discretion.'

Glenda's face was agog with curiosity as she nodded in agreement to the terms stipulated.

'How shall I put it? Two of us went to England... But there were three of us when we returned to Italy.' Adam paused for dramatic effect and was deeply gratified to see that the desired effect had been achieved.

'Adam! You mean that Rosaria is...? My goodness, you really have put the cat among the pigeons now.'

'And her name is Sofia,' added Adam with heavy emphasis.

'Wait a minute, Adam. You cannot possibly know the gender of the child so soon. You mean, you hope it will be a girl, don't you?'

'And...' said Adam as tantalisingly as possible, knowing that his sweet moment of revenge could not be protracted any longer. 'Sofia is twenty-seven years old.'

Adam had never experienced the sensation of having bits of tomato-sauce-covered pasta tubes flicked into his face before that moment. When he had stopped laughing, he filled in a few more essential details of their adventure in London. 'Let us say that a very lovely girl has been brought back to life,' he concluded.

But Glenda was not to be fobbed off so easily. She intuited that there was a more sinister side to the events that had taken place. 'I hope to goodness that Rosaria – or you, Adam – is not going to have to pay the price for any...assistance that you might have required,' she said seriously. And then, with a complete transformation of tone, she took *her* revenge on Adam.

'And *I* know something that *you* don't know, Mr Adam Knight.'

It did not make any difference what tack Adam took. Glenda refused to divulge more than a tiny fragment of the nature of her 'secret' information. Her perfect revenge, conceded Adam. She merely added that it was something that Daniele – the language school boss – had told her in strictest confidence.

'You'll find out soon enough, Adam. Not even Daniela knows.'

She could really be the most exasperating woman friend that Adam had ever known.

Three more unusual things happened to Adam before the end of June when his contract with the school and the landlord of his flat were due to expire. Two of these happenings were mildly disturbing and he failed to find an explanation for them that made any sense.

The first thing was that the *padrona* of his favourite coffee bar offered to read his palm – something that she had been threatening to do since he first arrived in Campanula. She was a large, jovial lady who never seemed depressed about anything, not even the economic climate. Adam was not in a hurry to go anywhere and he was thoroughly convinced, by that time, that he already knew what his future would hold. It would be nice, he decided, to receive confirmation of what he firmly believed would transpire – more or less directed by the hand of fate. He held out the palm of his hand for her inspection.

'No, A-damn,' she said with mock severity, 'your left hand, please.'

She took his hand in her plump, warm fingers and looked.

'I see you are deeply in love. But you will never get married again.' Adam looked so downcast that she added hurriedly: 'But you must see this relationship through to the end. It is very important for both of you.' She paused and looked again at his palm. She raised an eyebrow in surprise – genuine surprise, Adam noted. 'Your lifeline goes on for...I have rarely seen such a long lifeline.' She changed the angle of his hand. 'I see you have three children,' she added as an afterthought. Adam thanked her and told her she obviously had a gift. Instead of thanking him, as he had half expected, the *padrona* just shrugged, as if to say: 'I know.' One of the older 'regulars' said to Adam as he went out: 'She is always right, you know.' It was a disconcerting experience. She had been so convincing – except for one small detail.

And then, even more disconcerting, was the occasion when he had been walking home from school one night as he had always done without any sense of threat at all. Just after he had turned into the side street leading to his flat, he found himself surrounded by four silent figures who had appeared from nowhere. They looked no more than teenagers and were wearing anoraks with the hoods up and sun glasses, which effectively hid their faces. He was reminded all too poignantly of the events that had taken place in London only weeks ago. One of them spoke to him in dialect. As far as Adam could make out, he was saying: 'You're the man with the dog, right?' Adam shook his head. Surprisingly, he did not feel frightened, merely puzzled. None of them laid hands on him and neither were they carrying any weapons that he could see. 'Get rid of the dog. You understand?'

Adam said: 'You're making a mistake. I'm English.'

He expected the youth to say there had been some error and leave him alone. But another of the group took over, speaking in Italian 'It's time for you to leave Campanula, *signore! Capito?*' Then they disappeared just as they had appeared a few seconds earlier, melting into the shadows. 'What on earth was all that about?' wondered Adam.

Nothing is ever as it seems...

When Adam related what had happened to Rosaria, she reacted quite differently to what he had expected - smiling indulgently at the bar owner's 'guesswork' and glowering darkly and angrily as he related how he had been accosted in the street. She muttered something under her breath that sounded like a cross between an imprecation and the word *Benedetto*.

The third event that occurred belonged entirely to the 'real' world. Weeks beforehand, Rosaria had printed off application forms for an English teaching post at Lecce University on Adam's behalf. It had taken him hours to work out the convoluted steps involved in filling out the forms and photocopying the necessary documents to prove that he was who he said he was and that he really did possess the qualifications that he claimed to hold. With everything that had happened since that weekend, he had completely forgotten about the matter. It was with some surprise and great delight that he found an equally convoluted letter inviting him to attend an interview in Lecce in early September. He felt a twinge of conscience about deserting the 'English Academy of Salento' and Glenda. Rosaria was elated. She threatened to leave him if he did not go for the interview. 'Now I know you will come back to Italy,' she said. The problem of Adam's conscience was resolved easily. Glenda's 'big secret' turned out to be that the Campanula branch was to close this summer because it had proved to be financially unviable.

'It would be great to have a university teaching post,' said Adam to Rosaria. 'But we don't know yet whether I shall pass the interview.'

'Of course you will, Adam. You're a brilliant teacher.' He hugged her warmly and thanked her for her unshakeable faith. 'And think of the advantages, Adam. You will get thirteen months' salary throughout the year and a teaching job until you are sixty-five at least. It's great news, Adam.'

Adam began to believe he really did have a future in this part of the world, based on sound economics. It seemed to make the prospect of sharing a life with Rosaria far more feasible. Even her parents could not object to a union with a university 'prof' surely? 'Other brain' was not so confident about the future. 'Houses built on sand,' it muttered. Adam's enthusiasm was not to be dampened and he dismissed its objections with an airy wave of the hand.

He bid farewell to Daniela and they parted on good terms as the result of a pizza evening with Glenda, himself, Daniela and a more-or-less forgiven Claudio. Adam insisted on paying for everyone.

Adam looked back on the last few months in wonder at how his life had been transformed in such a brief period of time. Inevitably, the time came for Adam to return home to England for the months of July and August before his return in September. On a rational level, Rosaria appeared to accept this period of separation. Adam explained that he had to pay bills, decorate doors and walls that had been neglected by the previous owner, find a tenant, organise his return to Puglia on the basis that he would be staying there permanently. Through Glenda, who lived in the village of Sannicola, he had found a house to rent on his return. Lecce was only a thirty minute bus ride away and the village was near enough to Rosaria's town for what he assumed would be a short term arrangement.

On the evening before his departure, Rosaria and Adam decided to walk along the long sandy beach between Lido Conchiglie and Gravino to watch the setting sun together. They took warm clothes and beach towels to lie on. Due to the fact that Rosaria had run out of fuel on her way to pick him up – Adam had a moral heyday – and had had to send an SOS to her *papà* to come out and rescue her, they arrived at the beach as the last rays of the setting sun were already casting a glorious, copper pathway from the horizon to the beach. Twilight fell and darkness enveloped them. The lights of Gravino twinkled in the distance. They spread out their towels and lay down side by side gazing up at the stars in the black sky above them. The only sound was the gentle lapping of the waves on the shoreline in time with their breathing. Adam stretched out an arm and began, as gently as the waves, to caress her body from head to toe. He kissed her on every part of her body that remained exposed. She lay there motionless for a period of time before the intimate workings of her mind and body were awakened. Suddenly they were making passionate love, removing only the clothes that impeded their progress to sexual union. The eternal stars shifted around the heavens by a few degrees, resplendently indifferent to the act of love taking place on that insignificant lump of rock beneath them. Adam was powered by an unrestrained feeling of lust approaching anger as he moved deeply inside her with an urgent, steady rhythm. The mood was infectious and Rosaria came with him, uttering a succession of cries that accompanied her protracted climax. Seconds later, she whispered: 'Adam, what happened? Where am I?'

Adam did not need to specify a geographical location. They had been on a journey to the stars and back again. Only then did Adam think to check that their stretch of beach was deserted. He listened, but there was only the sound of the waves lapping somewhere in the darkness. They lay there hugging and kissing until the cold night air reminded them that it was time to return to reality. They stood up shakily and made their way back along the strand to Rosaria's car.

'And to think that I only put ten euros' worth of fuel in my tank,' she said in her beautifully modulated angel's voice. Adam groaned in mock despair at the unlikelihood of ever changing this endearing, yet irritating, idiosyncrasy.

The following morning, Rosaria drove Adam to the railway station in Lecce. They were very subdued during the forty minute journey. Adam rested his hand on her knee and she placed her hand on his, driving as she usually did with only one hand on the steering wheel, until the city traffic required her to use both hands. This was to be their first separation after the most emotionally intense six months of their lives. Adam swore that it would be the last time if it remained in his power to do so. They arrived outside the station and sat there squeezing each other's hands in a desperate last gesture. When Adam made a move to get out of the car, Rosaria broke into a flood of uncontrollable tears. Adam could not hold back his own tears as she clung to him and cried out: 'Adam, I'm frightened!' Adam attempted to console her, telling her that it would not be for long and that he would be back as soon as he could. She eventually calmed down enough to accompany him on to the platform.

'I'll phone you as soon as I get home,' he promised.

'No – even before you get home, Adam, please!'

She waved good-bye as the train pulled smoothly out of the station. He could see the tears running down her cheeks again. Never, but never before had he experienced the same feeling of desperation at having to wrench himself physically and emotionally apart from another human being. During his journey home, Adam accused himself of cruelty, insensitivity and a failure to understand the depth of her love for him. One thing was certain – he was truly in love for the first time in his life. Being in love, he had just discovered, was no easy thing to bear. He phoned her as soon as he had arrived at Brindisi airport to make sure she had arrived home safely.

'Adam,' she pleaded. 'Please come back soon. I am lost without you.'

He was painfully aware of experiencing the same deep sense of loss. He hoped and prayed that she would not weaken during his absence. Later on, he would have plenty of time to regret his untimely act of desertion. If he had known in advance what the next few years held in store for him, he would have acted very differently.

'But you *should* have known, Adam Knight!' This admonition came from 'other brain' which, Adam noted with curiosity, had changed camps; it appeared to be decidedly on Rosaria's side now.

20: Three Times Round the Sun

Oh Adam! My very own Adam! By what stroke of fate did I find you? Have you any idea how much I love you? You invaded my straightforward life and took it over completely. I've got you under my skin. Do you remember playing that Beatles song during the lesson? The time you told me off for speaking Italian. I really hated you for that, you know. It took me days to forgive you. Did you realise? Yes, I'm sure you did because you were especially nice to me after that. You were heaven-sent – just at the right moment in my life. I would never have dared go through with that crazy scheme in London if you had not been there by my side. You were my rock, just as I kept telling you. I was so afraid that you would think that I was using you just because I needed an Englishman to help me. But it wasn't like that at all, I promise. I truly believe that we are meant for one and other. But it has been wonderful, hasn't it, Adam? All the things that we have done together! You have become part of me. We are inseparable now – whatever happens to me in real life. You see? I dare not even put the unthinkable into words. You will always be my 'anima gemella'. How do you say that in English? My soul mate? My other half?

I don't know what I loved most about us; the way we talked together, the companionship, the funny little differences, the expression on your face when I threw that horrible green cardigan in the bin... Certainly it was the way you made love to me. I have never felt like that before...with ANYONE. It was just everything put together, wasn't it? I hope you feel the same way as I do. You do, don't you Adam? Please say yes!

When you left me at the station after all those months together, I felt abandoned. I was suddenly adrift – washed up on a strange shore with nothing to cling on to. I was frightened to death, Adam. I know you will be coming back because you said you would. But you have left me without my 'sostegno', my rock to hold on to as the currents try to drag me back into deep waters. You think I'm a strong person, don't you Adam? Everybody thinks I'm strong. Why? I don't know! But I'm not strong underneath. I lack the courage to do what is right for ME – Rosaria Miccoli. I'm a coward. You must believe me, Adam. And now you are in England, I feel that everybody is forcing me to do what I don't want to do.

It's so different over here. I know you think you understand my situation but it is quite impossible for you to grasp what it is really like, because you have never had to live with it, grow up with it being drummed into your head by the church, the schools, your parents. They brought me into this world so I have a moral obligation to please them, to 'do my duty'. All this must sound pathetic to you, amore, I'm sure. Your English mind believes that, if you're in love with someone, you have an absolute right to be with them, whatever anyone thinks. It's not like that down here. My parents tell me I have a duty to marry Benedetto because of the commitment I made when I was...all those years ago. And you know what my father is like, don't you? He has ways of making me do what he wants – like the house, MY house, OUR house. He would never sign it over to me if he knew that you were living there too. I know, Adam. It's called moral blackmail. But he truly thinks he is doing the right thing by me.

I love YOU, Adam. But my 'duty' is to marry Benedetto. For me, marriage and love are two separate things. I know that, for you, they both belong together. PLEASE try and understand. I don't want you to hate me. I feel I have to go through with this marriage to please everybody else. Afterwards, when it doesn't work out, I can say to

them all: *'There, I tried. I did as you wanted but it didn't work out.'*
After that, I promise you Adam, I shall only do what I want to do.

And then...O Dio mio! I didn't want to tell you this because I know
you will be angry with me. You were right when you warned me that
there would be a price to pay for the 'help' we received in London. HE
phoned me and told me that he needed Benedetto in the bank – to
'look after some special accounts' that he has at that branch. He said
it was important for Benedetto to be happy. He hinted darkly that I
should not marry a man whom my parents do not approve of, a man
who does not understand how things work down here. He sounded so
reasonable, Adam. No threats, but I understood. He had already
spoken to Benedetto about this before you left for England. You
remember the men with dark glasses and hoods who accosted you on
your way home that night? It was just meant to scare you, Adam. The
trouble was, you weren't really all that scared, were you? After what
we had lived through in London, it didn't seem all that serious to you.
But the next time, it would have been a bit more unpleasant. I know
how these people operate and I was scared for you.

Now comes the worst part, but I have to say it. I slept with
Benedetto after you had gone. I had to. He knew I didn't want to and
he kept on saying stupid things like: 'I'm just as good as that
Englishman, aren't I? How many times did you have him? What was
it like doing it with an old man?' I hated him. But he hated me
afterwards because I told him we only made love once but I said it
was beautiful. He was angry and nearly hit me. But I had to make
love to him, Adam. I know you think I have betrayed you. I have
betrayed you. But I did not mean to. I was scared. When you come
back, everything will be different. I cannot see into the future. You
know what I am like, Adam. You told me my 'future gene' is missing.

We will have to wait a while. Then you will have to decide my future for me, mio amore. But please! Don't hate me. I could not bear that.

Now I have to carry our secret to the altar. And it is going to be very, very hard for me for a long time.

Ti amo, ti amo, ti amo per sempre.

Tua Rosy xxxxxxxx

* * * * *

Adam was at home telling himself that he would rather be back in Italy. He had tried to phone Rosaria on his mobile but she was not answering his calls. He was only allowed to phone her on her parents' landline if she had texted him first to say the coast was clear. He had tried anyway but the mother had picked up the phone first. When he asked to speak to Rosaria, she claimed that her daughter was 'not available'. She sounded frosty as soon as she had realised who was speaking and hung up with a curt *'Arrivederla.'* It was not a reassuring sensation.

When he checked his e-mails and found the long letter from Rosaria, he was devastated. He read it through time and time again, looking for some hidden fragment of comfort that he might have missed; hoping beyond hope that the words were not telling him what he had feared might happen in his absence. Then came a sensation of anger; it was not directed entirely against Rosaria, but also against Benedetto for daring to encroach on *his* sacred preserve, against Rosaria's parents for the ignorance that led them to decide the fate of their daughter in this manner. He felt angry with the whole of Puglia for its blind adhesion to such narrow-minded traditionalism.

252

When he had vented his rage for a few days more, the self-doubts emerged, more terrible to endure than the anger. He accused himself of falling into precisely the same trap as in his previous relationships – choosing to pursue a romance with a built-in shelf life. He blamed his own lack of judgement for allowing himself to fall in love with a woman so much younger than himself. He even told himself that there was nothing more to their relationship than the usual crush that girls have on their teachers, despite this being blatantly not the case. For good measure, he added the consideration that he had tried to build a house on shifting sands without any thought for the 'real world' in which Rosaria lived. There was an undeniable element of truth in these self-inflicted accusations that made them all the more difficult to contradict. He often found himself a prey to the unexpected prickle of tears as haunting images of their times together came to mind during the wakeful early hours before dawn.

After days of mental and emotional self-flagellation, a calmer and better balanced frame of mind prevailed over the mists of despair. He had, he concluded, been painting too negative a picture of himself. He analysed himself and decided philosophically that the webs that we weave as we try to find a way through the tangled paths of our lives are never straightforward as we try to balance our own needs with the reality that the world, and other people, attempt to impose on us. He read the final lines of Rosaria's e-mail yet again and found a few crumbs of comfort. Maybe there was no need after all for their love to end in failure. It did not have to be a tragedy like Romeo and Juliet; Italy again, he thought ironically. There *was* a hint that the future could be redirected –

but it would need to be him that took the necessary steps, it appeared. The conquering of Rosaria and Puglia would take far more courage than he had displayed during his brief encounter with Enrico in London - and a lot of patience and perseverance too.

He had been debating with himself whether he should return to Puglia at all. The pain of knowing that Rosaria would be geographically nearby and yet untouchable was a serious consideration. In the end, he considered that it would be cowardly and defeatist not to return in September. Besides which, there was the prospect of an interesting teaching post at the University. It made sense to be in the same part of the world as Rosaria, should her situation change. No, he reminded himself forcibly – *he* would have to change *it*.

His attempts at phoning Rosaria drew no response. There was a brief e-mail from her apologising for the fact that she was not answering his calls. 'If I hear your voice, Adam, I know that I shall lose my resolve. I'm so sorry, *amore.*' And then there was silence.

* * * * * * *

Adam did get his lowly university teaching post – paid slightly less than a bus driver from Lecce. But that was of no importance – he was financially secure even without this post. All the students called him *professore* and displayed a degree of respect, the level of which he had never experienced before. They appreciated his unflagging attempts to bring the English language to life for their benefit. The mere fact of being undergraduate students, he quickly discovered, did not imply that their English was of a high standard. Most of them had been taught by native Italian teachers who had never set foot in England and whose contact with the living language had been minimal at best. For better or for worse, each student was expected to demonstrate a modest knowledge of English in order to pass their degree. With this in mind, it became Adam's mission in life to help them on their way.

Adam taught without any interference from his superiors. He was free to teach how he saw fit. Nobody doubted his competence to do the job for which he was being employed by the Italian State. Professionally speaking, Adam was delighted and positively looked forward to every new teaching day. He was paid through the lengthy summer break and received his 'thirteenth month' salary round about Christmas time. He even bought himself a car to travel between Lecce and Sannicola – another yellow FIAT Panda since there was no Rosaria to object. He was of the firm belief that it was the bright colour that warded off the other cars, for he never once had an accident in that accident prone country. The house that Glenda had found him was luxurious compared to the one in Campanula and had a garden and a working fireplace.

Yes, he was happy with his job. He had been greatly helped at the interview stage by being the only candidate. 'Yet again!' he thought ironically. He had been interviewed, in Italian, by three members of the University staff. After informal introductions, he was handed three envelopes and asked to choose one of them at random. He was told that the envelopes each contained a question on which he would have to give a short talk. Whenever Adam had to make a decision between even two alternatives, he inevitably made the wrong choice. If he had two keys in his hand to open one lock, he would instinctively try the wrong key first – like John Beardsley in far off Vicenza.

So it was that Adam chose the one question about which he knew next to nothing. 'What part do computers play in learning a language?' His immediate instinct was to answer: 'They don't.' But Adam had lived long enough in Italy to understand one of the fundamental principles which govern this country – never give a succinct response to anything when you can use a thousand words to say the same thing. If you attempt brevity, it will be construed as ignorance rather than honesty.

Thus Adam launched into a scholarly-sounding discourse about how languages are acquired, through a complex process of social interaction with ones fellow human beings. Computers, he conceded, could greatly help in learning the grammatical mechanisms of a language and even, he allowed, help with pronunciation.

He learnt afterwards that he had been awarded 17 out of 20 points, which is about as good as it gets in a country which believed firmly that awarding 20 points would represent an unobtainable level of Platonic perfection. 'How differently Italians view the world compared to Anglo-Saxons,' considered Adam – not for the first time.

This precept was born out in his subsequent dealings with Lecce University. He was asked to be present, in his capacity of native speaker, at an interview to appoint one single candidate for an administrative post. In the name of fairness, every single person who had applied for the post had to be interviewed. This amounted to over a hundred candidates. Not only that, but by law, every candidate interviewed had the right to attend all the other interviews – which were inevitably conducted in a public hall. It took three separate evening sessions to appoint one candidate. The Italians' concept of democracy is impressive, Adam conceded.

Their sense of the practical problems involved, considerably less so.

It was an identical situation when he conducted oral exams with his own students. It was a public examination therefore anyone could attend, in the name of impartiality. The corridor was filled with students craning their necks to get a good look at proceedings taking place in an office intended for a maximum of five people. 'Tell him about your time in London,' called out one spectator in encouragement, when his friend was floundering for words. Adam was inclined to admit that there was a measure of true justice in the system – albeit skewed in a very non Anglo-Saxon way.

Adam made friends – or 'free-ends' as Italians preferred to pronounce it – including the family of musicians who had performed the *pizzica* that fateful night in Campanula. He gave one or two private English lessons in and around Sannicola. Glenda had cornered most of the market, obliging Adam to pick up the remaining crumbs from under the mistress's table. Working from home after the closure of the language school suited Glenda well. By the time Adam had established himself in Sannicola, Glenda was mother to a pretty girl called Gemma, who had inherited her father's good looks and at least a small proportion of his wayward personality. There was a second child on the way. Pedro had fulfilled his mission in life and Glenda was encouraging him to take himself off. But he hung on doggedly if only, as Glenda explained bluntly, because she paid for the rent and the food when Pedro's wages as fisherman-cum-excavator were found wanting.

If Adam was ever likely to forget the ominous undercurrents in southern Italian life, he was reminded of them one day whilst walking along a road in his village, where a local builder was constructing a row of brand new dwellings. He recognised the builder because he had shown Adam round one of his houses. The man was hemmed in by three young men wearing identical sunglasses, whose furtive glances and hard faces told Adam exactly to which substrata of society they belonged. The builder was handing over a thick wad of €50 notes to one of the gang. 'He's paying his *pizzo*,' thought Adam, deeply shocked by what he had witnessed. It was a stark reminder of the darker side of the country where he aspired to live. He felt angry with the State and its agents who made little move to halt such blatant transgressions of the law. All too often, the self-same agents were part of the corrupt system.

There were exceptions to this rule, however. Occasionally, men and women, who dared to defy the clans, emerged from obscurity. Their defiance sometimes cost them their life. Adam was shocked by a report in the local newspaper about the mayor of a small town to the south of Gravino who had been found dead after an inexplicable 'accident'. The newspaper article suggested that the mayor had attempted to defy the local *boss* – perhaps refusing him planning permission for some dubious building project. The precariousness of life in this part of the world was brought home forcibly to the inhabitants of the town who had voted for their mayor. Adam shuddered at the thought of how his own life had been spared thanks to the 'protection' afforded by this same sinister individual dwelling in the shadow-lands of this beautiful country.

Adam's life was busy and even professionally and socially fulfilling. He kept his word and visited Sofia's family twice, making the lengthy overland journey by coach. The welcome was warm and genuine. The countryside, in sharp contrast to Puglia, was green and mountainous. When he returned the second time, Sofia had taken herself off to London to work for an Italian company that imported foodstuffs from the homeland. She acquired an English boy-friend and seemed set to continue her life far from home. The exact reverse of Adam himself, he pointed out to her in one of his e-mails to her. To Sofia's surprise, she had not heard from Rosaria for some time.

It was only when Adam was on his own or in the early hours of the morning that he became aware of his loneliness. In those moments, the sense of loss was acute. He would unexpectedly find himself staring down into the emotional void which his life was becoming. It was a sensation he had never felt when he had been with Rosaria. The importance of love, he realised, was that it gave life a purpose of its own. No, it was even worse than that; love, in whatever form it takes, *is* the meaning of life.

His attempts at contacting Rosaria always drew a blank. She must have changed her phone number. She had cut him off. Adam had had one or two 'near misses' with women he had met along the way during the period he and Rosaria had been apart. But the promise he had made in that extraordinary period of his life had held good and he had drawn back from sexual encounters. He knew that fidelity was strictly uncalled for. Rosaria would certainly not have remained faithful, at least not in any physical sense. But that was not the point. He felt, against all logic, that one day he would be glad that he had kept to the promise, made half-jokingly on bended knee between the towering cliffs of the Adriatic Sea.

The first intuitive stirrings that the time had come to don his warrior's gear once more began to make their presence felt at

Easter time almost three years after he and Rosaria had separated. The Earth had orbited the Sun three times, travelling an incredible two-thousand-eight-hundred million kilometres, dwarfing the aspirations of mankind, in its steady swing through the vastness of space. And Adam was becoming aware that he and Rosaria had made this incredible journey without each other's help. Glenda had lectured him only days before, during their frequent morning cups of coffee on the broad *piazza* of Sannicola, pointing out to him that Rosaria would never make the first move. Hadn't he, Adam, got it into his head yet that Rosaria was a southern Italian woman? She would never, in a lifetime, be the one to upset the *status quo* imposed by her circumstances.

But it was something more out-of-the-ordinary that gave Adam the *spinta* necessary to wake up from his three year trance. He was in the depths of oblivion at about two o'clock in the morning. It was Good Friday. For once, Adam had decided not to go home for the short, almost non-existent academic Easter break. He became dimly aware of people singing in the road that ran along above the level of his house, Sannicola being built on one of the rare hills in Salento. In his sleepy state, he thought it must be carol singers, until he remembered that it was not Christmas but Easter time. Besides which, they were not singing hymns, he worked out, but songs which sounded distinctly more like the *pizzica*. Yes, they were playing instruments as well. The insistent beat on the tambourines and the words sung in dialect evoked, not Christianity at all, but voices reminiscent of the older gods of the land. Now he was awake. The singing was right outside his window and, somehow, the words of the song contained the name Adam. Now there was somebody tapping on his window. He got up to investigate. Slipping into a track-suit, he opened the front door which gave directly on to the descending street. He recognised several villagers including the *Schiattacore* musicians. As he peered out of the half-opened door, there was a cheer and a rattling of tambourines enough to waken the dead. He raised a hand in greeting and asked: 'What's going on?'

'Oh, it's an old custom, A-damn. It used to be just the young men of the village who went round singing outside the houses of the pretty virgins to encourage them to come out and play,' explained one of the young men.

'Nothing to do with Easter, then?' asked Adam.

'Oh no! It's more to do with the coming of spring and the birth of new life,' explained one of the girls. 'Nowadays, of course, we just go round and call on anybody we know. Come on A-damn. Get dressed! Everybody we call on has to join in and do the rounds with us until daybreak.'

And that was it. Adam knew the time had come. He set out for Campanula for the first time in three years. For once, Adam and 'other brain' were in complete accord.

He headed for the house that they had visited together presuming that she would still be living there. Benedetto would be at work. For some strange reason, in this most Catholic of countries, Good Friday was not a national holiday. He sat outside the block of flats for half an hour or so. People came and went. There was no sign of Rosaria's distinctive *Cinquecento.* There was nothing for it. He would have to go and ring on her doorbell. He found their names on the brass entry-phone plate: 'Miccoli-Rocca'. A good job, he thought, that married women retained their maiden name. With quivering, fate-laden finger, he pushed the doorbell.

But there was no response. The sensation of anti-climax was disheartening. But there was no giving-up. Maybe she was out shopping. Or, more likely, she had gone into town to visit someone. The fact that she might be at work did not occur to him. He decided to walk into the centre and leave the car where it was. After all, it was a kind of pilgrimage that he was undertaking. It was appropriate that he should tread the cobbled streets of Campanula on foot. He reached the *piazza* in fifteen minutes. He was standing on the same spot where he had danced with her all that time ago. He smiled at the memory and went through the events of that tumultuous period of their lives. He shook his head to clear it of the images that besieged his mind.

At first, he did not recognise her because she was pushing a child's push-chair along the pavement and holding the hand of a little girl walking along by her side. It was just as it had been three years ago when she had been dancing the *pizzica.* There had been a veil over his eyes preventing recognition. Now she had almost reached the spot where he was standing. He remained still until she had drawn level with him before he spoke. 'Rosy!'

In the first instant, her face registered profound shock. She stood stock still clutching the hand of the little girl tightly in hers. And then Rosaria's face was transformed as the well-loved smile illuminated her face once again. 'Adam! Adam! *Mio* Adam!' She was laughing and the tears began to run down her cheeks. *'Finalmente, sei tornato!'* The little girl was looking anxiously from her mother to Adam and back again. For the first time, Adam looked properly at the child. She was a very pretty girl with olive skin, dark brown hair and wide brown eyes. There was something familiar about the shape of her face which reminded Adam of a photo he had been looking at recently.

'Adam, this is Anna,' said Rosaria.

Now the girl was looking at him unafraid. Instinctively, Adam crouched down to be on a level with the child. *'Ciao, Anna,'* he said. *'Quanto sei bella!'* Anna returned his gaze unperturbed. Rosaria was standing above them with something close to ironic humour in the happy smile that transfixed her expression. And then Adam remembered the photo he had been looking at. It was one of himself as a three-year-old child that he had dug up when he had last been in England. He had brought it back with him so that friends and students could enjoy a few lighter moments at his expense. In that instant, he understood everything that he needed to know. He stood up and looked at Rosaria with a joyous smile that spread all over his face and would not go away. There would be time for words later. The three of them joined hands and began to dance around in a circle while Anna giggled with mirth, her dainty feet barely touching the ground. And that, by chance, was how Benedetto found them as he emerged from the BPS bank, where he had been transferred that week.

For once, everything in Puglia was exactly as it seemed.

Epilogue: Loose Ends

If, like me, you would prefer to savour Rosaria and Adam's moment of revelation and joy without the details of how their lives proceeded after these tumultuous events, then it would be better to close the book at this point. I have added this epilogue for readers who need to have loose ends neatly tied up - if this is ever possible in our earthly lives. On the other hand, if you read this epilogue, it will lead you in the direction of the second novel, also set in Puglia: 'The Demise of Judge Grassi' in which Rosaria Miccoli plays a significant role as the astute private investigator in the mysterious case of a distinguished, retired judge in the city of Lecce.

Adam and Rosaria's life together could hardly be described as straightforward. The course of true love never runs smooth, they say. The main problem did not arise from any opposition from Benedetto. The worst moment was the immediate and public row which irrupted beneath the unperturbed figure of San Giovanni. Rosaria told Adam later that Benedetto had repeatedly begun to ask for a paternity test to be carried out to ascertain whether or not Anna was his daughter. The scandal that would have broken out as a result of such a test would, in any event, have brought the marriage to an end very swiftly. Benedetto had, soon after his marriage, begun an extra-marital affair with a girl he worked with at the bank. After due course, Benedetto divorced Rosaria and married his new partner, leading a more conventional life with an individual who was considerably more docile than Rosaria.

Neither did Adam have to walk around in fear of his life from reprisals by the Gentleman of 'virtue' and 'bravery'. In the first place, foreigners are very rarely, if ever, the target of mafia recriminations. After all, the 'man of honour' in question was still able to exploit his contact in the bank. The presence of an Englishman living with an Italian woman, mad enough to be in love with him, was a matter of no consequence. Adam was 'invited' to an audience with Don X to whom this act of courtesy was due. Adam set off in trepidation but excelled himself diplomatically speaking. He had quickly cottoned on to the fact that this powerful criminal needed his vast ego to be fed. Thus, Adam thanked Don X for being instrumental in avenging the life of an innocent woman and saving his and Rosaria's lives in London. When challenged to state what he understood Don X's role in Puglian society to be, Adam repressed any temptation to tell the truth, reminding himself that he had to consider the safety of Rosaria and Anna. He had replied that, as far as he could understand the complexities of life in Italy, Don X was responsible for nurturing and safeguarding the local economy. This description greatly pleased the gentleman concerned. Even Rosaria had been very impressed by the account that Adam had given her afterwards.

'You have become as artful with words as any Italian,' she said proudly and would have led him to the bedroom had it not been for the delightfully intrusive presence of Anna.

Rosaria had been terrified of admitting that she was expecting a child before her marriage to Benedetto. She did the only thing that she could to spare her family from what would have been a devastating scandal with consequences for her – both social and financial – quite impossible to predict. Adam did not need an explanation as to why she had not told him about their love-child. Never once did he ask her to justify her behaviour or chastise her for her act of concealment. She thanked him silently for his loyalty and trust, vowing that nothing else would come between them.

The relationship between Adam and his newly discovered daughter was established immediately. She accepted Adam without question. He couldn't be a bad man, she decided, because *mamma* seemed a lot happier than before. It was only later that she became puzzled as to why her new father had a few grey hairs just like her grandfather. She would go through a stage of telling her teachers and school mates that her new dad was nearly as old as her grandfather, but grew tired of this approach when she discovered that other peoples' reactions were not always predictable. In general, parents whom Adam met outside the school gates when he picked up his daughter accepted the situation without question. Most people took to Adam easily because of his post-youthful good looks and ready smile. He was obviously a man content with his life. Adam pointed out to anyone interested that, thanks to Rosaria, he had left his emotional and mental adolescence behind him and had the rest of his adult life to look forward to.

The real obstacle to complete happiness came from Rosaria's parents. Well, it boiled down to Rosaria's mother in reality. Umberto had developed a grudging respect for Adam after they had had a heated heart-to-heart argument in which Adam told him that he did not expect a single penny of the man's money, or a stone of his property to come his way. If ever there was any hint of reducing Rosaria's share of her rightful inheritance, he, Adam, would personally come back from the grave and haunt him till his dying day. Umberto had actually managed a brief chuckle.

The younger generation of Rosaria's family and, above all, Martina, felt at ease with the situation when they came to visit Rosaria and her reconstituted family unit. Adam, after all, never acted as if he was older than any of them and was always pleased to see them.

Rosaria's mother was the only stumbling block. If Adam, Rosaria and Anna came round to visit the parents, she would either not be there or she would develop a sudden dental appointment and take her leave as soon as possible. She refused point blank to acknowledge Adam's presence and hardly spoke to Anna. Her intransigence angered Adam to the point where he overtly expressed his exasperation. After that, it was made clear that he was no longer welcome in their house.

After a time, Adam and family moved nearer to Lecce where they bought a *villa* with a garden. Adam had to sell his home in England, virtually burning his boats should he ever have needed to return. Not a very likely scenario, he considered.

Being near Lecce, they were outside the radius of family influences. The inhabitants of the provincial capital were decidedly more progressive than their cousins to the south. A few eyebrows were raised at the outset, but nothing too daunting. Adam and Rosaria felt more at ease living near Lecce and Adam only had a short journey to the University. Rosaria began to work part time in the provincial council offices. The lifestyle suited Rosaria's taste for the bustle of town life with its abundance of fashionable shops, cinemas and theatres. They did not eat out very often except when the three of them felt like a pizza. Adam was the chief cook. Rosaria contented herself by telling Adam that he might be able to cook Salento *antipasti* properly one day. In exchange for his culinary skills, Rosaria agreed to do the washing up although, true to character, she would leave the task to the last possible moment – usually to the following morning if it was an evening meal. This would infuriate Adam so much that he often ended up washing the dishes himself. Rosaria still refused to put more than the minimum amount of fuel in her tank. To do otherwise seemed to contravene a law of nature.

Adam happily left the creation of a homely ambience to Rosaria. It was fun going shopping and decide how to furnish their real house, instead of fantasising about it as they had done before. There was just time enough to defy the predictions of a plump and friendly bar owner in Campanula, suggested Rosaria to Adam soon after they had moved home.

Even taking into account the ups-and-downs of a shared life and the slow cooling of passion, Adam and Rosaria stayed together in relative harmony but, above all, abidingly in love. They shelved the idea of marriage for the time being, thus appearing to fulfil at least a part of the prediction.

And that is as clear-cut as such a story as this can ever be.

R.W. May 2016 (Updated version)

Acknowedgements

My thanks to the following people who have been so kind as to read the whole story, offering encouragement and suggestions along the way.

Rina Culora, Beppe Tristano, Prof. Daniel Thomas and last but definitely not least, Rod Davis – of 'The Quarrymen' fame.

R.W. 2012

About the author

Richard Walmsley lived, loved and worked for eight life-changing years in Salento - the southernmost province of Puglia – in the 'heel' of Italy. From 2002 until 2005, he taught English at the University of Lecce until age forced him reluctantly into retirement. At present, he spends his time writing novels and short stories. His novels and many of the short stories are born of his vivid experiences during the time spent in this contradictory region of Europe. Apart from writing, the author loves Italian cuisine, all too often accompanied by wine, walking and classical piano jazz. He gravitates towards the countryside rather than towards city life.

Although written ostensibly as tales of intrigue, mystery, romance and the influence of the mafia, his stories are laced with humour. It is impossible, he maintains, to live in Italy without being struck by the Italians' anarchical relationship with the world around them. His modest ambition is to provide an enjoyable reading experience for as many readers as possible, regardless of race, age, gender or any other category you can think of.

Published by nonno-riccardo publications

Printed in Great Britain
by Amazon

66150510R00158